Izumo Takeda, Monzaemon Chikamatsu

**Chiushingura: The loyal league**

A Japanese romance

Izumo Takeda, Monzaemon Chikamatsu

**Chiushingura: The loyal league**
*A Japanese romance*

ISBN/EAN: 9783337196813

Printed in Europe, USA, Canada, Australia, Japan

Cover: Foto ©Andreas Hilbeck / pixelio.de

More available books at **www.hansebooks.com**

# 忠臣藏

## CHIUSHINGURA;

OR,

# THE LOYAL LEAGUE.

### A JAPANESE ROMANCE

TRANSLATED BY

## FREDERICK V. DICKINS, Sc.B.,

OF THE MIDDLE TEMPLE, BARRISTER-AT-LAW.

WITH NOTES AND AN APPENDIX CONTAINING A METRICAL VERSION OF
THE BALLAD OF TAKASAGO,

AND A

Specimen of the Original Text in the Japanese Character.

ILLUSTRATED BY NUMEROUS ENGRAVINGS ON WOOD, DRAWN AND EXECUTED BY
JAPANESE ARTISTS, AND PRINTED ON JAPANESE PAPER.

❖

" Est hic, est animus lucis contemptor, et . . .
Qui vita bene credat emi . . . . honorem."
VIRG.

❖

NEW EDITION

LONDON:
ALLEN & Co., WATERLOO PLACE.
MDCCCLXXX.

# ERRATA AND ADDENDA.

Appendix, p. 157.—"Meiji," translated "illustrious rule," is better rendered "enlightened rule."

Appendix, p. 164.—"We shall climb together the Shide Hill." The note here is erroneous. Mr. Chamberlain (Trans. As. Soc. of Japan, vol. vii., pt. iv., p. 293, n. 24) says: "Souls on their way to hell have to cross the river Sandzugawa, containing the waters of Avarice, Cruelty, and Envy, where a crone named Datsuiba despoils them of their raiment, which she hangs upon the branches of a willow tree."

For the preparation of the design on the cover, taken from a Japanese album of decorative art some two hundred years old, in the possession of the translator, he is indebted to his friend, Mr. T. W. Cutler, of Queen's Square, Bloomsbury.

# CONTENTS.

# ILLUSTRATIONS.

# LIST OF PRINCIPAL PERSONAGES.

---

N.B.—PRONUNCIATION. Vowels as in Italian, save "u" as in English "put,"
"full," "bull," &c. Consonants as in English, h being well aspirated.

---

Bánnai (Ságisáka), retainer of Moronaho.

Gihéi (Amagawa), agent of Yenya.

Goyémon (Hara), retainer of Yenya.

Heiyémon (Teraoka), a common soldier, retainer of Yenya.

Hónzô (Kakogawa), chief councillor of Wakasanosuke.

Íshi (or O Ishi), wife of Yuranosuke.

Íshido (Umanojô), one of the commissioners present at the *seppuku* of Yenya.

Kámpei (Háyano), a retainer of Yenya, husband of Karu.

Káru (or O Karu), wife of Kampei (Hayano), daughter of Yoichibei, sold on
his account to the teahouse in the Gion Street.

Kawôyo, wife of Yenya, beloved by Moronaho.

Konámi, daughter of Honzô, affianced to Rikiya.

Kitaháchi (Tákemôri), a retainer of Yenya.

Kudáiu (Ono), a disloyal retainer of Yenya.

Moronáho (Kô no), Lord of Musashi, superior and enemy of Yenya.

Náhoyóshi, deputy of the Shôgun.

Rikiya, son of Yuranosuke, affianced to Konami.

Sadákuro (Ono), disloyal retainer of Yenya, son of Kudaiu and murderer of
Yôichibei.

Tonáse, wife of Honzô.

Wákasanósuke Yasuchika, officer under Moronaho.

Yágoro (Sénzaki), retainer of Yenya.

Yákushiji (Jirôzáyemon), one of the commissioners present at the *seppuku* Yenya.

Yazáma Jiútarô, a retainer of Yenya.

Yénya Hánguwan Tákasáda, officer under Moronaho, husband of Kawayo.

Yóichibéi, a farmer, father of Karu, murdered by Sadakuro.

Yúranósuke (Óhobóshi), hero of the tale, chief retainer of Yenya.

# CHIUSHINGURA;

OR,

# THE LOYAL LEAGUE.

### TRANSLATOR'S NOTE.

THE "Chiushingura" is, or at least was, one of the most popular and best-known romances in Japan. It is easy to understand why such should be the case, the main object of the tale being to glorify "chiushin" or loyal-heartedness, the supreme virtue of the Bushi class under the old order of things that passed away with the year 1868. The story is, as a mere story, not unskilfully constructed, and the variety of its incidents is sufficient to interest even the reader of the sensation novels of the period; while to those who still preserve some lingering affection for the quaint and picturesque national life that ended with the last decade, to be replaced by the vulgar and commonplace existence of the day, the following pages, as descriptive of old-

world manners and already obsolete sentiments, a portion of a
curious mediæval system that has lasted down to our own times,
will not, it is hoped, be altogether unpleasing.

The title "Chiushingura" is hardly translatable, and is a notable
example of the Japanese love of a play upon words. "Chiushin"
may mean either "loyal-heartedness" or "loyal followers;" and
"kura" (gura) signifies a treasury or storehouse, while it is also
the first half of the name of the popular hero, Kuranosuke, of
the historical episode of the "Forty-seven Rônin," upon which the
romance is founded, and which has been so pleasantly told by Mr.
Mitford in his admirable "Tales of Old Japan." The translator,
therefore, without attempting to render the native title, has chosen
that of the "Loyal League," as fairly indicating the nature of the
story, and preserving as much of the spirit of the original title as
could be preserved in a single expression.

The translation, it should be premised, was made long since,
in Europe, without the possibility of assistance; and although it
has been revised with as much care as the limited leisure and still
more limited scholarship of its author have permitted, there are,
doubtless, numerous inaccuracies to be detected in it by those better
versed in the language and literature of Japan than himself; for
which an indulgent consideration is claimed.

The translation is made partly from the text of the abbreviated
form in which the story is more commonly met with, but mainly
from that of the "jôruri" (or musical romance) in which the tale is
amplified and adapted for theatrical recitation.

A few explanatory additions, necessary to make the story plain to the English reader, have been incorporated with the translation, which is throughout, and purposely, a free one; and in some instances it has been found advisable to leave untranslated, or to translate shortly, portions of the original.

## NOTE TO THE PRESENT EDITION.

The whole translation has been revised, and much of it rewritten. Errors in the earlier edition have been corrected, and the present version is, on the whole, a closer rendering of the text now followed than the former one. But it has not been the translator's aim to assist in any way the student of Japanese, and amplification, condensation, and, to some extent, combination and alteration have been practised where judged advisable to meet the exigencies of English readers.

It should be added that the revision has been made in England, without the advantage of the usual native assistance in its preparation.

The text employed differs to some extent from that which served for the previous edition. New notes have been added, and the former notes have been rectified and enlarged. The Appendix has been but little altered.

*London, December, 1879.*

## PREFACE OF THE AUTHOR.*

I F you don't eat of a dish, however savoury, you can't enjoy its flavour, they say; and so, in piping times of peace, the loyalty and bravery of valiant *samurahi* remain un noticed, like as the light of the stars, unseen in the day-time, becomes visible only in the darkness and confusion of night; whereof an example will be found in the following syllabary written pages.

* In the text the whole of the First Book is dignified by the name of "*daijo*" or "preface"; but the introductory sentence here translated alone deserves that title, the rest of the book being, in reality, a portion of the narrative.

鶴ヶ岡ノ場

高ノ師直

塩谷判官

桃井若狭之助

# BOOK THE FIRST.

FTER the Shôgun of the Ashikaga dynasty, Taka-uji kô, had overthrown Nitta Yoshisada, profound peace reigned throughout the land. His Highness built a palace at Kiyôto, and the fame of his achievements penetrated into every corner of the empire.

All the people yielded to his authority, bowing down before him as the grass bends to the breeze, and the imperial might spread its protecting wings over the realm.

In commemoration of his success, the Shôgun caused a shrine to be erected to the War-God Hachiman at Tsuruga-oka, and sent his younger brother, Ashikaga Sahiyôye no kami Nahoyoshi kô,[*] to act as his deputy at the inauguration of the newly completed building.

Towards the close of the second month of the first year of the *nengo* Riyakuô (A.D. 1338), Nahoyoshi accordingly arrived at Kamakura, and was received by the Lord Moronaho, Count of Musashi,

---

[*] The Lord Nahoyoshi of the Ashikaga family, Commander of the left Imperial Guard.

and chief representative of the Shôgun at the Eastern capital, a haughty nobleman, arrogant of carriage, and overweeningly proud of his position near the person of his august master; assisted by Wakasanosuke Yasuchika, younger brother of Momonoi, Lord of Harima, and Yenya Hanguwan Takasada, a baron of Hakushiu, charged by His Highness with the duty of receiving guests, and who were keeping strict ward within the curtain before the shrine. Nahoyoshi, taking his seat under the porch of the shrine, motioned Moronaho to a place on his left, while the two younger noblemen took up their position below the steps by the great maiden-hair tree there standing.* Pointing to a Chinese coffer, which the attendant had brought forward at his command, Nahoyoshi exclaimed :—" Among the helmets contained in this chest is one which belonged to Nitta Yoshisada, who was defeated by our brother Takauji, bestowed upon him by the Emperor Godaigo. Nitta, it is true, was our enemy; but he was a descendant, in the elder line of the Seiwa family, a Genji house, and it is commanded that the helmet worn by him should not be thrown aside, but placed in the treasury of the shrine."†

" His Highness's command surprises me," cried the Count of Musashi; "Nitta, no doubt came of the Seiwa stock, but thus to honour a helmet worn by him, seeing that scores of feudatories of high and low degree claim like descent, is hardly, I submit, a prudent policy."

"Nay, my Lord, not so," said Wakasanosuke; "it seems to me that His Highness hopes in this way to obtain the submission of the disbanded partisans of Nitta without having recourse to force, trusting to the effect which his generosity in thus honouring their chief will have upon them. Your counsel is lacking both in wisdom and respect."

The words were hardly out of his mouth when Moronaho exclaimed, angrily :—

" *Yah!* you dare to interrupt me and twit me, Moronaho, with lack of wisdom. Round the spot where Nitta was slain, forty-seven

---

* Still to be seen.                †  *I.e.,* As an offering to the God.

假名手本忠臣蔵大序兜改

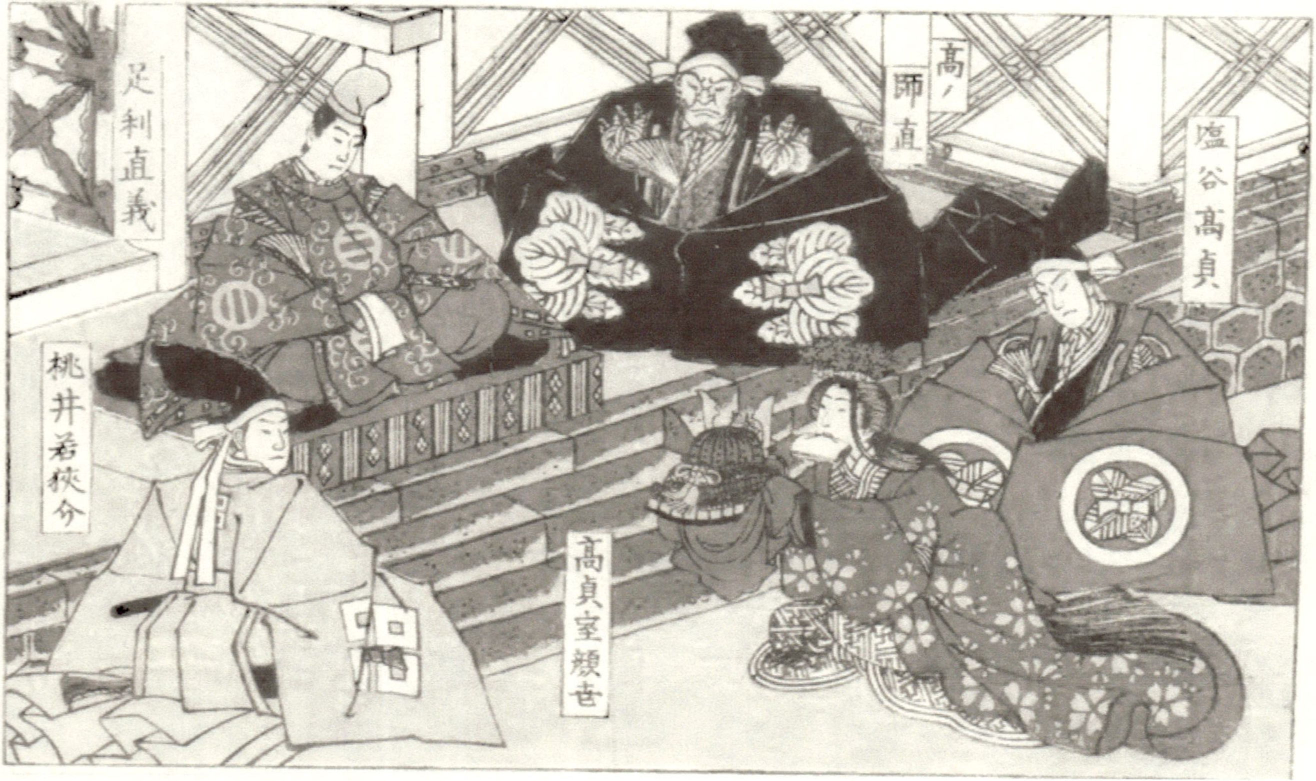

helmets that had fallen off the heads of their dead wearers were found; who shall tell which of them was Nitta's? and if the wrong one should be thus honoured, what ridicule would be incurred! Away with you* for an overmeddlesome raw youngster."

The colour mounted to Wakasanosuke's face; but Yenya Hanguwan interposed.

"*Kowa!* your lordship is no doubt right. Still, what Wakasanosuke says is worth consideration. His Excellency, perhaps," he added, glad to avert a quarrel, "will assist us."

"Let the wife of Yenya be sent for," replied Nahoyoshi, in answer to the appeal made to him.

A messenger was accordingly dispatched in quest of her; and after a short interval the Lady Kawoyo, the beautiful wife of the Hakushiu baron, presented herself. Her face was powdered, and the brilliancy of her appearance rivalled the lustre of a gem, as, with bare feet and long sweeping train, she modestly prostrated herself at a respectful distance from His Excellency.

"Lady Kawoyo," said Moronaho, who was an admirer of the sex, "we are much obliged to you. His Excellency has commanded your attendance, pray come nearer," assuming a soft manner as he spoke the latter words.

Nahoyoshi, regarding her, added:—"It is true that we have sent for you. Some time since, during the rebellion in Genkô (A.D. 1331), Godaigo Tenwô bestowed a helmet that His Majesty had himself worn, upon Nitta Yoshisada at the capital, and the latter doubtless wore it upon the day of his death. It is supposed to be among the helmets I have caused to be placed in yonder coffer, but there is no one here who can pick it out. We have heard that the wife of Yenya was, at the time we refer to, one of the twelve Naishi, and if she can recognise the helmet in question we bid her to point it out."

The Lady Kawoyo listened modestly to His Excellency's command, and replied softly:—

---

Lit. "Draw in your head as a tortoise does."

"Your Excellency's command honours me beyond my merits. Every morning and evening His Majesty's helmet was in my hands, and I was present at the bestowal of it upon Nitta. Indeed, it was from my hands that the latter received it; accompanying his grateful acceptance with the following declaration:—'Man lasts but one generation, but his name may endure for ever. When I go forth to battle I shall burn precious *ranjatai* perfume in the helmet thus graciously presented to me; and if I should die upon the battle-field, the foe to whom my head will fall a prize will know by the fragrance that he has taken the head of Nitta Yoshisada.'"

"Your answer, lady," exclaimed His Excellency, as the wife of Yenya ceased speaking, "is sufficiently clear. Ho! there; take out the forty-seven helmets in yonder coffer, and show them one by one to Lady Kawoyo."

The attendants hastened to obey; and, opening the coffer, brought out the helmets one by one. After a number had been examined, they came upon a five-fold helmet with a dragon crest, which the Lady Kawoyo immediately recognised by the odour still clinging to it, as the one bestowed upon Nitta by the Emperor Godaigo. The helmet thus identified was delivered to Yenya and Wakasanosuke, who were commanded to take charge of it, and see that it was duly placed in the treasury of the shrine. Nawoyoshi then rose and withdrew, followed by the two noblemen.

The Lady Kawoyo, thus left alone with Moronaho, addressed that nobleman with some embarrassment.

"My lord, pray excuse me. My duty being performed, and permission given me to retire, it would not be fitting that I should remain here longer. I beg, therefore, to take leave of your lordship."

Moronaho, however, coming close up to her, detained her.

"*Má*, an instant, pray. Your duties to-day are over, and I venture to ask you to look at something I have to show you. His Excellency's sending for you was a most fortunate thing for me,—just as if he were a god desirous of bringing us together. You know that I am fond of putting my thoughts into verse, and, day after day, I have

asked Yoshida Kenkô to assist me in composing some lines to you,
which were to have been sent to you. You will find them in this
paper," slipping a folded letter into her sleeve-pocket. "I hope you
will look upon them favourably. You might give me your answer
now, by word of mouth."

The letter was addressed to the Lady Kawoyo—different enough
in face and form from the Musashi stirrup,* from whom it purported
to come. And the wife of Yenya, as she read the address, trembled
with shame and confusion, yet feared to reproach Moronaho, lest
disgrace should attach to her husband's name. At first she thought
of shewing it to her husband; but recollecting that it would only
make him angry and might cause trouble, she simply threw the letter
back without a word.

Moronaho picked it up, quoting a line from the *Senzai* collection—

> "What thou hast spurn'd, is prized by me,
> For hath it not been touch'd by thee!"

and continued to press his suit, hoping by importunity to compel a
favourable answer—but in vain.

"Know you," he cried at last, "that I am Count of Musashi?
that on my will depends the weal or woe of the Empire? that your
husband's fate hangs upon your decision?—Do you hear me?"

Kawoyo could only answer with her tears, when Wakasanosuke
opportunely returned, and, seeing that some insult had been offered
to her, cleverly interposed.

"Lady Kawoyo, your duty is accomplished, and permission has
been accorded you to retire. Ought you not, out of respect to His
Excellency, to avail yourself of it?"—motioning her to withdraw as
he spoke.

Moronaho saw that Wakasanosuke suspected something; and,
determined not to show any weakness, cried angrily,

---

* Moronaho, as Lord of Musashi, had designated himself upon the cover of
the letter as a Musashi Stirrup. Musashi being famous for the manufacture
of stirrups.

"*Yah!* again you dare to thrust yourself in my way. If the lady Kawoyo withdraws it is by my permission, not by yours. Kawoyo desires me, according to her husband's secret wish, to instruct him how to discharge the duties of his office with perfect propriety, without which he would be helpless. And Yenya, though a Daimiô, seeks my aid; while you, a petty fellow who got your rank through the favour of nobody knows who, take care, and remember that a word from me will suffice to bring you into the clutches of the executioner."

The colour mounted into Wakasanosuke's face at this insolent speech, and he grasped the handle of his sword with force enough to crush it. Remembering that he was within the grounds of the War-god's shrine, and within the precincts of the palace, he had restrained himself when Moronaho had previously insulted him; but this last trial overcame his utmost patience, and he was on the point of making it a life and death quarrel, when His Excellency's fore-runners came rapidly up, clearing the way with loud shouts for their lord's passage.

In the confusion, Wakasanosuke was obliged to defer the hour, but still treasured the hope of vengeance. Thus, Moronaho, with a good fortune the reverse of merited, escaped destruction; and the next morning Yenya, ignorant of the ill-turn which his superior had played him, followed in his suite.

Nahoyoshi, meanwhile, returned at a slow pace to the palace, and his authority was everywhere reverently acknowledged; while his servants held their heads proudly erect, and the war-helmets were laid by arranged in peace-betokening order, according to the letters of the I-ro-ha.

Thus a profound tranquillity reigned in the land; throughout which, not to harm a head-piece became an universally observed rule.

 END OF THE FIRST BOOK.

# BOOK THE SECOND.

---

### THE RAGE OF WAKASANOSUKE.

N an evening in the *Yayoi** month, Kakogaha Honzô, a man of some fifty years of age, and of matured intelligence, *shikkenshoku* † of Wakasanosuke almost ever since the tall pines had overshadowed the courtyard of his lord's castle, was pacing to and fro before the *sho-in*,‡ while the servants, muttering together over their task, were sweeping up the dead leaves, and putting everything in due order.

"Yesterday, at Tsuruga-oka," said one of them, "our master was grievously insulted by the Lord Moronaho. They talk of nothing else in the servants' quarters. Indeed, it is said that violence was used towards him."

"*Yai, yai!*" cried Honzô, breaking in, "what is all this about—what have you to do with such matters? If your work is finished, away with you, every one."

---

* "Development month," the 3rd of the late national calendar, answering to the middle of our April.

† Chief Councillor is a sufficiently near rendering of the word.

‡ These appear to be anterooms on one or both sides of the *Genka*, porch, or entrance hall.

Honzô spoke good-humouredly enough ; and, just as he ended, the clatter of footsteps resounded in the verandah, and his only daughter, Konami, and her mother, Tonasé, came together out of one of the apartments.

"How is this ?" he exclaimed, in a sharp tone, "both of you absent from attendance on your mistress, amusing yourselves instead of looking after your duties. Shame upon you—ten thousand times shame upon you."*

"Nay, father," said Konami, "our mistress is more than usually well to-day, she is now quietly asleep ; is it not so, mother ?"

"Yes," replied the latter. "But, Honzô, our mistress has just been telling me a report she heard from Konami that our lord Wakasano-suke and Moronaho had words together after the close of yesterday's ceremony at Tsuruga-oka.† Our mistress is very anxious about it."

"Now, now, Tonasé," cried her husband, "why do you listen to such stupid rumours ? Have a care, have a care ! So our daughter here got hold of this rumour yesterday, did she ? How people talk, to be sure—but the whole thing is ridiculous ; I must go and put your mistress's mind at ease about what you have told her."

Just as he was quitting the spot, however, a warder came up and announced "Rikiya Sama, the son of Ohoboshi Yuranosuke."

"Ha !" said Honzô, "he will have brought instructions about the reception of the guests at court to-morrow. Tonasé, hear what he has to say, and inform our lord of his message. And stay, Rikiya and Konami are betrothed ; so treat him civilly. I must away to your mistress."

So saying, Honzô hurried off in the direction of the inner apartments.

"Ah," cried Tonasé, approaching closer to her daughter, "your father was always a punctilious man, but in this matter I am not at all of his mind. 'Tis you ought to receive the message, not I. You and

---

* Lit., " A thousand times ten thousand times."
† *I.e.,* " The Cranes' Hill or Mound."

桃井館 場

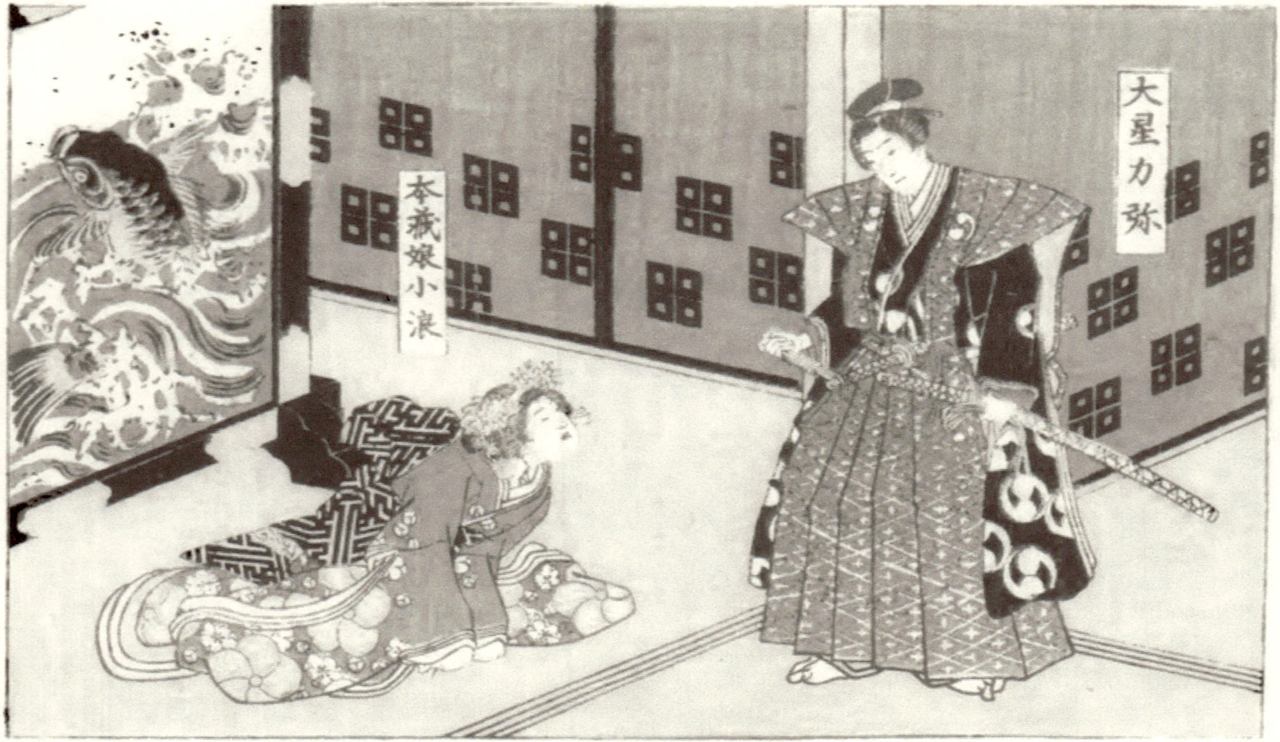


THE MEETING OF THE AFFIANCED

your affianced would, of course, like to see each other, and be with each other a little; therefore, you take my place and receive Rikiya—what say you?"

But Konami only turned red, and, although her mother repeated the question, gave no answer. The latter divining, however, her daughter's real wishes, immediately feigned an attack of hysterics.

"*Ai, ta, ta, ta,*—daughter,—rub my back, please; I have been fearing this ever since the morning. It is another attack of my usual spasms. Ah! it will be impossible for me to receive the messenger. *Ai, ta, ta, ta,*—daughter,—I must get you to receive him instead of myself. Take care to treat him civilly, and offer refreshments. This fit quite prevents me. Mind you offer refreshments; and, when Rikiya has partaken of them, take his message carefully and make my excuses to him."

With these words Tonasé hobbled off towards the inner apartments. Konami, bowing after her mother with an expression of entreaty, said to herself, "Of late Rikiya has become very dear to me, but what am I to say? How shall I act when I meet him?"

A timid blush dyed her soft cheek as she made these reflections, and her little heart went "pit-a-pat, pit-a-pat," like the tiny waves* breaking on the sea-shore.

Presently, Rikiya was announced, and immediately afterwards entered the apartment, saluting Konami courteously. He was a handsome youth; and, as he and Konami shyly interchanged glances, they were mutually charmed with each other. Neither could find a word to say, modesty dyeing her cheek with the hue of the plum-blossom, rivalled by the blush of the wild cherry that overspread the face of her betrothed; and, the pair being alone, there was no intermediary to bring them closer together.†

"Welcome, Sir," exclaimed Konami, with some embarrassment; "we

---

* A pun upon her name, "Konami," *i.e.*, "little wave."

† Lit.; "There was no *makura-giyôji* present." A *giyôji* is an umpire or director in a wrestling match—*makura-giyôji*, pillow-umpire, is a term for a *nakôdo*, or matrimonial go-between, who is supposed to bring together the pillows of the affianced, as the wrestling umpire (*sumô-giyôji*) gives the signal for the onset.

hardly know how to thank you for the trouble you are put to on our behalf. I am charged with the duty of receiving your communication. Pray let me know what it is"—approaching her betrothed as she uttered the last words.

Rikiya, however, drew back with an offended air. "Hold!" he cried, "this is scarcely civil. All the world knows that when a message is to be received, the forms of politeness ought to be rigidly observed." "My lord Yenya," he continued, "informs Wakasanosuke that His Excellency's order is, that both my lord and yours be at their posts to-morrow morning at the seventh hour precisely (4 A.M.), and in everything submit themselves, without failing in any particular, to the directions of Moronaho."

As the words flowed softly like water from the youth's mouth, Konami was struck with admiration, and could not find a word to say in reply: so completely was she under the charm of his address. At this juncture a partition was pushed back, and Wakasanosuke, who had heard the whole conversation from an adjoining room, entered the apartment.

"Oh, I understand—many thanks, messenger. Yesterday, when I took leave of His Excellency, I somehow missed Hanguwan. To-morrow morning, is it? At the seventh hour precisely? Good. You may assure your master I shall not fail to be there. Commend me to your lord, and thank him for me; and I must thank you, too, messenger."

"Your lordship, then," said Rikiya, "will permit me to take leave. And to you, lady," addressing Konami, "I beg to express my thanks for having received my message."

So saying, Rikiya courteously withdrew. Tonasé who had all this time remained hidden behind a screen, where, after leaving her daughter upon a pretended plea of illness, she had concealed herself, also slipped away unperceived. Hardly had she disappeared when Honzô entered the apartment.

"Ah, your lordship is here? I am very sorry to have to remind you that your lordship's presence at the palace is required so early as the seventh hour. It is already midnight. Will it not be well to take some rest?"

"Is it indeed so late? But hark ye, Honzô, I must have some talk with you, in private. Send your daughter away."

"Do you hear?" cried the *Shikkenshoku*, addressing his daughter; "If we want you we will clap hands. Away with you."

"I was desirous," pursued Honzô, after she had withdrawn, approaching his lord, whose face had assumed an expression of the deepest concern, "I was desirous of being allowed to inquire what was troubling your lordship? I pray you, tell me everything without any reserve."

"You must swear to me that you will attend to what I am about to say, whatever may be the results, without making a single objection."

"Surely, my lord, that is a strange request to your servant; whose duty it is to do whatever he may be directed."

"So, then, you will not give me your oath as a Bushi." *

"Nay, not so,—but first I would ask to hear the whole matter from your lordship."

"Then you will give me your advice! Nay, but perhaps you would oppose my wishes."

"Is not my lord assured of his servant's respectful attention and devotedness? I will not interrupt your lordship by a single word. I pray you, therefore, tell me all, now; and be not angry with this fellow Honzô, who will treasure up in his inmost heart whatever you may deign to confide to him."

"Well, then, I will tell you everything. As you know, the Kuwanrei† Nahoyoshi came down to Kamakura a short time since, to inaugurate the shrine that has just been completed at Tsuruga-oka. Yenya and I were charged with the duty of receiving guests, and were commanded by His Highness the Shôgun to put ourselves under the

---

* The general name of the military or two-sworded class; literally "warriors."

† Governor-General of the eight eastern provinces of which Kamakura was formerly, and Yedo afterwards, the capital.

orders of Moronaho, a nobleman of great experience in all ceremonial matters. Moronaho took to riding the high horse, and day by day grew harsher and stricter with me, who am one of the youngest and least experienced of all the *samurahi* in Kamakura. At last his insolence passed all bounds, and I would have ere now cut him in pieces, were it not that the respect due to His Highness has always forbidden me to give way to my passion, and wreak vengeance upon my enemy. But my patience is exhausted. To-morrow, come what may, I will throw back his insults in his face before the whole court. My honour as a *samurahi* is at stake. This hand shall strike the villain dead. And you, Honzô, beware of attempting to restrain me. My wife, and you too, have often remonstrated with me of late, because of my quick temper gaining more and more the mastery over me, and I know your counsel is good. But a *samurahi*, with the spirit of a *samurahi*, I can no longer brook these repeated insults. You will say, I am courting destruction, bringing grief upon my wife. Too true, perhaps; but the sword I wear, and the dread archer-god to whom I pray, command me to wipe out the insults to my honour. Even though I die not upon the battle-field, if I slay this Moronaho, a service will be done to the Empire, and the name of my house will be saved from infamy. I have spoken thus freely with you that my motives may be known, and that it may not be said of me afterwards that I rushed upon my fate in a mere fit of passion, like a mad fool or a stupid wild-boar."

"Most clearly have you put the matter, my lord. You have indeed acted with wisdom throughout,—a wisdom your servant could never hope to imitate."

"*Yai!* Honzô," cried his master, interrupting him; "what say you? I have acted with wisdom, have shown forbearance. What means this? Dare you to insult me?"

"Far from your servant any such thought. Street-folk, it is true, take the shady side of the road in winter, and the sunny one in summer, to avoid disputes; but *samurahi* follow no such coward's rule. I pray you excuse my ill-considered words. Search my heart, my lord, and you will find in it no thought of disrespect to your servant's master."

As he uttered the last words Honzô drew his short sword, and with a blow cut off a branch from a pine-tree that stood close to the verandah in front of the room where the conversation was being held : immediately returning the weapon deftly to its scabbard.

"Sa ! So let the enemies of my lord perish by his hand."

"Silence ! Look well, lest there be any one about who can hear what we say."

"And now, my lord," said the *Shikkenshoku*, after having peeped into the adjoining room to satisfy his master, "it is already midnight, pray take some rest: I will myself see to the alarm-clock. Do not delay, I pray you."

"I am glad you quite understand me. If I see my wife, I shall make some excuse for leaving her."

Bidding Honzô good night, Wakasanosuke then withdrew. For a few moments Honzô gazed after his lord wistfully ; then rousing himself, he bent his steps hastily in the direction of the servants' quarters.

"Ho, there, some of you," he cried in a loud tone, "saddle a horse for me, quick."

The order was obeyed without delay, and Honzô at once swung himself into the saddle.

"Follow me, I go to the mansion of Moronaho."

As he spoke, Tonasé and Konami came out of an apartment, and hurrying up to him, hung upon his bridle, exclaiming—"Where are you going? We have overheard everything. How, Honzô! You an old man, and yet you do not endeavour to moderate our lord's anger by your wisdom—what can this mean? Stay, stay !"

And the two women clung beseechingly to his bridle.

"Silence, both of you," cried the *Shikkenshoku*, angrily. "Our lord's life—the existence of his house—are at stake. Mind you do not utter a word about my departure to your master. If you betray me, you, daughter, shall be turned out of my family, and you, Tonasé, shall be divorced. Ho, there (to the servants), I will give you your orders on the way."

Tonasé and Konami uttered an exclamation of alarm.

"You are too importunate," repeated Honzô, sharply. "Delay not (to the servants), but follow me." So saying, he hastily rode off, clouds of dust marking his rapid passage. Tonasé and her daughter immediately afterwards betook themselves with heavy hearts to the inner apartments.

**END OF THE SECOND BOOK.**

# BOOK THE THIRD.

---

USPICIOUS events were the completion of the Palace at Kamakura, and the arrival of Nahoyoshi Kô, the Governor-General of the eight eastern provinces; brilliant was the throng of courtiers of high and low degree, in splendid attire, that crowded the spacious apartments on the morrow of the day of which the events have been already narrated. It was as if the moon and the stars* had combined to shed their radiance on the hills around Kamakura. About the Rear-gate were waiting the *nô* performers, who had been summoned to display their talents before the assembled court, while round the Great Gate were gathered the officials charged with the reception and entertainment of the guests.

As the seventh hour struck the assembled nobility and gentry presented a gorgeous appearance. Now loud cries of "Hai, hai,

---

* The Governor-General (*Kwanrei*) is the moon. the courtiers the stars—a complimentary extravagance.

hai !" from the warders of the western gate, gave notice of a fresh
arrival. Immediately afterwards, the glimmer of numerous lanterns
shone in the dusky dawn, and the lord Moronaho, Count of Musashi,
a proud and haughty nobleman, appeared, dressed in a court suit
of blue silk, ornamented with a large *mon** and wearing a tall
*yeboshi*† cap on his head. His retainer, Sagisaka Bannai, causing
some of the attendants to herald his master's approach, and ordering
the remainder to betake themselves to the proper quarters, squared
his elbows in a superb manner, for all the world just like a stork,‡
and, puffed up with his lord's dignity at secondhand, thus addressed
the great man :—

"Your lordship's arrangements are excellent, most excellent. As
to Yenya and Momonoi, however, strut about as they may with
awkward pride, they are as clumsy in their attempts to carry out
their duties as puppy dogs struggling to keep their footing upon a
slant roof. It makes one laugh to watch them. As to that fellow
Yenya,—by the by, his wife, I hear, has not yet answered your
lordship,—your lordship must not let yourself be disturbed by that.
Pretty though she is, she is beneath your lordship's notice ; and as to
her husband, it is wrong to mention him in the same breath with
your lordship, now made *Shiuttô* by His Highness."

"Yai ! don't speak so loud, Kawoyo is a married woman. Pretending to be a teacher of poetry, I have again and again expressed
my passion for her in verse, but hitherto without success. She has
lately, however, got a new maid, I hear, named Karu ; I must see
if I cannot bribe the wench to assist me. I don't abandon all hope ;
for if she really disliked me she would have spoken to her husband,
which she has not done."

While Moronaho and his follower thus conversed together familiarly

---

* Badge or device on the sleeves and back of the *haori* or mantle worn by
*Samurahi.* An interesting essay on Japanese heraldry by Mr. McClatchie will
be found in the Transactions of the Asiatic Society of Japan.

† Such as are shown in the first and second plates.

‡ A punning allusion to Bannai's surname " Sagisaka," *sagi* meaning a stork.

under the portal of the four-pillared gateway, one of the *Samurahi* on guard came up hurriedly to them, exclaiming :

"Just now, as I was sitting on the bench by the gate, Kako-gawa Honzô, the retainer of Wakasanosuke, rode up hastily and asked for an immediate audience of the lord Moronaho; saying he had been to your lordship's house, but had been told that you had gone to the palace early. He seemed most anxious to have an interview with your lordship; and was accompanied by a number of followers on horseback. What answer shall I make him?"

"My lord Moronaho is on His Highness' service," cried Bannai indignantly; "such a request for an immediate interview is monstrous. I will see the man myself."

"Stay, stay," broke in Moronaho, detaining his follower. "I understand it perfectly. Wakasanosuke does not come himself to wreak his revenge upon me for what took place the day before yesterday at Tsuruga-oka, but sends this fellow Honzô instead, to flatten my nose for me. Ha, ha, ha! Don't stir, Bannai, it is some minutes yet short of the seventh hour. Bring the fellow here, I will make short work with him."

"If that is your lordship's will," answered Bannai. "But look out, fellows," turning to the attendants. Moronaho and his obsequious follower then wetted with spittle the pin that held the blades of their swords in the handles; and rubbing the muscles of their arms, waited for Honzô, who presently appeared advancing slowly as he arranged carefully the folds of his dress. He was followed by several retainers bearing presents, which he caused to be set down before Moronaho; while he himself fell prostrate, at a respectful distance, from that haughty nobleman.

"Hah, if it please your lordship—His Highness the Shôgun Takauji lately honoured my master, Wakasanosuke, by entrusting him with the discharge of the duties of an office of great dignity; a good fortune far beyond my master's deserts, who is young and inexperienced in the duties of his post. Under these circumstances, I venture in my perplexity to request your lordship to act

c

as my master's instructor, and to advise him in the execution of his duty, so that he may perform it satisfactorily and without failing in any point. We shall all, from our master and mistress down to your servant, be overjoyed should this request be granted, and I dare to ask your lordship's acceptance of the presents, paltry though they be, which are enumerated in the list I hold in my hand, as a slight mark of respectful gratitude, a condescension we should treasure the memory of to our dying day." With these words the speaker handed a paper to Bannai ; who wonderstruck at the whole proceeding, received it without uttering a word, and unfolding it with circumspection,* read out, after a short pause, as follows :—

"Memorandum, 30 picture rolls and 30 Ôgon. These are presented by the wife of Wakasanosuke."

"Item, 20 Ôgon. These are presented by the chief councillor, Kakogaha Honzô."

"Item, 10 Ôgon. These are presented by the retainers of Wakasanosuke."

As Bannai finished reading the list, Moronaho opened his mouth wide with astonishment, unable to utter a word, and staring in a dazed way before him, while he and his follower looked at each other with the foolish expression of men who had just been told that the great mid-year feast had been put off, and were at their wits' end what to do. †

---

* Lest perchance a dagger were wrapped up in it. The story is here alluded to of the Chinese Emperor Shin-no Shikuwô (*vide* Appendix) and Keika, the minister or envoy of the King of Yen, with whom Shikuwô had been at war. The envoy presented the latter with a rolled-up map of his master's kingdom, in token of its cession. But the roll contained a dagger wrapped up in it, which, on it dropping out, Keika seized, and attempted, though fortunately without success, to plunge into the Emperor's heart.

† Probably the "Great Purification" *Minadzuki no haraye* or *Nagoshi no haraye* is referred to. Such a postponement would of course excite as much astonishment, and cause as much confusion, as a sudden adjournment of New Year's Day would give rise to. In the Calendar of Old Japan (Japan Mail, June 29th, 1878), Mr. Satow says with respect to this festival, " The liturgy used. . . . is to be found in the ' Yengi-shiki.' Its object was to get rid of and appease evil gods, says the *Yakumo Goshô*, whence the name *nagoshi* (appeasing) *no haraye* (sweeping away). The

Moronaho at last found utterance :—" Really, we are ashamed to have put you to this trouble. Bannai (in a whisper), what does all this mean ? "

" Well, it seems to me that to decline these gifts would be too harsh a reception of this gentleman's polite intentions. As to assisting his master, too, in the discharge of his duties, doubtless under present circumstances, Wakasanosuke Sama* would be put to great distress by a refusal."

" *Iya !* " said Moronaho, addressing Honzô ; " I am not capable of instructing your master, who is a clever man enough : he wants no assistance from me, I am sure. Ho there, Bannai, see that these presents are put away in a secure place. But (turning to Honzô) I had forgotten to offer you tea after your journey. Pray pardon my rudeness."

Honzô, who, in the space of a turn of the hand, had divined † the

Festival is of extremely ancient origin, and can be traced back to the very dawn of Japanese History. In its earliest form it was a means of fining those who had committed offences, or in other words, had contracted pollution, under which term all crimes and sins were at first included. The meaning of the ceremony was almost forgotten in later times, and the chief rite until lately seems to have been jumping through a hoop or ring of plaited grass, which was supposed to act as a charm against pestilence. It was also the custom to cast into a river human images made of grass or hemp, a survival of the primitive symbolical washing in order to get rid of pollution. This practice is mentioned in the famous romance entitled ' Ganji-Monogatari,' and also in verses by Teika, the well-known poet of the 13th century, and others. Orthodox Shintôists trace back the various rites which go by the name of *harae* to the washing in the sea which Izanagi-no-kami performed after his return from the region of the dead, whither he had followed his wife Izanami, to purify himself from the uncleanness there contracted. In this legend we can only recognize a myth unconsciously invented in later times to explain why death in a household was supposed to pollute the surviving inmates. The ' Great Purification ' is now held on the 15th June and 15th December, in consequence of the change of calendar.

" It is worthy of notice that the Japanese work from which we extract the principal parts of these notes (*Nen-chiu-ko-ji-yô-gen*) says that a similar ceremony of Lustration used anciently to be performed by the Chinese twice a year, in the spring and in the autumn."

* An honorific, appended to names, and answering to our Mr., Mrs., and Miss. It probably relates to the same root as *samurahi.*

† Lit., " to arrive at a result by mental arithmetic."

importance of the favourable acceptance of his gifts, prostrated himself more respectfully than ever.

"It is already the seventh hour (4 A.M.), and I must ask leave to retire. To-day the inauguration festivities take place; and I venture once more to entreat you to assist my master with your advice."

With these words Honzô rose to his feet and prepared to depart, when Moronaho detained him by the sleeve.

"Nay, nay; would you not like to be present at to-day's festivities?"

"Your servant is but an inferior follower,* and dares not venture into His Excellency's presence."

"Oh, for that matter have no fear, have no fear. No one will dare to say a word to you in my company. Besides, your master, Wakasanosuke, has some sort of a post at Court. You may look on safely, quite safely."

Thus urged, Honzô complied.

"In that case I shall be glad to be allowed to accompany your lordship. I am at your lordship's orders."

"Honzô followed Moronaho, congratulating himself upon having purchased his master's life by plastering the latter's face with money and gifts, and overjoyed at the precision of his mental arithmetic, which had brought out a result as accurate as if the calculations had been worked out upon the *soroban*,† without one slip of peg or ball. So the Councillor of Wakasanosuke, crafty, white-haired old rat, kept straight on in the path of fidelity, loyalty and devotion, and passed with Moronaho through the Great Gate.

Almost immediately afterwards Yenya came up in a norimon. His retainers remained behind, while Hayano Kampei, his hereditary vassal, caused the norimon in which his master was seated to be set down, and rustling in his yellow, figured, wide-pocketed, hemp-cloth trousers, made for the Great Gate, exclaiming in a loud voice, "I have to announce the arrival of Yenya Hanguwan Takasada."

---

* Lit., "follower of a follower."
† The Japanese abacus or calculating board. *Vide* Appendix.

"Wakasanosuke Sama," said a gateward, coming forward, "has just gone in, as well as Moronaho Sama. Both asked after your master. Be pleased to enter at once."

Yenya, alighting from his norimon, exclaimed,

"How, Kampei, am I the last to arrive? How unfortunate that I should be so late!" and hastened through the gate as he spoke, followed by Kampei.

Meanwhile the sound of singing was heard from the interior of the palace, where the festivities had already commenced; and the words of the old song,

> " Harima's sandy beach we touch,
> Takasago's noted shore,"

were borne towards the Great Gate, wafted on the breeze which lightly rustled amid the branches of a willow tree that grew hard by. More graceful than the willow itself, a maiden, over whose head some eighteen * or nineteen springs † had passed, with eyebrows slender as the young shoots of a pine tree, who had been brought up in a strict household, and was no less modest than beautiful, came up to the gate, accompanied by a number of servants carrying lanterns that bore the device of the house of Yenya.

"Ho, there ! men," cried the young girl, "dawn is breaking, and as you cannot enter within the gate, you may retire. . . . . Kampei, Kampei," she continued, looking round after the servants who had accompanied her had withdrawn, "where can you be? I have a message for you; pray don't delay."

While she was still peering about, Kampei, coming forward in the half-gloom, caught sight of her.

---

* There is a sort of pun, or rather rebus, here in the original text as unsusceptible as unworthy of translation. It is one of a kind not unfrequently met with in Chinese books, and may be thus shortly explained. The character for "pine tree" consists of three parts, two meaning the numbers 10 and 8 respectively, and the third pronounced "*ku,*" equivalent to "*k u,*" "*nine.*" Herein is involved the fact of the girl being eighteen or nineteen years of age.

† We should say "summers." summer being our most agreeable season : but in Japan, spring is the most, and summer the least, agreeable of the seasons.

"What, O Karu, you here?"

"Oh! I am so glad, I wanted so much to see you."

"But what does this mean? While it is yet dark, without a servant—all by yourself?"

"Nay, some servants came with me, but I have just dismissed them, and so am left alone. But I have a message for you from my mistress." And presenting a letter box * to Kampei, the girl continued: "She said I was to tell you to hand this to your master, and to ask him to be good enough to give it to Moronaho as my lady's answer, with her excuses and compliments. At first, fearing there might be some mistake in the middle of all this feasting, my mistress told me to put off giving you the message for the night. But I wanted to see you, and said, had not the letter better be given at once? and so I was allowed to come, and I have run here so quickly that I am almost dead for want of breath,"—panting as she spoke.

"Good! my master shall hand the letter-case to Moronaho. I will go and deliver it; wait for me.'

As he uttered the last words, a voice cried loudly from within, "Kampei, Kampei, your master, Hanguwan, is calling for you. Kampei, Kampei."

"*Hai, hai*, I come. *Yeh !* have a little patience."

And quitting † the girl, the youth hastened towards the palace. He had hardly gone when Bannia Sagisaka came up with a stealthy gait, like a heron trampling upon lampreys in a rice swamp.

"Hah, O Karu," he cried, "how love sharpens one's wits. Just as the youngster was babbling in your ear, to shout out 'Kampei, Kampei, your master is calling for you !'—a capital idea, was it not? My lord Moronaho has a favour to ask of you, pray accompany me. You will let me have just one. . . . .

---

* Letters in Japan are sent in oblong lacquered boxes (often called and used as glove-boxes by foreigners), which are tied with silk cord or paper string, and sometimes seal-impressed as well.

† Lit., " shaking off and separating sleeves."

THE BRUTALITY of SAKISAKA BANNA.

And the fellow, as he spoke, endeavoured to embrace her.

" Let me go," exclaimed the frightened girl; "how dare you use me thus rudely—within the precincts of the palace, too.  Away, villain," escaping from his grasp, "away ruffian."

" Don't be so hard," replied Bannai.  "Come it is still dark enough to prevent any one seeing us—just for a moment."

And seizing her hand, he was on the point of dragging her away, when loud cries of " Bannai, Bannai, the lord Moronaho is calling for you.  Bannai, Bannai," interrupted him, and two men came forward through the gloom, looking anxiously around.  They were not long in catching sight of Bannai, with whom Karu was still struggling, and exclaimed, angrily: "What are you about, Bannai? the lord Moronaho has been asking for you some time.  What! ill-treating a woman, within the precincts of the court, too?  Shame on you, you ill-bred villain !"

" *Yeh!* what are you fellows saying?" muttered the wretch; and quitting the spot, the crestfallen* scoundrel made his way hurriedly towards the palace.

Kampei appeared immediately afterwards: "Hah, O Karu, did you understand my device?  That Bannai is well tricked now.  I knew that if I were to shout out that his lord wanted him, that he would cry 'stale trick;' and to avoid such a result I bribed those two fellows with a little *saké* to shout out instead of me.  He will own the trick is not a stale one for this once, I think; ha, ha, ha!  And now that this Bannai's affair is settled, will you not stay and let me talk with you for a little while?"  And the youth took her hand as he spoke.

"No, no," said the girl; "you take my breath away.  Why, what have you got to say to me, I wonder; cannot you wait?"

" Wait!" replied the youth; "why, it will be daylight in a few moments.  Come, you must not refuse me."

After some further show of reluctance, the girl yielded to her lover's entreaties, exclaiming, however, half repentantly,

---

* Lit., "with swollen features."

"But, suppose some one should pass by here?" As she spoke, a verse of the old poem, "Takasago," was again borne by upon the breeze—

"'Neath the pine tree will we sit."

"Hark!" exclaimed Kampei, "are not the words apt? let us, too, sit down here." And seizing the girl's hand in his, he led her gently away.

Meanwhile the guests were being entertained with various musical and recitative performances, in which the praises of Nahoyoshi, together with felicitations on the prosperity of the Empire, were sung to the sound of drums and kettledrums, while his Highness' continued well-being was the desire of every heart.

Momonoi, who had for some time been on the watch for Moronaho, seeing that the latter did not arrive, rambled about the palace in search of him. The long trowsers of his court dress were well girded up; his ears were open to every sound; his sword-blade was loose in its sheath; while he held his breath, bent upon cutting down his enemy the moment he appeared.

Moronaho, ignorant of Momonoi's presence, approached the spot where the latter was standing; and while yet some distance from him, recognised the wrathful noble.

"Ho, there! Sir Wakasanosuke,* cried the lord of Musashi, "you are early at your post ; nothing, to be sure, can exceed your attention to your duties. I have a favour to beg of you, but hardly dare put my request into words." As he spoke, the wily courtier took both his swords out of his girdle and threw them on the ground at Wakasanosuke's feet. "To tell the whole truth," he continued, "I was most rude to you the other day at Tsurugaoka ; and, doubtless, you were very angry, as indeed you had good right to be. I cannot understand how I came to address such rough words to you. I hardly know what they were; but I shall regret my ill-breeding all my life. See, I, a wearer of two swords, am your suppliant. You are a man of the world and will understand me. Were you an

---

* Momonoi Wakasanosuke.

桃井若狭之助 高ノ師直

塒ノ服立井桃

THE APPEASEMENT OF WAKASANOSUKE.

ignorant fellow, I should doubtless have to dread being cut down
by you. I tried to follow you, clasping my hands and begging your
forgiveness. Ah, I am an old man, of little use, now. You must
show some favour to my years. See, I, a *Samurahi*, have cast my
swords at your feet, and am a suppliant before you; it cannot be
that you will not listen to me. I know that I have been wrong:
wrong in every way and repeatedly; but I and my follower, Bannai,
entreat you to let your anger cease."

Wakasanosuke, as he listened to this bribe-bought flattery, thought
he was dreaming. His threatening arm hung irresolute;* now was
the moment to draw weapon, but he could not unsheathe his freshly
whetted sword, and found himself obliged to hold it in the reverse
attitude to that of fighting. Honzô watched the scene with anxiety
from behind a neighbouring bush, without so much as winking, so
intense was his suspense, while his master let his head fall upon
his breast in dumb wonder.

"Ho! Bannai," added Moronaho, "that fellow Yenya! what
means his delay? This gentleman," turning to Momonoi, "gives
a different attention to his duties. As to Yenya he is nothing less
than an ill-bred clown, not to have shown his face yet. Like master,
like man; he has clearly no councillor wise enough to urge him to
perform his duty with propriety. Come, Sir," turning again to
Wakasanosuke, "we will go to his Excellency. Pray forget my wrong-
headedness, and do me the honour to accompany me."

"I think I must ask your lordship to excuse me, I am not very
well; pray do not wait for me."

"I am sorry to hear you are not well, pray what is the matter?
Bannai, rub this gentleman's back, and send for some cordial."

"Nay, there is no need I should give such trouble."

"But at all events you will do well to rest awhile. I will look to
all arrangements being properly carried out. Bannai, conduct this
gen'leman to an apartment."

---

* Lit., "out of tune with the opportunity."

Wakasanosuke felt as much embarrassed by this excessive attention as if he had been suddenly invited to enter the Mikado's car. However, he accompanied Bannai, to the delight of Honzô, who thanking earnestly heaven and earth for the success that had attended his scheme, contentedly withdrew.

Immediately afterwards Yenya appeared, making his way towards the palace. Moronaho, who was standing under the verandah, saw him passing by and called out angrily, " You are late, you are late ! what is the meaning of this carelessness? You were to have been here at the seventh hour (about 4 A.M.) precisely. Did you not receive my message to that effect?"

" It is true, my lord," replied Yenya, "that I am later than I ought to be. I must ask you to excuse me; but I am still in time, I think." So saying he took a letter-box from his sleeve pocket, and handed it to Moronaho.

"One of my servants," he added, "came to me with this just now, asking me to give it into your hands. It is from my wife, Kawoyo."

" Is it so?" said the lord of Musashi, taking the box. " Ha ! I understand; your wife knows that I am fond of verse-making, and has sent me some lines of her own for correction."

With these words the Shiuttô* opened the case, and taking out a paper, began to read it :

> " Thus in truth it may not be,
> That over the heavy day-dress
> A night-garment should be thrown.
> O'er a bordered robe (day-robe)
> Who would throw a borderless one (night-robe)? †

---

* Lit., the chief—as of a department—here, probably, equivalent to High Commissioner.

† There is a word-play here. The last two lines mean also,

> " To one who is not my spouse,
> How may I, a spouse, be united?"

the word "*Tsuma*" meaning either a married person or the hem or border of a garment.

"Ha! from the New Selection of Ancient and Modern Poems. No correction of mine wanted here, it would seem."

Moronaho understood that his suit was rejected, and felt sure that Yenya had opened the box. Angry at the idea, he yet managed to conceal his ill-humour; and with an appearance of unconcern, asked Yenya if he had read the paper.

"I saw it just now for the first time."

"H'm, well, you heard me read—oh, your wife is a model of virtue. See what she sends me. 'One who is not my spouse.' A model of virtue! a model of virtue! what a fortunate man you are! That is the reason probably of your inattentiveness. You stick at home tied to your wife's apron, and give no thought to your duties here."

All this invective was really occasioned by the refusal of Kawoyo, but Yenya, who did not know of this, could not understand Moronaho's conduct. He managed, however, to restrain his indignation.

"Ha, ha, ha! your lordship is merry; doubtless your lordship has been passing the bottle round a little."

"Passing the bottle; passing the bottle; what does the clown mean? Passing the bottle or not, I manage to attend to the duties of my office. As for you, you neglect them. Explain that to me. Have you been 'passing the bottle,' or sticking at home glued to your wife's side? You had better take a leaf out of Wakasanosuke's book. Oh, your wife is a model of virtue, eh? a charming woman! writes most elegantly! You may well be proud of her. Nay, don't look angry, man; what I say is all true enough. Now, your wife's verses here—— If you have such a treasure at home, we cannot expect you to come to court. You fellows who remain at home remind one of *funa*\* in a well. These tiny fish—are you listening to what I say?—think that neither in heaven nor on earth is there any place comparable with the miserable hole, some three or four feet across at the most, in which they live. They have never seen any other

---

\* "Funa" (*Carassius Langsdorfi*).

place, and when they are brought up from the bottom in a bucket, and then thrown into the stream, they cannot make out where they are, and flounder helplessly about, until at last they knock their heads against the posts of some bridge. You, and such as you, are just like these carplets. Ha ! ha ! ha !"

Yenya, at this insulting speech, lost his patience, and exclaimed, angrily :

" You must be out of your senses—you must be mad, Moronaho."

"Pshaw, fellow ! darest twit me with being mad ? Me, the *Shiutto !* the Lord Moronaho !"

" H'm, then, your insults are meant as such ?"

" *Kudoi Kudoi !* what a troublesome fellow it is. And if meant, what then ?"

"Why, this, then ;" and drawing his sword, the enraged noble-man aimed a stroke at Moronaho, which the latter tried to avoid by ducking his head and leaping nimbly aside. The blade, however, cut through his tall cap, and inflicted a wound on his forehead between the eyebrows. His assailant again raised his weapon, but Moronaho managed to shuffle out of reach, and made his escape ; while Honzô, who had witnessed the whole scene, ran up and caught Yenya's arm.

" Restrain yourself, Sir, I pray you." Yenya struggled to free him-self from his detainer's grasp, glaring after his enemy, who was making off as well as he could, stumbling at every step.

"That fellow Moronaho," exclaimed Yenya, "will get away ; let me go, Honzô. He shall feel the weight of my arm. Let me go, let me go."

Meanwhile, the scene of the quarrel became rapidly thronged with nobles, high and low ; some making towards where the dispute had taken place, their hands on their swords ; others flying to the assistance of Moronaho. Indescribable confusion ensued ; the gates were closed, and lanterns began to flash about in all directions.

Hayano Kampei, hearing the uproar, was filled with anxiety ; and running up to the Rear Gate, knocked at it as if he would shatter it into pieces, crying loudly : "I am Hayano Kampei, clansman of

THE QUARREL BETWEEN YENYA AND MORONAHO.

Yenya Hanguwan. My lord may be in danger, and I must be at his side. Open, open, quick."

" This is the Rear Gate," cried the Gateward; " you must go round to the Great Gate if you are in the suite of some nobleman."

" No. no;" exclaimed the vassal of Yenya, "this gate will do well enough. Besides, the Great Gate seems besieged by such a crowd of retainers that it would be impossible to get at it even if mounted on a good horse. What is the meaning of all this disturbance?"

" The disturbance is at an end," replied the Gateward. " Yenya grievously insulted the Shiutt Moronaho, and for this offence is to be confined to his house, where he is now being carried in a net-covered norimon."

" *Namu sambo,** conveyed home a prisoner?" cried Kampei.

He was on the point of hastening after his lord, when he was arrested by the thought, that the sentence of confinement would entail a closure of the gates of the castle. Pacing up and down, uncertain how to act; in the midst of his embarrassment he was joined by the maid Karu, whom he had left behind when he hurried to the gate to see what was the cause of the uproar.

"Oh, Kampei," cried the girl, "I have heard all about it. What is to be done? What is to be done?"

The girl clung to her lover, sobbing as she spoke.

Kampei, however, thrust her aside, saying : " *Yeh!* what is the use of puling? Listen! my honour as a soldier and a clansman is gone. Gone! do you hear? And now nothing remains for me but this ;" grasping, as he spoke, the handle of his sword.

" Kampei, not that, not that, I implore you. You do not know what you are doing in your bewilderment."

" Bewilderment! I may well be bewildered, to find that I have been absent from my lord's side in the hour of danger; that men are conveying him away, a prisoner, in a net-covered norimon, like

---

* A portion of a Buddhist prayer, commonly used in former days as an exclamation.

a criminal; that the gates of his castle are closed upon him; while I, his born vassal, have been spending my time in toying with you. How can I ever again wear two swords before the face of men? Let me go: let me go."

The girl, however, continued to cling to him, exclaiming: "If only for a moment, listen to me. You must listen to me. What you say is quite true; but whose doing is it that your honour as a clansman is tainted? Is it not mine, mine? 'Tis for me, then, not for you, to die. If you should die now on this spot, how will any one know your motives? And not knowing your motives, how will any one be able to praise your deed as that of a true clansman?

Oh! Kampei," the girl continued, "be guided by me; come with me for a time at least to my village, where my father and mother are still living. They will do everything they can for you. Kampei, let our common misery plead for me; let your affianced wife's words persuade you"—bursting with a loud sob into a flood of tears as she spoke the last words.

"Well, perhaps that were best," said Kampei, irresolutely, "our lord's chief councillor, Ohoboshi Yuranosuke, is away at one of our master's estates—you could not know this, being but lately come among us. I can wait for his return, and then implore pardon for my disloyalty and neglect. Come, let us away."

They were on the point of departing, when Sagisaka Bannai suddenly made his appearance, followed by several armed men.

"Yeh! Kampei," he exclaimed, "your master has been employing himself in heaping insults upon Moronaho, His Highness' Shiuttô, and has actually dared to wound him within the court precincts; for which offence, strictly forbidden as you know, he has been confined to his house, and no doubt ere long his head will be made to fly from his shoulders."

"Sah!" continued Bannai in a loud voice, turning suddenly to his attendants, "seize this fellow, bind him, and prepare to hew the scoundrel in pieces."

"Yeh!" cried Kampei, "nothing could be more opportune. Come

Sir Stork,* you are not equal to gobbling me up without assistance, it seems; but here is my arm thin as an onion stalk. Come and try what it tastes like, all of you."

"Silence!" shouted Bannai. "Upon him, men."

"At your service, gentlemen."

Bannai's attendants, four in number, rushed upon the follower of Yenya, and attempted to seize him; Kampei, however, eluded their onset, and grasping a couple of his assailants by the arm, twisted them suddenly round, and spurned them with his feet right and left. They returned to the attack, but he parried their strokes with his scabbard, and hurled them on either side with the hilt and point of his sword, on the top of each other, like skewered *dengaku* cakes.† Daunted by his prowess, his assailants did not attempt to renew the fight, but made away in panic-struck confusion. Bannai, beside himself with rage, then flew at Kampei; but the latter avoided the blow, and, seizing his antagonist, hurled him to earth with such violence that he turned head over heels as he fell. The victor, placing his foot on his prostrate enemy's neck, exclaimed: "Shall I stab you or slash you, or hew you in pieces?" raising his weapon as he spoke.

Karu, however, ran up to her lover, and laid her hand upon his arm. "Hold!" she cried. "To kill the wretch may destroy your chance of pardon. The fellow has had sufficient."

Bannai, meanwhile, had wriggled from under his enemy's foot and made off as hard as he could, crestfallen enough, and in mortal fear for his life.

"Yeh!" cried Kampei, "it is a pity the rascal should get away, too; but, as you say, it might be adding disloyalty to disloyalty to slay the wretch just now. Well, we must away and hide ourselves, and wait for an opportunity of procuring pardon."

The sixth hour was now long past, and the low clouds on the eastern horizon were whitening with the dawn, while the crows* were leaving

---

* Alluding to the name Sagisaka; "Sagi" meaning a stork.

† A sort of thin cake of baked bean-curd.

their perches, filling the air with their mournful caw as they flew by the lovers, who hastened on their way towards the girl's home, their hearts heavy with grief as they bemoaned the evil days that had come upon their lord's house, and tremblingly asked themselves what fate was reserved for him.

---

\* There is a sort of appropriateness in mentioning the crows here. The caw or croak of these birds is supposed to resemble in sound the repetition of the word *Ka-uai* (pronounced "kah why"), "love."

END OF BOOK THIRD.

THE MEANNESS OF KUDAIU.

"Ho there, young sir," cried the chief of the retainers, "you are early in your attendance."

"It is my duty, as you know, sir," replied Rikiya, "to be at hand from morn till night until my father returns from the provinces."

"And well you perform that duty." So saying, Goyemon prostrated himself, and addressing the Lady Kawoyo, exclaimed, "We venture to inquire after our lord's health."

"I thank you heartily, gentlemen," said the wife of Yenya. "Of late my lord has looked far from well, and I am in sad trouble lest some illness should declare itself. Night and morning he keeps his eye fixed upon yonder mound, now brilliant with flowers: and seems to take so much pleasure in the contemplation of their bright hues that I have caused rare cherry blossoms to be sought out, and have had them arranged as you see, in the hope of affording him some distraction."

"Ah! lady," cried Goyemon, "I understand your thought. As the flowers open out so will the gates be thrown open, and the order of confinement rescinded. It is well thought of. Would that your servant, Goyemon, too, were a less clumsy fellow, and could hit upon some such mode of alleviating our lord's distress. However, lady, I would ask your attention for a moment. I have something of importance to communicate to you. I understand that commissioners are to come here to-day, and I do not doubt but that their orders are to set our lord at liberty. What do you think, Kudaiu?" turning suddenly to his companion.

"Well," answered the latter, "if you ask my opinion, Goyemon, why—do you see those blossoms there? they are pleasant enough to look upon just now; but let a puff of wind come, and their beauty is all blown away in a moment. So too with your words. They are pleasing enough to hear, but think you it is fitting that you, a *samurahi*, should utter such honeyed phrases, as devoid of meaning, if stripped of their show, as mere New Year's compliments? You know what I mean. You know the gravity of our lord's offence, how, honoured by His Highness with a post at Court, in connection with the festivities at Tsuruga-oka, he yet dared to lift his hand against the *Shiuttô!* Within the palace precincts too! The punishment for such a crime is banishment, if viewed leniently; if not, an order of self-dispatch. What but misfortune can be expected to result from opposition to the Lord Moronaho?"

"Enough, enough," broke in Goyemon. "You talk of banishment and self-dispatch as if you rather desired our lord should be so punished————"

"Not so! *iya!*" exclaimed Kudaiu, in some haste; "I desire nothing of the kind. But I am a man of plain speech, and speak the plain truth. And let me tell you, Goyemon, that all this trouble is caused by your own parsimony. If you had but plastered Moronaho's face with gold, things would never have come to this pass;" trying to dissimulate the mean expression of his face, that displayed so plainly his true nature.

"No, *samurahi*," said Goyemon; "no one wearing the two swords of a gentleman could condescend so to grovel before any one. Rikiya will bear me out in what I say."

Desirous of keeping matters smooth, Kawoyo interfered :—

"Pray let there be no quarrelling, gentlemen. It is I, in truth, who am the unfortunate cause of my husband's distress; and I only. Some few days ago, at the festivities at Tsuruga-oka, Moronaho, who is an unmannerly fellow, dared to speak to me, a wedded wife, of unlawful love. Pestered by his importunity, but without saying a word to my husband, I tried to make him understand how shameful was his conduct, and how vain were his attempts, by a few lines from a well-known song which I sent to him. Enraged by my refusal, he wreaked his vengeance upon my husband by covering him with insults, and Yenya, who is of a hasty temper, at last lost command of himself, and so committed the offence for which he is now confined."

The cause of their lord's disturbance of mind was now plain to Goyemon and Rikiya, and their faces betrayed their concern. At this juncture the sound of voices was heard proceeding from the parlour by the entrance porch, and presently the arrival of the Commissioners was

announced, who were demanding, to be at once conducted to the inner
apartments. The Lady Kawoyo upon this came down into the body
of the apartment, and with Goyemon and Rikiya advanced to meet
the Commissioners, who presented themselves the next moment. The
Commissioners—there were two of them—were an esquire of Moronaho's
named Ishido Umanojô, and a *samurahi* called Yakushiji Jirôzayemon.
As they were on duty they did not return the salutations offered them,
but seated themselves at once at the upper end of the apartment.
Hardly had they done so when a partition was moved back, and
Yenya Hanguwan entered the room with dignified composure.

"Ha! Ishido dono, you come officially? I am ashamed of being
the cause of so much trouble to you. Ho, there! offer *saké* to the
gentlemen. There can be no harm in a draught to chase away bad
spirits; and the purport of your visit can meanwhile be explained
to me."

"Capital!" cried Yakushiji; "I have no objection, I am sure.
But," he continued with a sneer, "if you knew the purport of our visit,
I think the *saké* would stick in your throat."

Ishido now said : "We are ordered to make an official communication to you, to which we demand your attention."

So saying, the Commissioner drew a paper from his breast, and
unfolded it, while Hanguwan arranged himself on his mat, and assumed
an attitude of respectful attention. Ishido then read out the paper,
which was to the following effect:—"Lately, Yenya Hanguwan
Takasada, following the promptings of private malice, drew his weapon
on the Shiuttô, the Lord Moronaho, and created a tumult within the
precincts of the palace, on account of which crime his estates are hereby
ordered to be confiscated, and himself is decreed to commit self-
dispatch."

As the Commissioner concluded, the Lady Kawoyo and the
assembled retainers were filled with sudden terror, regarding each
other with trembling amazement. Hanguwan, however, remained
unmoved. Without changing a muscle of his countenance he exclaimed, quite calmly, "I understand perfectly. But now, gentle-

THE MESSAGE OF DEATH.

# BOOK THE FOURTH.

———

## THE SEPPUKU OF YENYA.

IN accordance with the sentence of seclusion pronounced against Yenya Hanguwan, that nobleman was strictly confined in his mansion of Ogiga-yatsu, all communication with which was rigorously prohibited. While things were thus, the ladies of the household in the inner apartments passed the time in all manner of elegant diversions. One day, shortly after the event mentioned in the Third Book, young Rikiya was in attendance upon the Lady Kawoyo, and in the hope of cheering his lord had brought a basketful of rare eight and nine-fold wild-cherry blossoms, gathered upon the hills around Kamakura; himself more pleasing for the eyes to dwell upon than the flowers themselves. Presently Hara Goyemon, the chief of the retainers, passing under the verandah in front of the willow-room,* followed by Ono Kudaiu, approached the son of Yuranosuke.

———

* The partition-slides of which were ornamented with paintings of willow-trees. Similarly decorated apartments were common in the mansions of the old nobility, doubtless in imitation of the "willow halls" of the Imperial Palace at Kiyôto.

Meanwhile a confused sound of knocking in the partition resounded from the adjoining apartment, and the voices of a number of clansmen were heard clamouring for permission to look once more upon their lord's face while in life, and begging Goyemon to obtain that favour for them. Goyemon, accordingly, asked the condemned nobleman to allow the retainers to enter.

" What is this?" cried Yenya. " Yet their request is proper enough! But they must wait until Yuranosuke returns."

Goyemon bowed assent, and addressing himself to the clansmen, exclaimed : " You have heard our lord's will. You cannot enter yet; not one of you.

They did not utter a word in reply, and complete silence reigned in the apartment in which they still remained assembled. Rikiya, meanwhile, at a sign from Yenya, had placed the sword with which the self-dispatch was to be accomplished, and which had been pre- viously got ready, before his lord, who, after composedly throwing back the shoulder-folds of the *kamishimo*, arranged himself in a suitable position.*

" And now, Sirs," said Yenya, addressing the Commissioners; " I call upon you to be witnesses to my obedience."

He drew a three-cornered stand towards himself as he spoke, and taking up the short sword that lay upon it, lifted it respectfully to his forehead.

" Rikiya, Rikiya."

" My lord."

" Yuranosuke?"

" He is not yet returned, your lordship."

" Alas ! and yet I wished so greatly to see him once more in life. There is so much to be arranged—but now—— "

As he uttered the last words the unfortunate nobleman grasped the sword, point downwards, in his bow-hand, and with one movement ripped himself open.

---

* So as to fall forward in the death-agony. To fall backwards was considered ignominious.

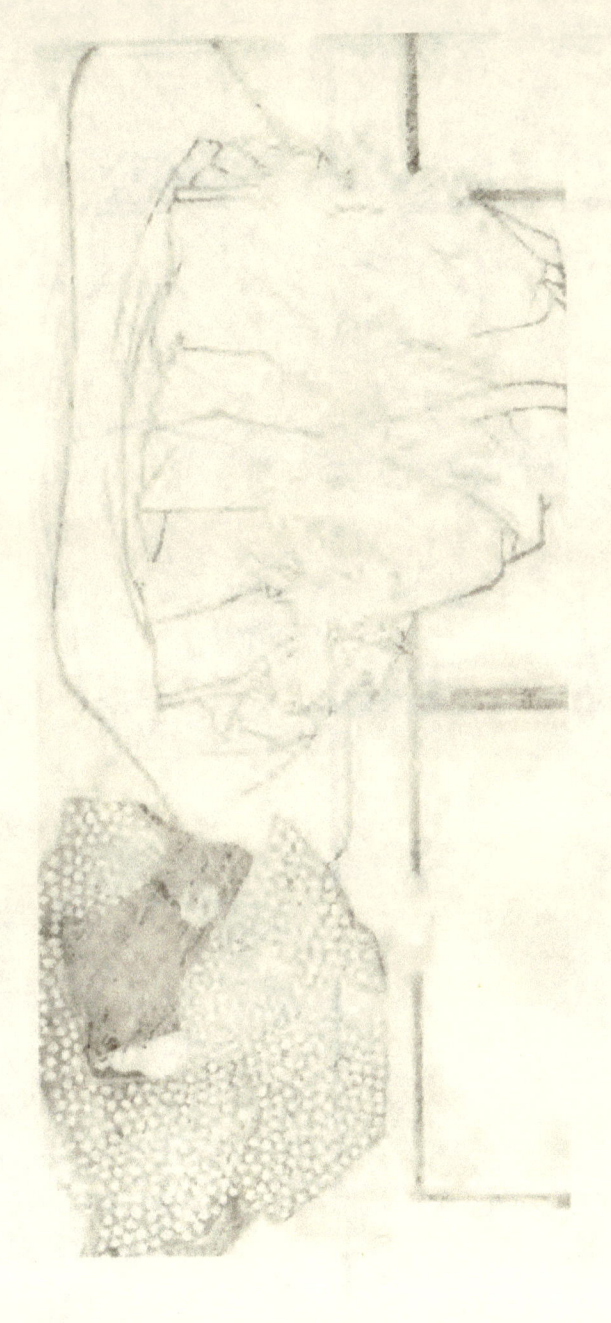

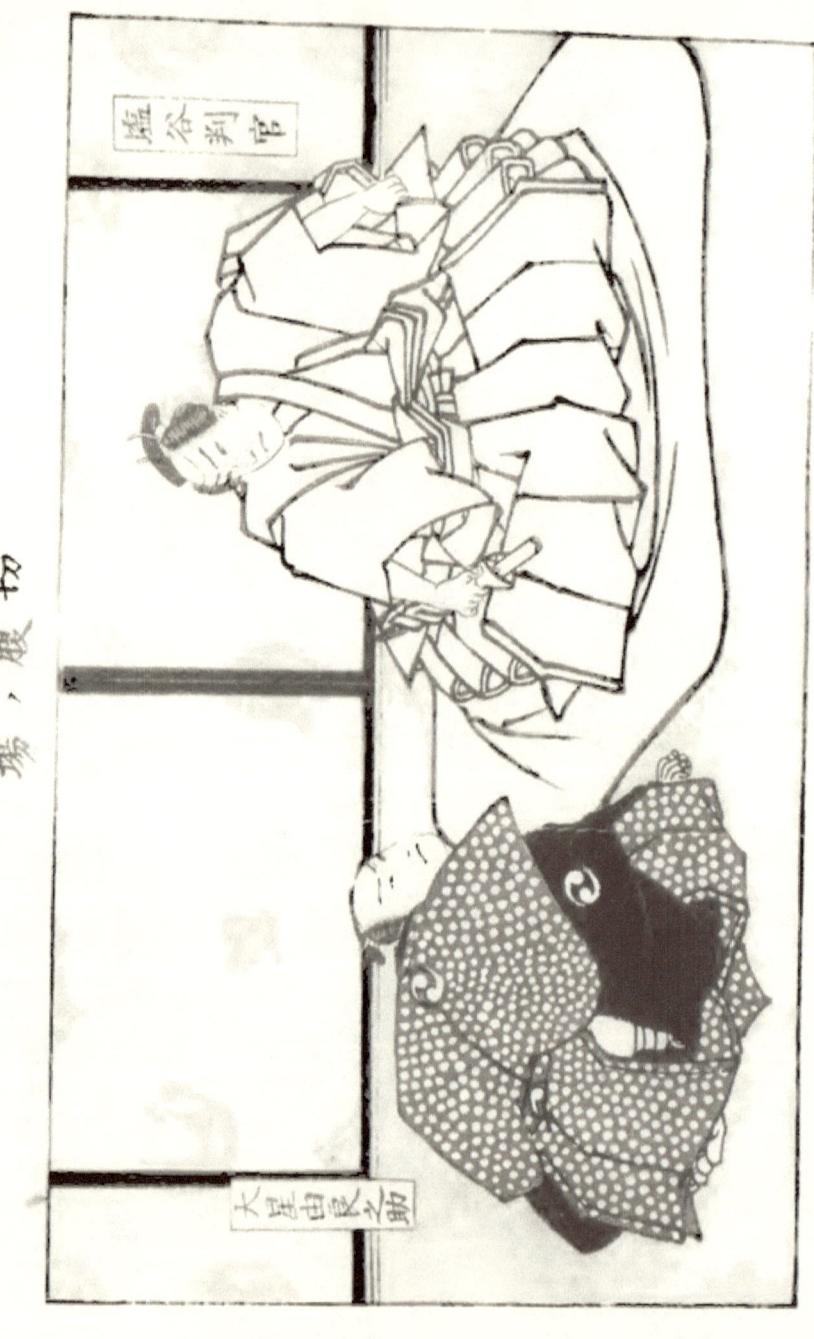

傷ノ腰切

塩谷判官

大星由良之助

The Lady Kawoyo closed her eyes with horror and anguish; and with the tears streaming down her cheeks, muttered to herself a Buddhic prayer for the dying.

Presently a panel of the partition that separated the apartment where this scene was being enacted from the outer corridor, was pushed suddenly back, and Ohoboshi Yuranosuke burst into the room, followed closely by Senzaki, Yazama, and a crowd of other retainers. As soon as he saw his lord's plight he started, and then made his obeisance.

"Hah, Yuranosuke!—you see I could not longer delay."

"At least I am thankful that I am in time once more to look upon my lord's face in life."

"And I, too, am glad to see you, Yuranosuke, ere I die. You know all, doubtless. 'Tis a pitiful story enough of unsatisfied vengeance."

"Ay, my lord, I know all. But this is not the time to dwell upon the details of what has happened. My only prayer now is, that my lord's death may be such as befits a brave *samurahi.*"

"Do not fear for that," cried Yenya, and, seizing the sword with both hands, he widened the gash he had already inflicted upon himself. Gasping for breath he continued, speaking with difficulty: "Yuranosuke —this sword—my dying gift to you—you will exact vengeance. Then stabbing himself in the throat, he threw aside the blood-stained weapon with a last effort, and Yenya Hanguwan Takasada rolled over on his face—dead.

The Lady Kawoyo and the retainers present started back in affright, closing their eyes horror-struck at the terrible sight; while their sobs and the grinding of their teeth showed the grief and rage that were in their hearts.

Yuranosuke meanwhile dragged himself* close to the corpse, and grasping the fatal weapon, lifted it reverently to his forehead. Fixing his eyes earnestly on the blood-stained point, he clenched his fist

---

* Lit., shuffled—a peculiar theatrical gait.

convulsively; while in a flood of tears he gave vent to the sorrow and passion that consumed him.

The misery of his lord's agony had penetrated to the inmost depths of his retainer's heart,[*] and it was at this moment that there arose in Yuranosuke's breast those sentiments of unswerving devotedness and loyalty to his dead chief's memory, that have made the name of Ohoboshi famous for ever.

Yakushiji, springing suddenly to his feet, exclaimed:

"Now, my masters, Hanguwan is dead and done for. You can take yourselves off. Away with you."

"You are too hasty, Yakushiji," said his colleague. "Yenya Hanguwan was a lord of province and castle; and proper arrangements must be made for the funeral rites. Therefore," turning to the clansmen, "pray understand that there is no intention of driving you hurriedly away from the castle. I will myself draw up a brief report showing that I have, in the execution of my duty, witnessed the self-dispatch of your master. And now, Sir Yuranosuke," addressing himself to the *Karô*,[†] "I fully understand your distress. If I can render you any service pray do not forget to avail yourself of my assistance."

As he concluded, the Commissioner courteously saluted the retainers of Yenya, and composedly took his departure.

"For my part I want this dead body removed, at any rate," cried Yakushiji. "Meanwhile I will snatch some repose within yonder. Ho! Some of you, throw these fellows' rubbish out of doors. As to Yenya's property—and you," turning to the clansmen, "away with you and turn into *rônin*[‡] as fast as you please." Glaring fiercely round, he then strode out of the apartment. As soon as he had gone the Lady Kawoyo suddenly lifted up her voice and exclaimed in a piteous tone:—

"Alas! alas! my friends, was ever condition more distressful than

---

[*] Lit., wrung his five entrails and six viscera—an expression borrowed from the Chinese.

[†] Lit., "house-elder;" the title of the chief councillor of a Daimiyô.

[‡] Clansmen dismissed from, or who had abandoned, the service of their master: lit., "Wave-men;" *i.e.,* "Vagabonds."

yours! Oh! that I had said all that I wanted to say to my lord in his agony! But I did not know what to do. I was afraid of exciting the contempt of the Commissioners; and so I have forborne from speaking until now. I cannot tell you how miserable I am." And falling upon the corpse, her grief overwhelmed her, and she burst into a flood of tears.

Yuranosuke now called to his son: "Rikiya, you will accompany our mistress, and at once convey the body of our dead master to the family burying-place at the Temple of Kômyô. I shall follow close after you, and charge myself with the ordering of the funeral ceremonies. Hori, Yazama, Odera, Hasama, and the rest of the retainers will go with you as escort."

A norimon was immediately brought forward, and the body reverently lifted and placed within, amid the tears of all present.

Yuranosuke tried to console the Lady Kawoyo, who was beside herself with grief, while the clansmen strove each to be one of the bearers, or, at least, to accompany the corpse. At last all was ready, the more fortunate bore off their dead lord, while their comrades, who remained behind, looked wistfully after them. As these seated themselves, Kudaiu, who was amongst them, exclaimed:

"Well, Ohoboshi, the office of *Karô* has been hereditary in your family ever since the days of your ancestor Hachiman Rokuro. And I, too, have been accorded a place at the right hand of him whom they are bearing off yonder. But now we are all made *rônin*; and as we have to find food for our wives and children, why should we not lay hands upon the treasure amassed by our lord, divide it amongst ourselves, and leave the castle without further delay? For Yakushiji is sure to be offended if we stop here much longer."

"I think quite differently from Kudaiu," said one of the clansmen, Senzaki by name. "It seems to me that as long as our enemy, the Lord Moronaho, lives, vengeance is our care. Let us wait here until he comes to dislodge us; and die, if necessary, upon our own ground."

"I say, No," cried Sadakurô, son of Kudaiu. "The notion of dying upon our own ground is a silly one. I am of the same opinion as my father, let us ransack the place, divide what we find, and then get away. That would be really sensible conduct."

Yuranosuke quietly intervened:—"I am quite of Yagorô's opinion. We ought, according to old custom, to slay ourselves for the sake of our dead lord. But instead of a cruel self dispatch, would it not be better to await the force which Ashikaga may send against us, and die in resisting it with our utmost determination?"

"*Yah!* what say you there?" said Kudaiu. "Is that your sage counsel? What, we miserable *rônin* puff ourselves up with the notion of drawing bow against Ashikaga! A silly proceeding enough that would be, and one in which Kudaiu, at all events, will have no part."

"You are right, father," chimed in his son, "you are right. What these gentlemen propose is to me unintelligible. However, what need to prolong this discussion? It is waste of time to remain here. Let us away, father."

"We will, we will," replied the latter. "And you, gentlemen, remain here if you choose! It won't be for long," he added derisively. Kudaiu and his son then took their departure together.

"Pah!" cried Senzaki, "what a covetous wretch that Kudaiu is! The pair were anxious to beat a retreat the moment they heard us talk of resistance. Cowards! But we need not concern ourselves with them, let us prepare ourselves to meet the attack."

"Ah! not so fast, Yagorô," broke in Yuranosuke. "What have we against Ashikaga that we should draw bow against him? What I said just now was only to find out the real sentiment of the precious pair who have just left us. Let Yakushiji take possession of the mansion, and bitter though it be to leave this place, let us make our way to Yamashina near Miyako; there I will unfold to you my designs, and we can then arrange upon some plan of carrying them out." The last words were hardly out of his mouth, when Yakushiji suddenly made his appearance.

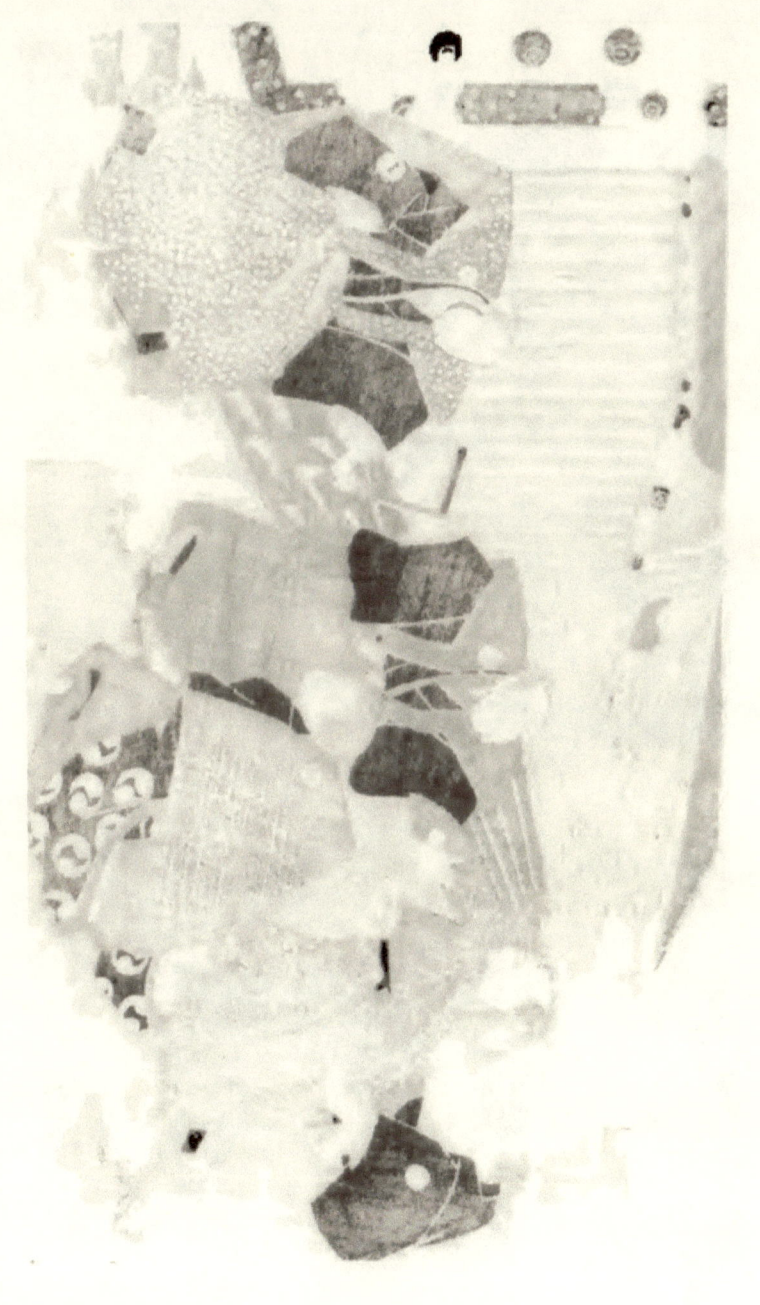

撥　渡　橋

大星由良之介

原郷右エ門

片山源右エ門

大星力弥

大鷲文右

THE OATH OF VENGEANCE

"Ho, there!" he said with a snarl, "your conference seems long enough. If the body has been removed, what do you linger here for? Leave the place at once without further delay."

"Hah!" broke in Goyemon, "your lordship cannot wait, it would seem? Well, there are our dead lord's arms, armour, and horse gear, look them well over and take them. Come, Sir Yuranosuke, let us withdraw."

Yuranosuke signified his assent; and rising to their feet, their hearts heavy with the thought that they were quitting for ever the castle where for generations their ancestors, and where they themselves for so long a time, had night and day done their duty as *samurahi*, the retainers of Yenya slowly and reluctantly, and with many a wistful look back, passed out through the castle-gate. Hardly had they turned their faces from their old home when they found themselves confronted by Rikiya, Yazama, Odera, and Hori, who, after escorting their lord's body to the temple of Kômyô, had hastened back to the castle.

"Ah!" exclaimed the latter simultaneously, impetuously arresting as they spoke the progress of Yuranosuke and his companions, "has the castle then been taken possession of? We thought we were to make our last stand here against the force that Ashikaga might send to expel us."

"Not so, not so," said Yuranosuke; "we will not die here. Look, comrades," displaying the short sword which Yenya Hanguwan had made him a dying gift of. "With this weapon our dead lord let out his lifeblood; with this weapon he gave escape to his indignant spirit; and with this weapon will I take the head of Moronaho, and thus fulfil the last command of our lord."

"So be it! so be it!" they all exclaimed in a loud voice.

Yakushiji from within the gate heard the gallant cry, and, noisily putting up the bars, shouted out derisively:

"Your lord's crime against Moronaho has met with its proper reward. You are in a pretty plight now. Ha! ha!"

His satellites backed up the fellow's sneer with loud laughs, which so enraged some of the younger *samurahi* of Yuranosuke's party, that they would have retraced their steps, if their leader had not prevented them by reminding them of the necessity of sacrificing everything to the accomplishment of vengeance upon Moronaho. Still they could not help often glancing back with angry looks upon the castle they were leaving in the possession of Yakushiji and his crew.

END OF THE FOURTH BOOK.

# BOOK THE FIFTH.

———

### THE NIGHT ADVENTURE OF KAMPEI.

NOT unmindful of the example set by the falcon, that even in the last extremity of hunger, will not peck at a single ear of grain, Hayano Kampei, as the dark nights and the bright days passed by, continued to dwell in poverty and seclusion near the village of Yamazaki, mourning over his youthful error, and gaining his livelihood by tracking the monkey and the wild boar along the narrow mountain paths — narrow as were his means of existence.*

One night he was out among the hills a-hunting, when the thunder began to roar, and the lightning to flash, and the ground to tremble with the storm —a veritable July tempest,—and his sleeves were soon wet through with the pouring rain.

He sought shelter under a pine-tree, holding his matchlock in readiness, until the storm should be over; but hardly had he got

———

* Such is the sense of a play upon words occurring here in the original text, and incapable of anything like a literal rendering.

there when he saw the glimmer of a light coming towards him through the darkness.

It proceeded from a small paper lantern, carried by a man, who seemed to be a *samurahi*, and who held it by its bow-shaped handle under the folds of his dress, which, partly to shelter himself from the tempest, partly to prevent the light from being blown out by the wind, he had drawn close round his person.

" *Iya !* there," cried Kampei.  " Pardon me for stopping you, but will you be good enough to give me a light?"  With these words he approached the wayfarer, who, as soon as he saw him, assumed a posture of defence, exclaiming :

" I know the risk of journeying alone on this road, but you must not fancy I have any fear of you, highwayman though you look like; you will get nothing out of me—try your tricks elsewhere." And suddenly turning towards his questioner, the traveller scanned him narrowly.

" What !" said Kampei, "you take me for a robber, your eyes deceive you, but I can excuse your mistake.  I am a hunter of the neighbourhood, and the rain has so damped my match that I can make no use of it.  You can understand my plight.  See, I will give the gun into your own hands, while you can light the match for me yourself."

The hunter spoke in an honest accent enough, and the traveller once more regarded him attentively.  After a slight pause, he exclaimed suddenly:

" Why, you are Kampei, Hayano Kampei, are you not?"

" I am; and you?  You must be Senzaki Yagorô."

The two friends greeted each other cordially after their long separation, and clenched their fists firmly as the memory of the ruin of their lord's house again stirred their hearts in the undying hatred of his enemy.  Kampei, letting his head fall mournfully on his breast, could not for some time utter a word.  At last he found speech, exclaiming:

" Yeh! I am so stricken with shame—my honour as a Bushi is

THE RENCONTRE OF KAMPEI AND SENZAKI.

so entirely gone—that I hardly dare show my face even to so old a comrade as yourself. I ought to have been at my lord's side when the event that resulted so cruelly for our master's house took place; but my ill-fortune was such that I was not where my duty called me, nor was it possible for me to return to the castle. While waiting for a favourable moment for begging that my fault might be overlooked, I was overwhelmed by the news of our master's self-dispatch. *Namusambô!* that fellow Moronaho is the cause of all this; and thinking that at least I could accompany my lord on the dark path, I laid hand upon my sword, when I was arrested by the reflection that my lord would ask me what high deed I had done to entitle me to follow him, and that I could do nothing but hang my head with shame in reply. Heartbroken, I gave up the idea of self-dispatch; and it coming to my ears that it was intended to avenge the death of our master, the design originating with the Ohoboshis, father and son, and Sir Goyemon, and as I have never been formally thrust out from the clan, I thought that if means could be found of getting me a favourable hearing from Yuranosuke, I might be permitted to add my name to the list of conspirators, and should then never fear to face the world as long as I lived, while my name would remain bright for ages after my death. In our chance meeting to-day, I am as fortunate as if I were to come upon the Udonge* in bloom. I adjure you, as an old comrade, as a fellow-*samurahi*, give me your aid, and help me to regain the honourable position I have lost." So saying, Kampei prostrated himself, full of remorse for his disloyalty, and burst into tears. Truly pitiable it is to see a man weep. Senzaki felt that his friend's repentance was sincere, but thought it right not to reveal the whole plot, seeing how important a matter it was.

"Come, come, Kampei," he said, after a pause; "you are speaking at random. Your talk about a list of conspirators is all moonshine; as far as I know, no one has dreamt of any such scheme

---

* Udonge. *Vide* Appeudix, and below.

as you refer to. I am on my way from Yuranosuke to Goyemon
with a message about erecting a monument over our lord's grave.
True, we are all mere *rónin* now; yet we wish to put up a monument
that will last for ever, so that his memory may not be lost, and are
trying to collect the money necessary for the purpose among those
who do not forget the benefits they have received from our dead
master; whose disposition, however, we ascertain before we unfold
our scheme to them. You, of course, are among those who keep
a grateful memory of our lord."

The story about the monument was a fiction; Senzaki, who was
moved by his friend's distress, meant to hint what Yuranosuke's
real design was.

"You are very good, Senzaki. A rumour had reached me of
your intention to get funds for a monument. I understand you
perfectly. I shall move heaven and earth to get money somehow,
so that I may join in the subscription. Senzaki, what a shameful
position I am in; fit punishment for my disloyalty to our master.
There is not a single soul to whom I can apply for aid. However,
my father-in-law, Yóichibei, is a good-natured old man, a farmer of
these parts. My wife is as much grieved as I am at the remembrance
of my fault, and the old people are full of compassionate desire to
see me restored to my former rank by some means or other. I
shall tell them of my fortunate meeting with you to-night; and, if
I let them know of this chance of my regaining my position, they
will, for the sake of their daughter, sell some of their land. I know
they will not refuse to do so, and I would beg of you to take the
money for me to Goyemon."

Senzaki could not resist Kampei's pleading tone, and replied,
"Well, I will tell Goyemon all that you have said, and will see
what can be done by petitioning Yuranosuke on your behalf. The
day after to-morrow you shall hear from me without fail. And
here, by-the-bye, is Goyemon's itinerary," handing over a paper, as
he spoke, to Kampei, who lifted it respectfully to his forehead.

"A thousand, thousand thanks; no danger of my being behind-hand with the money. The day after to-morrow I hope to see you. If you should want to look me up you must go to the ferry at Yamazaki; turn to the left, and then inquire for the house of one Yôichibei; you will have no difficulty in finding it. And now, ere it gets too late, I think you had better continue your journey. Remember that the road you will have to travel over is somewhat dangerous, and therefore do not cease to be on your guard."

"Good, I understand. Until the monument to our dead lord has been erected, no flea shall taste this body of mine; and be of good cheer, you will get the money, I make no doubt. Fare you well, fare you well."

Kampei and Senzaki then took leave of each other.

The rain continued to patter down, amid the sound of which the clatter of wooden pattens betokened the approach of some wayfarer. Presently, Yôichibei, not fearing the darkness, for he knew the paths well, came tottering by, leaning on his staff, honest stouthearted father, only fearing for his child, Karu, whose surviving parent he was.* As the old man struggled forward through the storm, he was startled by some one behind him shouting, "*Oi, oi,* old gentleman, let's travel together."

This was no other than the son of Kudaiu, Sadakuro, whose home was no more fixed than the white crest of a wave, and who had betaken himself to night work on the highways, a heavy sword hanging by his hip.†

"How, old fellow, art deaf?" cried Sadakuro; "I've been shouting after you for some time. Perilous task for an old man like you to travel alone, and by night, along a dangerous road like this. Come, I'll keep you company." So saying, he got in front of Yôichibei, and stared at him rudely. The latter started, but with the craft of old age, replied:

---

* This portion of the text is stuffed with puns, of which a full rendering is impossible.

† That is, not stuck in his girdle, as was usual, but pendent by his side, so as to be readier for use.

"Well, well; you don't look young, and so I suppose I need not fear you.* True, indeed, it is perilous for an old man like me to be out on such a night, and all alone; but there is no help for it. Money, you know, is what people are always in want of, everywhere; and as I am behind with my taxes, I have been round among my relations to ask assistance, but without getting a cash from one of them; and so, as none of them seem inclined to help me, I did not trouble them with a long visit, and am now on my way home again."

Sadakuro broke in rudely: "*Yai!* don't try to fool me with your nonsense about being behind with your taxes. Just listen to what I've got to say to you. That bag in your bosom there, to judge by its bulk, must contain some forty or fifty *riyô.* I caught a sight of it just now, a striped bag—hand it over. What! must I ask it with clasped hands? Of course, you will howl about your poverty, and the money being for your family. I care nothing about all that; you can't help yourself, that's clear, so let me have it if you please, and at once."

And with a sudden movement he snatched the bag out of the old man's bosom.

"Ah! sir," cried the old man, "I implore you, that bag——"

"That bag, that bag—— Well, it seems I was right as to its contents."

And the robber grasped the bag more firmly as he spoke.

"No, no; it only contains some cash left after buying a pair of straw shoes at the last village, together with the remains of some rice balls I had for my dinner, and some emollient physic and stimulant lozenges my daughter gave me before leaving home, to use in case of an attack of flux. Pray let me have it back."

And with a quick movement the old man repossessed himself of the bag and made off with it. Sadakuro, however, soon overtook him.

---

* For the young, so think the Japanese, not without justice, are commonly more cruel and violent than the old.

"*Yeh!* you will be a fool then. I did not want to hew you in pieces, but gentle means, it seems, only make you harder to deal with. Hand that to me without more ado, or I'll have at you."

So saying, he drew his long sword and raised it high above his head, and ere one had time to cry mercy he aimed a blow at the old man, sweeping down with his sword as if it was only a bamboo he was splitting. But Yôichibei, whom some swerve of arm or weapon saved for the moment, convulsively seized the naked blade with both hands, crying :

"What, would you murder me?"

"Ah! I knew I was right," exclaimed the robber, "I felt sure you had money about you. It is your money kills you. Come, no more nonsense, but die and make no noise about it."

And the villain pressed the old man with the point of his sword as he spoke.

"*Ma, Ma!* I pray you a little patience. Alas! is there no escape for me! true, aye, true! I have money on me, but this money belongs to my only daughter. She has a lover, dearer to her than life itself, and the money is for him. For certain reasons he became a *rônin*. My daughter told me he had become a *rônin* through her fault, and begged us—her mother and me—that she might be allowed to help him to get back his lost rank. Night after night she begged this. But we are very poor bodies, and could hit upon no plan of bringing about what she wanted. At last, however, her mother and I, after talking over the matter, agreed upon a means of aiding her, and got her to consent to it. We took good care, however, that her lover should know nothing of our plan, and told her to be careful to say nothing about it to him. Oh, this money has cost tears of blood to us—my only daughter, her mother and myself. What shall we do if you take it from us? O, sir; I ask you, with clasped hands, to be merciful to us. You, too, sir, look like one who has been a *samurahi* and will sympathize with us. Without this money my daughter and her lover will never be able to hold up their heads again. He is affianced to my only daughter ; how pitiable, how

cruel to separate them.  Oh, sir, consider their hard case.  I beg
of you to afford us your merciful help.  Yé, yé, you are young yet,
sir; you have no children.  Bye-and-bye you will have children, and
then you will understand why I plead with you so earnestly.  You
cannot refuse to help us in our miserable lot.  My home is but one
league farther on; let only the money be given to my daughter's
lover, and do your will with me.  Let me but see my daughter's face
happy, and I will gladly die.  Have pity! have pity!"

But loud as the old man's entreaties were, the far-off echoes
of the hills alone responded to his cries.

"O pity, pity," sneered the robber; "what stuff you talk; your
doing a kindness to me will not harm your son, nothing evil can
come out of doing a kindness."

"Have mercy on me," groaned the victim as, pierced by Sadakuro's sword, he fell down and rolled in his death agony on the
ground.  The murderer, kicking the body aside, exclaimed coolly,
"Wretched piece of work!  Well, I am sorry for it; I didn't do it
out of any malice; but, you see, you had money.  That killed you.
No money and you'd be alive now.  Your money was your enemy.
I can't help pitying you, too.  Which prayer are you for?  *Namu-
amida butsu* or *Namu miyôhô renge kiyô?** Choose one, and let all
end."  And he buried his sword still deeper in the quivering form.
The blades of grass were red with dewlike drops of blood, and the
feeble breath passed away from the old man full of years and misery.
His murderer immediately possessed himself of the bag of money,
and tried to estimate its contents in the dark by feeling it with his
hand.

"Capital," he cried, after a pause; "fifty *riyô* here; it's a long time
since such a sum and I have been face to face.  I am much obliged to
you."  Casting a glance towards his victim, he then hung the bag
round his own neck and threw the corpse to the bottom of a neighbouring ravine, little thinking of the retribution that was awaiting him.

---

* *Vide* Appendix.

浴定九郎

百姓与一兵工

THE MURDER OF YÔICHIBEI.

He had not gone far on his way when a wounded boar came dashing up behind him. He stood aside to let the animal pass, that rushed straight on, heedless of roots and stones. At the moment Sadakuro stood back, startled, out of the animal's way, just as the boar was flying past him through the mud and bushes, he was struck by a double shot, which passed from his backbone through the side of his chest, and rolled him over dead before he could even utter a groan—a fit end for the villain.

Kampei meanwhile, for it was from him that the fatal shot proceeded, thinking he had hit the boar, came towards the spot, holding his gun muzzle downwards, and searched for the animal's carcase. Seeing something on the ground, he raised it up, and found to his horror and astonishment that it was a human corpse.

" *Yai, Yai!* 'Tis a man. *Namu sambo*, what an unlucky shot !"

It was so dark it was impossible to tell who the man might be, but Kampei put his hand inside the breast to see if his victim's heart still beat. In doing this, his hand came upon the purse of money, which seemed by its bulk to contain some forty or fifty *riyo*. Overjoyed at his luck, he lifted the bag gratefully to his head, and made off with the speed of a bird, distancing the boar itself.*

---

\* " Shishi yori saki he Issan ni tobu no Gotoku ni isogikeru."

END OF BOOK FIVE.

# BOOK THE SIXTH.

---

## THE HEROISM OF KAMPEI.

" All the old folks, hand in hand,
Haste to watch the joyous band,
Mingling in the harvest-dance *
'Neath the old folks' kindly glance."

UCH was the country snatch the corn-threshers greeted the morrow's dawn with at the village of Yamazaki,† which, as you will guess from the name, lay in the shadow of the hills.  Here stood the mud and wattle cabin of Yôichibei, who tilled some few roods of land around ; and it was here that Kampei had retired after his disgrace with his affianced Karu, who, up betimes, was combing out her disordered hair—of a truth, its dishevelled state seemed to show her indescribable anxiety for her lover's return—and restoring to it its beautiful dark gloss, managing at last to arrange it so charmingly that it was a pity there were none but country boors to admire her.‡  As she finished her task, wishing she had a friend to talk over her fears with, her mother, leaning on a stick, came hobbling up the country path.

---

* *Misaki-odori, i.e., misaki-*dance.  *Misaki* is the name of a place near Kiyôto.
*Misaki* means also the maturing of the ear, fruit or crop.
† " Before the Hills."
‡ In this passage, the sense of which is given with considerable closeness, are

" Ah, daughter, so you have finished doing your hair.   How prettily you have put it up.   Well, the wheat harvest is being gathered in, and you see nothing everywhere but people as busy as they can be.   Just now, as I passed by the bamboo copse yonder, I heard the young fellows singing, as they threshed the corn, the old snatch—

> ' All the old folks, hand in hand,
> Haste to watch the joyous band,
> Mingling in the harvest-dance,
> Neath the old folks' kindly glance. '

Your father is long in returning; I have been as far as the end of the village to look out for him, but without seeing the least sign of him."

" I wonder at that," replied her daughter; " I can't understand it; what can make him so late? Shall I run out and see if he is coming."

" Why, no; young women cannot go wandering about all alone. Don't you remember how you hated walking about the village when you were a little girl? and so we sent you to service at my lord Yenya's; but now, our grassy moor seems to have drawn you home again.   Ah, daughter," after a pause, "if Kampei were but here your face would soon lose its anxious look."

" Yes, mother, of course it would.   When a girl has her lover with her, however dull and stupid the village may be, all seems joyous to her. And soon we shall be in the *Bon* month,* and then Kampei and we shall be the ' old folks ' of the song, and go ' hand in hand ' to see the dancing—shall we not?   You don't forget your own youth, mother."

The girl spoke in a sprightly tone, wishing to spare her mother any anxiety, but her trembling limbs showed the distress she could not completely hide.

" *Nambo;* you talk merrily enough, but in your heart, in your heart——"

---

various word-plays and a character-rebus, the explanation of which would be out of place in the present translation, and would, besides, require the use of Chinese signs.

* *Vide* Appendix, " Bon month."

"*Iye, iye!* mother," said Karu, "I am not troubled. Is it not for my husband's sake that I have engaged myself at the tea-house in the Gi-on Street at Kiyóto? I am quite ready to go; and it is only the thought that I shall not any longer be able to look after my father's comforts that grieves me. My brother, who, though of mean condition, has been permitted to become a retainer of our lord Yenya, will be taken up by his duties——"

Their talk was interrupted by the arrival of Ichimonjiya, the master of the tea-house in the Gi-on Street, accompanied by two coolies bearing a *kago.* "This is the place," he cried. "Is this the house of Yóichibei?" he added, as he came up to the door, entering as he spoke.

"Pray come in, sir," said the mother of Karu. "You have had a long journey, to be sure. Quick, daughter, bring the gentleman tea and tobacco."

The two women were so anxious to please their guest that they would have covered the walls of their house with beaten gold, if they could have done so, to gratify him.

"Well, mistress," said the master of the tea-house, "last night I gave your good man a vast deal of trouble. Has he got back all right?"

"Got back—did you say?" cried the mother of Karu. "Why, sir, has he not come back with you, then? What can this mean? Since he went to see you he has——"

"Not come back yet?" broke in Ichimonjiya; "well, that is strange. Perhaps he has been carelessly passing by some shrine of Inari, and been bewitched by some crystal-pawing fox.* However that may be, here am I, come to take away the girl according to agreement. An engagement of five years for one hundred *riyô;* that was what we clapped hands on. Your husband said he had a pressing need of the money, and begged me with tears in his eyes to advance him half of the price,

---

* The fox, much dreaded on account of his supposed influence over human beings, is generally represented as holding a crystal ball in his forepaws, without which he is said to be powerless.

which at last, after he had sealed the paper, I agreed to do, bargaining that the girl should be given up on the payment of the remainder. He seemed beside himself with joy when I counted out the fifty *riyô* to him, and set out on his return there and then, although it was late, about the fourth hour (about 8 P.M.) I should say, and I warned him that it was unwise to travel by night with money about one. He wouldn't listen to me, however, and hurried off. Perhaps he has stopped somewhere in the road."

"But there is no place he would be likely to stop at, mother," said Karu.

"Stop, indeed!" exclaimed the wife of Yôichibei, "he would be sure to hasten homewards with all speed. He would never rest until he had got back and gladdened us by the sight of the money. I cannot understand his being so long, at all."

"Understand it or not," cried the tea-house master, impatiently, "that is your affair; here is the balance of the purchase-money, and now I should like to take the girl with me."

The fellow took fifty *riyô* from his bosom as he spoke, and offered them to Karu's mother, saying, "This makes up the hundred *riyô;* come, take them, and let me have the girl."

"But I can't give her up," cried her mother, "spite of what you say, until her father shall have returned."

"But you must, you must, I tell you," shouted Ichimonjiya; "why waste time? Look, here is the agreement with Yôichibei's seal upon it— it speaks for itself. The girl is mine from this day, and for every day of her service I lose I will make you pay well. Go with me she must, and shall."

Seizing Karu by the hand, he was about to lead her away when her mother interrupted him, catching her daughter by the other hand, and exclaiming, "Nay, nay, a little patience."

Ichimonjiya, however, pulled the girl towards him, and got her to the *kago*, in spite of her mother's resistance. At this crisis, Kampei, with his straw cloak over his matchlock, suddenly made his appearance, and, seeing how matters stood, hastened into the house, exclaiming:

"What is all this about, Karu? tell me. What is this *kago* here for? Where are you going in it?"

"Ah, Kampei!" cried the girl's mother, "I am so glad you have come. You are just in time."

Kampei could not understand his mother-in-law's delight. "There is some mystery here. Mother, wife, tell me, what is the meaning of all this?"

Further conversation was interrupted by Ichimonjiya, who strode into the apartment, and squatting down, exclaimed angrily, "O! let there be an end to this. You are my servant's husband, are you?" turning to Kampei. "Husband or not, matters little to me. The agreement provides that no one (husband or other) shall prevent the contract from being carried out. See, Yôichibei's seal is on the paper; is not that enough for you? Come, old lady," he resumed, speaking to Karu's mother, "let me have the girl without more ado."

"Oh! son-in-law," exclaimed the wife of Yôichibei, "what am I to do? Our daughter told us some time since you were in great need of money, and begged us to give her some for you; but how could we, poor folk, without a cash! At last, her father said the only way was to send our daughter for a time to service; but that this must be done without your knowledge, because he thought that perhaps you would not like money to be got in such a way. In case of need, you know, they say a *samurahi* may rob and steal;* and as it was for her husband's advantage, there was nothing shameful in parting with her. So her father went yesterday to Kiyôto and settled terms with this gentleman here, the master of the house in the Gi-on Street, and ought to have been back ere this, but has not yet returned, which makes us feel very anxious about him. In the midst of our uncertainty this gentleman appears, and says that he gave half the hiring-money to Yôichibei last night, and has brought the other half with him, which he offers to us in exchange for Karu. I have asked him to wait until her father returns, but he refuses. What are we to do, Kampei?"

---

* Allusion to the proverb, "Kiritori gô-tô-wa, bushi no narahi," *i.e.*, Slaughter and rapine, *samurahi's* daily deeds.

"Really my father-in-law is most kind," said the youth. "I have had a windfall, but more of that bye-and-bye. There can be no doubt, I think, that Karu cannot be given up until her father shall have returned."

"Cannot be given up," cried Ichimonjiya; "and why not, I should like to know?"

"Well," said Kampei, "this is Yôichibei's seal, no doubt, and perhaps you really have paid the fifty *riyô*, but . . . . "

"*Iya!*" broke in the tea-house master; "why, I could buy up all the women in Kiyôto and Ohozaka, for that matter; indeed, the whole population of Nyogo island;* and it is not likely I should say I had paid half the money down if I had not done so—is it? Besides, I can prove that I paid it. When I had counted out the money to the old fellow he wrapped it up in a cloth, which he was about to tie round his neck, when I showed him how dangerous it was to carry money in that way, and lent him a purse made of stuff just like my dress here, both in stuff and pattern. He tied the purse round his neck and started off at once."

"What do you say," broke in Kampei, "a purse made of striped cloth like this of which your dress is made?"

"Yes, yes, that will be proof of the truth of what I say, will it not?"

A terrible thought rose up in Kampei's mind as he heard this, and he furtively but closely examined Ichimonjiya's dress. His scrutiny convinced him that it was exactly of the same stuff and pattern as the purse he had taken the previous night, which was made of a sort of striped cotton cloth, shot with silken threads, and he could only conclude that the man whom he had accidentally slain was no other than his own father-in-law. "Would that the slugs had shattered my own breast-bone," he thought to himself; "it would have been a less miserable affair than this."

"Come, Kampei," cried Karu, impatient at her lover's silence,

---

* *Vide* Appendix.

"don't stand there hesitating, but speak out and decide whether I am to go with this man or not."

" Ah, well," said her lover, "you see—what this man tells us seems to be true. There appears to be no help for it, and you must go with him."

" What, before my father returns ? "

"I forgot to tell you that I saw your father this morning. It is uncertain when he will return."

" How! you saw my father this morning! Why did you not tell us, then, at once, and put an end to our anxiety ? "

Ichimonjiya, taking advantage of the pause, exclaimed : " They say if you search for something seven times without finding it you may suspect some one. However, now we know where the good man is, we need trouble ourselves no more about him. So pray don't let us be at sixes and sevens * any more about the girl, or faith, we shall begin to quarrel. Cheer up, all three of you ; and if ever you, sir, or the old lady, should visit Kiyôto, I hope I shall have the pleasure of a call from you. Now, my girl, into the *kago* with you ; up with you, quick."

"*Ai, ai,*" cried the girl. "O Kampei, must I, then, go? I leave my father and mother to your care. You will not fail to be kind to them, will you? to my father especially, for he is very infirm." The poor girl, of course, had not the least notion that her father was no more. Sad and pitiable situation ! Kampei was on the verge of confessing everything upon the spot, but the presence of a stranger restrained him, and he was forced to endure his misery in silence.

" Son-in-law," exclaimed the wife of Yôichibei, " you and your wife must now take leave of each other. It is a bad parting for you, daughter, but do not be faint-hearted."

" Do not fear, mother. It is for my husband's sake that I am sold into service for a time. I have no cause whatever to be unhappy. I

---

* Lit., at fours and fives.

山　帰ノ場

女房おかる

大　星　力　弥

早　野　勘　平

THE DEPARTURE OF KARU.

shall have plenty of courage—it is only going without seeing my father that troubles me."

"Your father shall come and see you as soon as he returns, I promise you that. Take care of yourself, daughter; apply the moxa occasionally, and bring us back a healthy face. Have you all you want,—nose-paper and fan? Mind you don't stumble and hurt yourself."

The girl then got into the *kago* with her mother's help, and the last farewells were exchanged.

"Ah me!" cried the wife of Yôichibei, "what ill-fortune has come upon us! why was the child born to such misery as this?"

The poor woman ground her teeth in an agony of distress, and burst into tears, while her daughter, grasping convulsively the sides of the *kago*, managed, but with difficulty, to stifle her sobs and restrain her tears so as to hide her grief. Pitiable sight!

The bearers now made a start, and the *kago* was borne rapidly away, the poor girl's mother gazing after it wistfully.

"Ah!" she cried, "I have not comforted her at all; how wretched, how wretched!"

"Son-in-law," she added, turning to Kampei, "you see I am her mother, yet I have forced myself to let her go. You must not let your grief overcome you. You spoke just now of my husband's return being uncertain, and said you met him this morning."

"Ha! did I?"

"Yes. Where was it you met him? where did you part from him?"

"Where did I part from him, you say? I think it was at Toba or Fushimi, or perhaps Yodo, or it might have been at Takeda."

The words were hardly out of Kampei's mouth, when a shuffling of feet was heard outside, and three hunters of the neighbourhood, Meppo Yahachi, Tanegashima no Roku, and Tanuki no Kakubei, immediately afterwards thronged the entrance, bearing on their shoulders a door, on which was laid a corpse decently covered with a straw rain-cape.

"As we came back from hunting among the hills last night," exclaimed one of them, "we found the body of Yôi-chibei, who has evidently been murdered ; and we have brought it here."

Overwhelmed at the sight, the mother of Karu for a moment could not find speech.

"O, son-in-law," she exclaimed at last ; "whose work is this? who is the villain who has thus slain my husband? Son-in-law, son-in-law! you must not rest until this cruel murder has been amply avenged, amply avenged. O my husband! my husband!" Her complaints and reproaches were, however, of as little avail as the tears which flowed freely from her eyes. The hunters, shocked at the sight of her misery, exclaimed together, "Dame, dame, this is a terrible misfortune truly. But had you not better lay a complaint at once before the magistrate? A sad business, a sad business." With which words they laid down the door with its burden upon the matting, and took their departure.

The mother of Karu, restraining her tears for a moment, marched up to Kampei : "Son-in-law," she cried, "what can all this mean? The more I think the less I understand. *Samurahi* though you are, how can you look upon your father-in-law's corpse without a start? You say you met him this morning. Did he not give you some money? Did he say nothing to you? Speak, speak! What, you have not a word to say? Ah! I understand, this explains everything."

She thrust her hand suddenly as she spoke into Kampei's breast, and dragging out the purse, continued :

"I saw you looking at this furtively just now. Ah! there is blood upon it,—it is you, you who have murdered my husband."

"*Iya!* That purse is——"

"That purse—ah! you thought your foul deed would remain hidden, but it is plain as sun at noon, in spite of you. You have killed him for the money that was in this purse—did you know for whom it was? Yes, of course you did, and murdered him because you thought he might not give you the whole of it, and hide some on his way back. Poor husband, poor husband! was it for this you sold your daughter? Wretch, we had always thought you a man of honour; and all the time you have been a villain,—oh! that I could kill you on the spot; you are a monster, not a man. The horror has dried up my tears, and I cannot weep. Alas! my poor husband! you little knew what a brute of a son-in-law it was in whose behalf, anxious as you were to help him to regain his position as a *samurahi*, you, an old man, gave up your rest and travelled by night and on foot to Kiyôto; gave up your treasure and your only daughter for one who sought to harm you in return for the good you were doing for him; like a dog that bites the hand that feeds him. Was ever such a vile crime dreamt of as this? Monster—devil. Give me back my husband, I tell you—bring him back to life!"

Blind with rage and grief, the poor woman threw herself upon Kampei, and seizing him by the side hair, dragged him towards her, buffeting him the while with all her might.

"Wretch," she continued, "if only I had the strength I would hack you in pieces, though even that would not glut my vengeance."

She went on loading him with reproaches, until at last, exhausted with grief and passion, she fell down in a faint; while Kampei, in an agony of remorse that made the sweat stand out upon his body,[*] threw himself upon the ground, gnawing the matting in his dread that the judgment of heaven had overtaken him.

Now two *samurahi*, wearing deep-brimmed bamboo hats that concealed their features, knocked at the entrance.

"Does Hayano Kampei live here? Hara Goyemon and Senzaki Yagoro desire an interview with him."

Ill-timed as the visit of the two *samurahi* was, Kampei nevertheless rose to his feet, and, tightening his girdle, snatched up his side-arms and thrust them hurriedly in.

---

[*] Lit., " Throwing off boiling hot sweat in his distress."

He then went to receive his visitors, exclaiming: "Well, well, gentlemen, who could have expected the honour of a call from you at this poor hut? I am sure I do not know how to thank you sufficiently;" bowing his head low as he spoke.

"But perhaps," cried Goyemon, "we are interrupting you in some family engagement; you seem occupied."

"Oh! nothing of any importance; some small private matter, of no moment, I assure you. Pray do not trouble yourselves on that point, but do me the honour to enter."

"In that case," cried the two *samurahi*, "we will accept your invitation." And passing to the upper end of the apartment, they seated themselves upon the matting.

Kampei, kneeling before them with the palms of his hands upon the ground, exclaimed: "Lately I was absent from my lord's side upon an important occasion; a failure of duty for which it would be vain for me to try to find any excuse. Nevertheless, I implore you to procure my crime to be pardoned. I entreat you, gentlemen, most earnestly I entreat you, to intercede for me, that I may be permitted to join with the other retainers of my lord's household in honouring the anniversary of his death."

As he spoke the unfortunate youth was overwhelmed with shame at the recollection of his fault. Goyemon at once replied:

"Listen. Though a *rônin* without resources, you have offered a subscription of a large amount towards the expense of erecting a monument to our dead lord. Yuranosuke has been informed of this, and is full of admiration of your conduct. The monument will be placed in the family burying-ground of our lord. But your disloyalty makes it impossible for our chief to receive your subscription. The spirit of our dead lord would be indignant with us were we to accept your money for such a purpose, and we have been ordered therefore to return it to you."

As he concluded Senzaki drew forth from his bosom a paper packet containing the money which Kampei had thought himself so lucky in finding, and had shortly after handed to Senzaki, and placed the packet before the youth, who, wild with grief and despair at the ruin of all his hopes,* was unable to utter a word.

"Ha, villain!" cried the mother of Karu, weeping and pointing to Kampei; "you are now reaping your reward. Listen, gentlemen: this fellow's father-in-law, a man stricken in years, but regardless of his age, sold his daughter into service for the sake of this wretch before you, who, lying in wait for the old man as he was returning home, murdered him and robbed him of the money. The deed was done in darkness, that none might know of it. Sirs, can you accept the assistance of such a man, a parricide, whom, if the gods and Buddha do not punish, they must surely be deaf to all entreaties. You see the wretch,—a son, a murderer of his father. Hew him in pieces, sirs, I implore you; for I am but a woman, and have not the strength to avenge myself with my own hands."

Overcome with her feelings, the unfortunate mother of Karu threw herself, in a flood of tears, upon the ground, while the two *samurahi*, aghast at the tale, laid hands on their swords.

Senzaki, his voice choked by indignation, exclaimed: "Kampei, villain! you dared to come to us with your murderer's booty in your hand. Is this the way to atone for your disloyalty? Inhuman monster! How dare you call yourself a *samurahi?*—horror. A parricide and a thief, you deserve instant crucifixion; and I should be well pleased to spit you with my own hands upon the tree."

"Like the philosopher Kōshi (Confucius)," added Goyemon, "who declared that he would rather die of thirst than drink of the water of a fountain so ill-named as that of Tô-sen (*i.e.*, the Fount of Robbers), so no man of honour could hold intercourse for a moment with such a wretch as you. How could you dream of offering us your ill-gotten gains for the service of our dead lord? Yuranosuke, with his rare sagacity, must have divined what a disloyal and treacherous nature yours was, when he ordered us to return you the money. Bloodthirsty wretch, your name will be handed down to posterity

---

* Lit., "Felt his senses turned upside down."

THE DISTRESS OF KAMPEI.

"Goyemon," he cried to his companion, "come here. This at first looks like a gunshot wound, but it is really a sword cut. Kampei, you have been over hasty."

The mother of Karu was so astonished by the discovery that she could not utter a word.

Goyemon, across whose mind a sudden recollection flashed, exclaimed: "Now I remember,—you too cannot have forgotten,—the corpse we passed on our road here, with a gunshot wound in it. We went up to it, and found it was the body of Ono Sadakuro, whom his father—that covetous wretch, Ono Kudaiu—tired of the fellow's evil course of life, had turned out of house. We had heard that the son, not having a mat to bless himself with, had taken to highway robbery. Without doubt, Kampei, this Sadakuro was the villain that murdered your father-in-law."

"What?" cried the mother of Karu, bending over the corpse and examining the wound, "Kampei then was not the murderer of my husband? O! son-in-law!" turning to the unfortunate youth, "I pray you with clasped hands to forgive me. I am but a silly, stupid old woman, and you will bear with me and pardon me for all that I have said. Kampei, Kampei, you shall not, must not die," turning her face, streaming with tears, to him as she spoke.

"Now that what seemed evil in my conduct has been' explained, mother," cried Kampei, "I can face the dark path in peace. Soon I shall be with my father-in-law, and we shall climb the Shidé Hill and pass by the triple cross-way together." *

Goyemon, interrupting Kampei, who had seized the sword which still remained in the wound with the purpose of hastening his death, exclaimed:

"Ah! Kampei, yet a little patience; without knowing it you have slain your father's murderer. Fortune has not been all against you, and, by the favour of the Archer-God, you have been enabled to take a glorious revenge. But I have something to shew to you ere

---

* *Vide* Appendix.

you die. Look here," drawing a paper from his bosom and spreading
it open before the dying youth; "at the foot of this is a list of the
*samurahi* who have sworn to take the life of our enemy Moronaho."

Goyemon began to read the paper, but Kampei, who felt his agony
coming on, broke in, saying:

"Tell me the names of the conspirators."

"We are forty-five in all," replied Goyemon; "but now that I
have come to know how truly loyal and devoted a retainer you have
been, I shall add your name to the list, and I give you this paper
that you may take it with you on the dark path, and reverently
offer it to our lord Yenya."

He then took an ink-horn from his bosom, and after writing down
Kampei's name, handed the paper to him, exclaiming:

"Seal it Kampei, seal it with your blood."

Kampei obeyed, pressing his bloody hands upon the paper.

"I have sealed," he exclaimed. "Comrades, I cannot thank
you enough; you have enabled me to obtain what I most wished
for in the world. Mother, do not grieve, my father's death and
my wife's service will not now be of no avail. The money will be
used by these gentlemen who have sworn the death of the enemy
of our house."

The mother of Karu, her eyes filled with tears, placed the packet
with the purse and the money which Ichimonjiya had brought, before
the two *samurahi*.

"Pray accept this purse as a token of my son-in-law's share
in your enterprise: and consider that his spirit is with you in your
plot against your enemy."

"We will; we will," replied Goyemon, taking up the purse.
"We will prize this purse of striped cloth as if it were full of barred
Ôgon.* Sir," turning to Kampei, "may the perfection of Buddha
be yours."

"Alas!" said Kampei, "the perfection of Buddha is not to be

---

* *Vide* Appendix. *184*

dreamt of by such a wretch as myself. The hand of death is upon me, but my soul will remain on earth that it may be with you when you strike our enemy."

His voice was rapidly failing, and the mother of Karu, seeing the end was near, burst into loud lamentations.

"O! Kampei, Kampei! my daughter is away, and knows nothing of all this misery. If only she were here to look upon you once more ere you die!"

"Nay, nay, mother; let her know nothing of her father's death, nothing of my death. She has gone to service for the sake of our lord Yenya; and if she were told of all that has occurred, she might neglect her duties, which would be like disloyalty to our dead chief. Let things remain as they are. And now," he resumed, "my mind is at ease;" and thrusting his sword into his throat, he fell back and died.

"Son-in-law, son-in-law!" exclaimed the mother of Karu; "alas! alas! he is dead! Is there any one in the world so wretched as I? My husband murdered, my son-in-law, to whom I looked for support after my man's death, a corpse before my eyes, my darling daughter separated from me, none but myself, a poor old woman, left,—why should I live all alone in the world? what have I to hope for? O, Yôichibei, Yôichibei, would that I were with you!"

Her sobs prevented further utterance for a time. At last, mastering her emotion for a moment, she struggled to her feet.

"Son-in-law, son-in-law," she exclaimed, "take me with you;" and falling upon his body, she embraced it convulsively, the tears raining down from her eyes as she gazed now on the corpse of her daughter's husband, now on that of Yôichibei, until at last, exhausted by grief and despair, she sank on the ground, unable to utter a sound.

"Come, mistress!" cried Goyemon, "do not grieve so much. I know it is very hard to bear; but it may comfort you if I tell you that I shall inform our chief Ohoboshi of the manner of Kampei's death. You had better keep this money, a hundred *riyô* in all. 'Twill buy a hundred masses—fifty for the repose of your husband's soul, and fifty for that of your son-in-law's ; you will see that all the funeral rites are decently conducted. And now," continued Goyemon, "we must take our leave of you. Fare you well, mistress."

"Farewell !" repeated Senzaki.

The two *samurahi* then took their departure, their eyes suffused as they gave a farewell glance back, and the tears falling as they became lost to view.

END OF THE SIXTH BOOK.

SATISFACTION IN DEATH.

# BOOK THE SEVENTH.

---

### THE DISCOMFITURE OF KUDAIU.

THE Gi-on Street in Kiyôto was crowded with pretty girls, flitting hither and thither, a very Paradise of Amida, beauty upon beauty showing their dazzling charms, bewildering and staggering the dullest and dreamiest of the passers-by.

"Hallo, there!" cried Kudaiu, making his way through the throng, followed by Sagisaka Bannai, to the entrance of Ichimonjiya, the tea-house of Ichiriki; "no host here? host, host——"

"Wait a moment, whoever you may be," cried a voice from within. "Who are you?" the voice continued, after a pause, the speaker opening the gate as he uttered the last words. "Yeh! what,—Ono Kudaiu, can it be your honour! with a gentleman too; pray enter, sirs, pray enter."

And the servant—for the speaker was none other—bowed respectfully as he spoke.

"Iya!" exclaimed Kudaiu; "this gentleman comes here with me for the first time. You seem to be deuced busy just now, but I suppose you can let us have a room where we can have a quiet drop together."

"Plenty of rooms," replied the servant, "but a rich gentleman named Yuranosuke has had a fancy to get together all the best known women of the place, and occupies the whole of the ground floor; however, there is a small room at your service."

" Full of dirt and cobwebs, I dare say."

" Still as sharp-tongued as ever."

"Sharp-tongued ? no, but I am getting old, and must look out lest I become entangled in women's webs."

"At least you are as pleasant a gentleman as ever. Well, I can find you a good room upstairs.—Hallo, some of your there," continued the servant, calling loudly for attendants; " light a fire, bring *saké* cups and tobacco, quick, pipes and *bon...n...n...n ;*" uttering the last word in a loud ringing tone, that chimed in well with the ding of *samisen* and drum that came from the apartments were Yuranosuke and his crew of laughing girls were revelling. " What do you think of all this, Bannai?" cried Kudaiu, turning to his companion. " You see how Yuranosuke spends his time."

"Well, sir, the man must be crazy, I think. Your private letters to my lord hinted at something strange about him, but my master had no idea things had come to this pass. I was ordered to come here and make inquiries, and if I saw anything suspicious I was to send word at once; but, faith, it is clear to me that I shall have my trouble for my pains. His son, that lout Rikiya, by-the-bye, do you know what he is about?"

" The lad seems to show himself here occasionally," replied Kudaiu; "a couple of dissipated scoundrels they are, 'twill be strange if they don't come to harm ! What I am here to-night for is to try and find out if there is anything at the bottom of it all. Speak low, speak low, and come upstairs with me."

" I follow your honour."

" Well, then, come."

  .  .  .  .  .  .  .

> " False, false your heart, I know it well,
>   You swear you love me, love me, while
> Your lips a flattering tale do tell,
>   Your heart is ever full of guile."

So sang a voice within, as Kudaiu and Bannai made their way to an upper story.

Meanwhile Yazama, accompanied by several other clansmen of Yenya, came up to the tea-house.

"Senzaki, Kitahachi, sirs," he cried, "this is the place where Yuranosuke, our chief, passes his time; it is called Ichirikiya. Ha! Heiyemon," addressing one of his companions, who seemed to be the follower rather than the equal of the rest, "you can remain in the servants' quarters; at the proper time I will send for you."

"I am much obliged to your honour," said the latter, hurriedly; "I venture to ask your honour to do your best for me."

Heiyemon then withdrew.

Yazama, knocking at the side entrance, now asked for admission. A girl's voice answered from within, exclaiming: "*Ai, ai,* there—who are you, what is your name?"

"*Iya!*" cried Yazama, as he entered with his comrades; "go and tell Sir Yura that Yazama Jiutarô, Senzaki Yagoro, and Takemori Kitahachi are here, and desire to speak with him. Tell him we have sent messenger after messenger praying him to return, but without success, and we have therefore come ourselves to see him and talk over matters."

"I really am afraid, gentlemen, that you have taken all this trouble for nothing," cried the girl; "for the last three days his honour has been feasting and drinking, and has got into such a muddled and confused state that it will be some time before he is himself again."

"Can this be true?" cried Yazama: "however, never mind, give the message all the same."

The girl, nodding assent, obeyed; and Yazama, turning to one of his companions, continued: "Did you hear what the girl said, Senzaki?"

"I did," replied the latter, "and she astonished me not a little. I had heard something of our chief's dissipation, but thought it was merely put on to lull our enemy into a false security. But this looks like reality; he seems to have given himself up entirely to pleasure. I cannot make it out at all."

"You see it is just as I told you," broke in Kitahachi. "Yura's disposition seems to have completely changed; the best thing we can do will be to rush in and slay him on the spot."

"No, no," cried Yazama, "let us have some talk with him first, and then——"

"That will be best," chimed in Senzaki, "and therefore we must wait here a little until the girl returns."

Just then, Yuranosuke, with his eyes bandaged, appeared, staggering towards where the three *rônin* were standing, and surrounded by a number of girls, with whom he was enacting the part of devil in a game of blind man's buff. "This way, devil, this way," cried the girls, shouting with laughter as they frolicked about the drunken fellow. "This way, where you hear our hands clapping."

"Caught, caught."

"Not yet, Yura, not just yet, devil."

"When I do get hold of one of you, I'll make her gulp down a good draught of *saké;* she shall have a good pull, I promise you; ha! I've got some one," seizing Yazama as he spoke; "bring the *saké* pot, quick, quick."

"*Iya,*" cried Yazama, disengaging himself; "Yuranosuke, I am Yazama Jiutarô, don't you know me? what can all this buffoonery mean?"

"*Namu sambo,*" muttered Yuranosuke; "I have done, the game is all up now."

"What kill-joys those great hulking fellows are, Sakaye-san," said one of the girls; "*samurahi,* I suppose, friends of our Yuranosuke!"

"I suppose they are," was the reply; "a horrid-looking trio, too."

"Pray excuse us, ladies," broke in Yazama, "we have some matters to talk over with this gentleman, and we must ask you to be good enough to leave him with us for a little time."

"Of course," cried a number of the girls together, "we knew you

THE GAME OF BLINDMAN'S BUFF.

dispatch of our lord.  *Namu sambo!* I turned my steps homeward
without a moment's delay, but the news reached me, while journeying
south, of the destruction of our lord's house, and of the dispersion of
the clan, and I was beside myself with grief and rage.   Though a
common soldier merely, I could not forget that I owed everything to
our lord's favour, and a burning desire to revenge the destruction of
our house took possession of me.   I went to Kamakura, and for three
months lived in the greatest wretchedness, dogging Moronaho's movements continually, in the hope of finding some opportunity of striking
the fellow dead at a blow, but he took such care of himself that I could
never get at him.   In despair I thought there was nothing left
but to commit self-dispatch, but then the recollection of my old
parents at home prevented me, and I went to see them.   On the
road, I heard a rumour (perhaps it was dropped from the sun) that
a plot was being set afoot to revenge our lord's death,—your honour
can imagine how delighted I was at the news ; and, leaving everything
behind me, I sought out the route of you gentlemen," turning to
the three *rōnin,* "and followed you here, trusting that you would
have the infinite kindness to listen to my humble request, and intercede for me with his honour for permission to add my name to
the list of conspirators."

"Ha!" cried Yuranosuke, "you're quick of tongue, it seems, as
well as quick of foot—you ought to be clown to some strolling company.
As for me, my desire for vengeance is hardly strong enough to make
me smash a flea, if I had an axe ready in my hand, to satisfy it ; it
would be strange, then, if I should take the pains to get up a conspiracy
with forty or fifty comrades.   Why, look you, if the plot failed, my
neck would pay the penalty ; if it succeeded, self-dispatch would in-
evitably follow ; death any way.   Where would be the use of seeking
vengeance if I could not live to enjoy it ?—one does not swallow
*jinseng* medicine one moment to get strangled the next.   Besides,
you were but a common soldier, getting your five *riyô* a year, and
three rations a day ; why should you trouble yourself about our
lord's misfortunes?   Your pay was hardly more than a begging

priest's dole of rice; for you to throw away your life in order to revenge Yenya would be as absurd as if a man were to give a high Kagura feast* in return for a morsel of laver. If you are bound to take one head, I, with my appointments of 1500 *kokus*, ought to take a bushel of heads at least. There need be no talk of seeking revenge, do you understand,—better do as the rest of the world. Come, *tsu-tsu-ten, tsu-tsu-ten*, don't you hear the joyous note of the *samisen?* away, and make merry."

"Your honour cannot be in earnest," exclaimed Heiyemon. "My wage, true, was small enough, and your honour held a high post, but did we not both draw our livelihood from one and the same source? There is no question here of high or low. According to custom I know well enough I have no right to ask that the form of a fellow like me should be seen among you great gentlemen, but, oh! let your honour, though our lord's representative, listen to my entreaty, and pardon my blunt speech! I am really nothing but an ape in the likeness of a man, 'tis true, still I implore you let me follow you; if only to tie your sandals or carry your burdens, take me with you; you cannot refuse me this boon, you . . . —ha! he has fallen asleep."

"Asleep, aye, so he is," cried Kitahachi, "miserable wretch. You need waste no further words with him; Yuranosuke may be looked upon as a dead man. Yazama, Senzaki, sirs, you now see what this brute's real disposition is; shall we make an end of him, as was our intention?"

"Yes, yes," responded his companions, "his fate will serve as a warning—upon him then." They again laid their hands on their swords, but Heiyemon a second time interposed, and restrained them from giving way to their anger.

"Sirs," exclaimed the foot-soldier, drawing near, "if you will carefully turn over the matter in your mind, you will see that Yuranosuke's conduct may be explained. Ever since our lord was taken from us, His Honour has been harassed by the thought of vengeance upon our

---

* *Vid:* Appendix.

clan's enemy, and none can know what cares have been heaped upon him, or what anxieties he has had to pass through, in the exact performance of the duties* devolving upon him. Look, too, how he has been compelled to bear in silence the contumely of men, and restrain his just indignation. If he did not, now and then, force himself to drink a bottle of *saké*, he would die, worn out with trouble and vexation. Wait till he wakes up, and you will see him again in his right mind."

Yielding to the justice of Heiyemon's address, the three *rónin*, attended by the foot-soldier, withdrew, and the good and evil of Yuranosuke's conduct remained to be cleared up.

*     *     *     *     *

Now the waning moonlight began to merge in the breaking dawn, and Rikiya, breathless with the haste with which he had made his way from Yamashima, peeped through the paper screen, within which Yura was lying in a heavy sleep, and, fearful of rousing some of the other inmates of the house, gently approached his father's slumbering form, and clashed his sword slightly. The *Karó* instantly rose to his feet, as if awakened by the clang of bridle-ring.†

"*Yah*, Rikiya," he exclaimed, "the noise of your sword has awakened me; what need presses now? Softly, softly."

"Here is a letter from the Lady Kawoyo, which I was ordered to bring to you without a moment's delay."

"Have you any verbal message to give as well?"

"Our clan's enemy, Moronaho, has obtained permission to return to his lands, and in a few days will be ready to start. Details will be found in the letter."

"Good. You can return home now, and at nightfall send me a *kago*; away with you."

Rikiya bowed assent, and at once left the apartment.

---

* Lit., " Scrutiny of each tree and bush " (to see if an enemy were lurking there).

† Alluding to the saying, " Yúshi wa kutsuwa no oto de ne wo sam asu," *i.e.*, " at clang of bridle-ring the sleeping hero wakes."

THE DISSIPATION OF YURANOSUKE.

Yuranosuke, eager to learn the contents of the letter, was in the act of opening it when Kudaiu appeared.

"Ha, Sir Yura," cried the new-comer; "I am Kudaiu; I hope I do not intrude upon you."

"Far from it," replied Yuranosuke, concealing his vexation; "it is quite an age since we met; a good year at least, and we are older than we were, older than we were. But you are here to rub out the wrinkles in your forehead, no doubt? a sad dog, I fear."

"*Iya!* Sir Yura," replied Kudaiu; "one must not pick holes in heroes' coats, they say, but to begin your enterprise by idling in a tea-house, careless of men's blame—faith, it looks promising."

"Ho," exclaimed the *Karô*, "you are hard upon me, hurling words at me like stones from a catapult."

"Now be frank with me," broke in Kudaiu, "this dissipation of yours, you know, is a mere blind to cover your revengeful designs against Moronaho——"

"Not a bit of it," cried Yura, "obliged as I am to you for the idea. Here am I, over forty years old, and do you think I should run the risk of being twitted with hankering after girls, called an old fool, and laughed at as crazy, to cloak any such designs as you hint at? a pleasant notion to be sure!"

"Then you have really no intention of revenging the death of Yenya?"

"Not I; not a whit of it. When our lord's castle and lands were confiscated, I spoke of dying upon our own ground, but this was merely to flatter the dowager. You remember you said that to fight with the government was the same as declaring oneself a public enemy, and so all at once left us to ourselves. Afterwards we talked a good deal of nonsense, but nothing came of it at all. Then something was said of committing self-dispatch at the tomb, but . . . . we made our way out by the Rear Gate, and now, as you see, are anything but wretched, thanks to your example. Old friends must not forget each other, and so—take my advice—shiver the past, let it care for itself."

"Ah!" said Kudaiu, "as I think of old days, I feel as wild as if I

were changed into the fox Shinoda.* So let us have a draught, Yura ;
come, it's long since we had one together; let me offer you a cup."

"Willingly. Now for a bout."

"Give me the cup; let me have a drain."

"Here it is ; drink."

"Won't you have a bit of fish with your *saké* ?"

Kudaiu, taking a piece of cuttle-fish with his chopsticks from a dish
beside him, offered it to Yuranosuke, who accepted the morsel,
exclaiming:

"Ah, a bit of the creature who salutes by throwing out his hands
and carrying his feet to his head.† Thanks, thanks."

Yuranosuke had lifted the morsel politely to his head, preparatory
to swallowing it, when Kudaiu seized his arm, saying :

"How! Yuranosuke, on the eve of the anniversary of our lord's
death, have you the heart to swallow that piece of cuttle-fish ?"

"Why shouldn't I, why shouldn't I ? Have you heard that our
master, Yenya, has been changed into a cuttle-fish ? *Yeh !* what nonsense has got into your head. It was his stupidity that has made you
and me *rōnin*. We have all of us good reason to detest his memory ;
and as to fasting, I cannot see that we are in the least bound so to
mortify ourselves for his sake. What a delicious morsel this is you
have handed me !" concluded Yuranosuke, swallowing it at one gulp
without changing a feature, and causing such astonishment to his
cunning interlocutor that the latter could not utter a word.

"Ah !" resumed Yuranosuke, "it is but ill eating,‡ after all. I will
order a fowl to be stewed; come, meanwhile, with me. Here, you
women there," he added ; "sing, sing ;" and beating time gaily with
his feet, he continued, "*teretsuku teretsuku, tsutsuten tsutsuten,* keep up

---

* One of seven celebrated fox-goblins. The other six were named Kurosuke,
Reita, Sansuke, Osuke, Yatsuyama, and Kudsunoha.

† Alluding to the Japanese custom, which is just the reverse, of acknow-
ledging a gift by lifting it to the forehead.

‡ Lit., "does not tempt one to eat." *Sakana*, the common term for fish
when used as food, originally meant anything eaten with *saké*, perhaps even simple
vegetables (*na*).

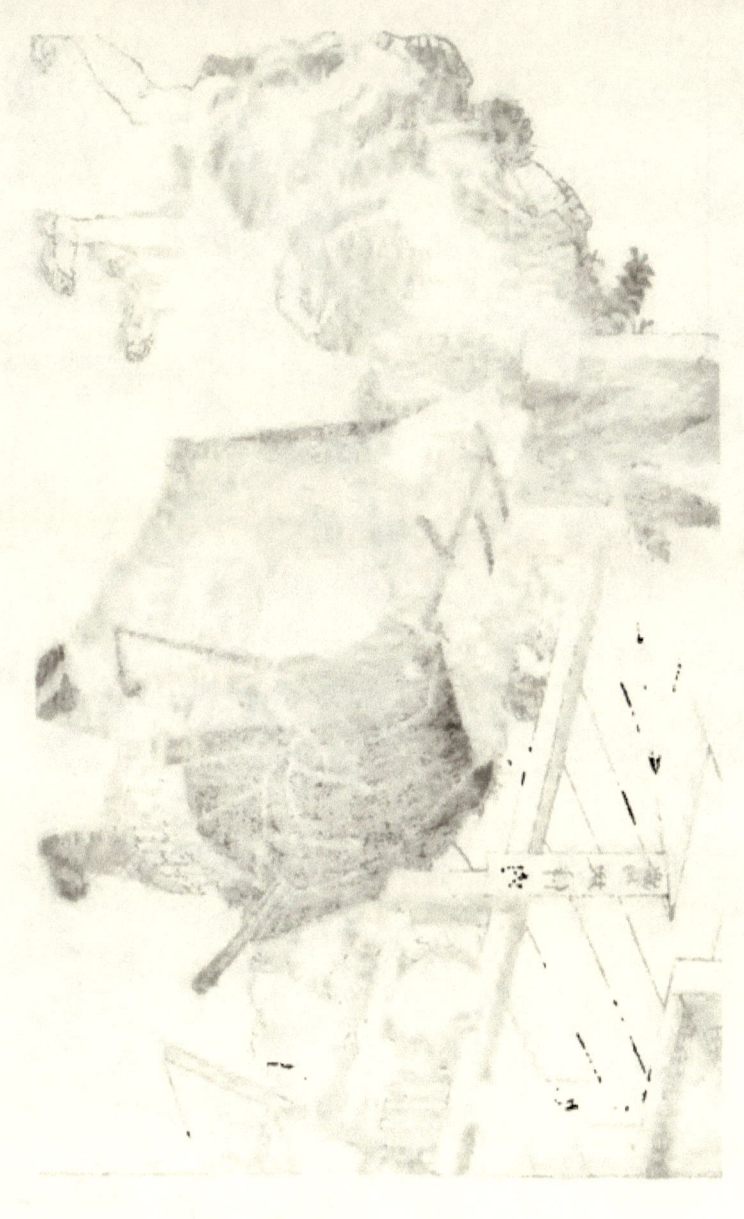

the merriment there," while he led the way, affecting a drunken gait, towards the inner apartment.

Bannai, coming down from the room where Kudaiu had left him, now made his appearance.

"It is clear enough, Sir Kudaiu," he said, "that the man has no thought of vengeance in his mind, or he would have been careful not to eat flesh on the anniversary of our lord's death. I shall inform Moronaho of this, and end his anxiety."

"In truth," replied Kudaiu, "it does not look as if anything was to be dreaded from such a fellow—and see!" he continued, pointing to a corner of the room, "he has left his sword there, plain proof that he is nothing but a spiritless brute; the blade is all red with rust as a rotten herring. We know the true character of the man at last, and need trouble ourselves about him no further. Ho, there! bearers, my *kago* here; quick, get in, Bannai."

"Nay," said the latter, "you are an old man; pray take it."

"You will permit me, then," replied Kudaiu, making as if to enter the *kago*, but deftly concealing himself under the raised floor.

"By-the-bye," continued Bannai, "I have heard that Kampei's wife, O Karu, is in the house; you remember her, Kudaiu, do you not?"

Surprised at receiving no answer, Bannai drew aside the blinds of the *kago*, and, looking in, was astonished to see nothing but a huge stepping-stone,* out of the court-yard.

"*Kowa!*" he exclaimed, "this is strange. Has Kudaiu met with the fate of the Princess Sayo of Matsura?"†

As he looked round with a perplexed air, he suddenly heard himself addressed by Kudaiu from beneath the flooring.

"Bannai, Bannai, this is but a device of mine. Just now, Rikiya brought his father a letter which has caused me some anxiety. I want

---

* Such as are generally found in courtyards of Japanese houses, for use in wet weather.

† Said to have drowned herself from disappointed love; and to have been turned into a stone.

to find out what its contents are, and as soon as I do, I shall let you know. Meanwhile, accompany the *kago* as if I were in it."

"I understand, I understand," answered Bannai, nodding his head, as he obeyed his companion's directions.

Meanwhile Karu was inhaling the fresh air from an upper verandah close by, trying to dispel the fumes of the *sake* she had been drinking, and chase away the gloom that settled upon her, as she compared the simple life of her village home with that she was now forced to lead.

Presently Yuranosuke appeared and said to her : "I must leave you for an instant. I have forgotten, *samurahi* though I be, a valuable sword, and must away at once to fetch it. You can arrange the hanging pictures on the wall and put fresh charcoal on the hearth by the time I return."

Re-entering the room where he had had his conversation with Kudaiu, he was surprised to find the latter had gone.

> "Hearken how the childish voices,
> Father, mother dear, repeat :
> Now the wayworn spouse rejoices,
> Wife and little ones to meet."*

"*Yah !* what is that ?" cried Yura, as the words fell upon his ear ; "cease, cease."

Then looking around for a light by which to read the letter Rikiya had brought him, he caught sight of a lantern hanging by a small doorway in a corner of the court, and went up to it. The dowager's letter, which was about Moronaho, was a pretty long one, and it took the *Karô* some time to wade through it, crammed as it was, like all women's epistles, with "and so-you-know's"† and sentences

---

* Lit., "As one hears in childish tones, Father, Mother, the words tell of the return home of husband or wife."

† Lit., with "*masassero's.*" In Japanese correspondence the word "*gosasero,*" a polite epistolary form of the copula or substantive verb, is constantly occurring. For "*gozasero,*" the expression "*ma'ra'esoro*" (lit., to cause to come or go) is commonly used by women and others not well versed in the complicated mysteries of Japanese letter-writing.

turned upside down. Karu, who was looking down from above, thinking the letter might be from some rival, leant over the balustrade, straining her eyes in the vain attempt to make out what it was about. A way of satisfying her curiosity, however, suddenly suggested itself. She disappeared for a moment, quickly returning with a bright metal mirror in her hand, by the aid of which she managed to read the letter from beginning to end.

Meanwhile Kudaiu, who had all this time lain concealed under the flooring of the adjoining room,* by furtive glances at the long slip of paper† which Yuranosuke, not being a god, could not suppose was within the ken of other eyes than his own, and had allowed to fall upon the ground as he unrolled it, contrived, by the help of the moonlight, to make himself master of the contents of the missive, and further managed to tear off a portion, which he intended to keep as a proof. Just then a metal ornament fell from Karu's hair upon the stones below, and Yuranosuke, startled by the noise, looked suddenly up, instinctively hiding the letter behind his back. A cunning smile crossed Kudaiu's face, while Karu, confused at being detected, hastily shut up the mirror, exclaiming, " Is that Yura ? "

" What ! O Karu, what are you about up there ? "

" Why, the *saké* you made me drink has overcome me, so I came out to see if the cool air would revive me a little."

" Oh, you came out to see if the cool air would revive you, did you? *Iya !* O Karu,‡ I have something to say to you. I cannot say it to you up there, I might as well be talking to you on the bridge of Heaven;§ come down to me, and you shall hear it."

" You have something to say to me? Why, what can you want with me?"

" Come down, and I will tell you."

---

* The flooring of a Japanese house is always raised above the ground, and is open, more or less, all round.

† A letter, if of any length, is always written upon a long, narrow slip of paper, which is afterwards rolled up and fastened in various ways.

‡ See Appendix. Names of women.

§ See Appendix.

" Well, I will go round by the stairs and come to you."

" No, no ; if you go round, some of the servants will get hold of you and make you drink more *sake*. Is there no other way ?—ha ! here is the very thing ; see, you can come down this ladder."

And seizing a small ladder that stood close by, Yuranosuke placed it against the eaves of the verandah.

"I cannot come down that way," cried the girl; " I should be frightened, I know ; I should be sure to fall."

" There is no danger," exclaimed Yuranosuke, " none whatever ; you need not fear, a strapping girl like you."

" Don't be so silly; it is like being in a boat, I know I shall tumble."

The girl, however, got upon the ladder, and began to descend, but very reluctantly. " Quick, quick," cried Yuranosuke, " or I will pull you down."

Frightened at his tone, she descended a few steps and then again hesitated. Irritated at her slowness, Yuranosuke sprang upon the ladder, and, seizing the girl, lifted her to the ground.

" What did you see from up there ? tell me," he added.

" See ? Oh, I did not see anything."

" You did, you did ; tell me."

" Why, what should I see ?—the letter seemed to please you."

" You read the whole of it from up there."

" I have told you I saw nothing—you are troublesome."

Yuranosuke, persuaded that she had read the whole, could not conceal his vexation. Karu, coming softly up to him, exclaimed : " What is it, Yuranosuke ; what is annoying you ? "

" O Karu, you know I have long loved you ; I want you to be my wife."

" Don't say that ; you know you are not speaking the truth."

" Truth has come out of falsehood. I am now in earnest. Say yes, say yes."

" No, I will not."

" Why ? "

" You are not in earnest; your 'truth has come out of falsehood' should be reversed. You have never wanted me, and now you only pretend to."

" What if I purchase you ? "

" Eh ! "

" To show that I am in earnest, I will see the proprietor of the house at once."

" I hardly know. I . . . . . "

" If you have a lover, I will assist you both afterwards."

" If I could be sure of that—but are you speaking truly ? "

" I am, on my honour as a *Samurahi.* Remain with me but three days, and then you shall be quite free."

" I should like that immensely, but you are only joking with me."

" Far from it; I will see the proprietor of the house, and make arrangements at once. Do not trouble yourself about the matter, but stay here quietly for a little time, until I return."

" Well, then, I will do so; you may trust me."

" Above all, do not stir from the place until I come back; you are mine now, you know."

" But for three days only."

" Of course, of course."

The girl was overjoyed at the prospect held out to her, and loaded Yuranosuke with thanks, as he hastened away to fulfil his promise. As she stood there, full of glad thoughts, she heard some one singing

" All the wide world cannot show
Grief the like of mine;
Endless is the weary woe,
As for him I pine."

" *Yah !* what is that ? cease ! "

" List'ning thro' the lengthen'd night,
To the shore-bird's * shriek;
Sad I mourn my lonely plight,
Sleep in vain I seek."

---

* *Chidori,* a small bird found in flights on sandy shores.

And depressed by the words, she fell into a melancholy mood, in the midst of which she was surprised by the unlooked-for appearance of her brother Heiyemon.

" How ! sister, is that you ? " said the new-comer.

" My brother ! " exclaimed the girl, in confusion, covering her face with her hands. " O, what a shameful thing, to be seen by you in this place ! "

" Nay, sister, not so," answered her brother, gently. "On my return from the Kuwantô,* I heard the whole story from our mother ; 'tis for your husband's sake, for our lord's service, that you have been sold ; do not be ashamed, sister, you have acted nobly."

" O brother, your kindness has made me quite happy—but I have got something to tell you, that will gladden you too. This very night, a gentleman is to take charge of me from the proprietor : the offer was altogether a surprise to me."

" That is most fortunate ; who is he ? "

" You know him very well ; it is Ohoboshi Yuranosuke."

" What ! Yuranosuke has promised to take charge of you ; is he really fond of you ? "

" No, I don't think he is ; he has only treated me several times during the last two or three days. He says, afterwards he will let me join my affianced, and let me go to him if I like. I could not meet with a better chance, could I ? "

" Does he know you are betrothed to Hayano Kampei ? "

" No, he does not. How could I tell him ? My being here might seem a shame to my father and my husband."

" H'm ! he seems to have become really a dissipated fellow. It looks very much as if he had given up all thoughts of revenging our lord's death."

" Nay, you are wrong there, quite wrong, I can assure you, brother ;

---

* The eight eastern provinces, of which Kamakura at first and afterwards Yedo were the capitals.

but—don't speak so loud—listen." And the girl whispered to him the contents of the letter.

" Are you sure that you read the letter correctly ? "

" Yes, the whole of it. Afterwards, he came close up to me and began to joke with me, and at last asked me to let him take charge of me."

" All this took place, then, after you had read the letter ? "

" Yes ; but why are you so solemn ? "

" Ah ! I understand it now. Sister, your days are numbered ; you cannot escape. You must let me decide your fate."

As the youth spoke, he suddenly drew his sword and aimed a stroke at his sister, who escaped it by a quick movement.

" Brother, brother," she cried, " what have I done wrong ? Both my betrothed and my parents are alive ; they should punish me if I have done wrong, not you. But if Yuranosuke takes charge of me I shall soon see both Kampei and my father and mother again. It was the thought of that made me so glad,—brother, do not be angry with me, even if I have done wrong."

And she clasped her hands in entreaty as she spoke. Her brother, flinging the naked blade away, threw himself upon the ground in an agony of grief, bending his head down to hide his tears.

" Poor sister ! " he cried, " you do not know, you do not know—our father is no more. He was cut down and murdered, on the twenty-ninth of the sixth month."

" Murdered ! my father ! "

" Aye, murdered. But that is not all. Oh, sister, try to bear the ill news ; your betrothed, Kampei, whom you hope soon to rejoin, he too is gone ; he has committed self-dispatch."

" O, brother, it cannot be true ! O me ! O me ! my betrothed Kampei, he too dead !—tell me, brother, it is not true," she cried, clinging to the youth's arm as she spoke, and bursting into tears.

" Too true, sister, alas ! But it would be out of place to tell you the sad story just now. Our poor mother was beside herself with grief, and her tears flowed constantly as she spoke to me of our loss. She begged me not to say anything about it to you, lest you should weep yourself to death at the terrible news. And I should have still kept silence did I not know that you cannot now escape your fate. Yuranosuke is immovable where his duty as a loyal retainer is concerned. Knowing nothing of your relation to Kampei, he never had any intention of taking charge of you; still less did any thought of love for you cross his mind. The letter you read contained matter of great importance, and it is quite clear that he only wanted to get hold of you to put you to death, and so keep his secret. You know the proverb, ' walls have ears.' * If the contents were to get abroad, even if not through you, your fault would still be as great. You were wrong to read a secret letter, and cannot escape your fate. Better to die by my hand than by that of some other man; and if I slay you, and tell our chief that, though you were my sister, I could not pardon you, as knowing what ought not to be entrusted to a woman, he will let me add my name to the list of conspirators, and I shall share with him the glory of the enterprise."†

"What makes the meanness of my condition so intolerable is, that unless I show the world that there is in me what makes me superior to the mass of men, I cannot hope to be allowed to take part in our chief's undertaking. You understand me, sister; give me your life, let yourself die at my hands."

The unfortunate girl, sobbing, sobbing all the time, could not at first make any reply; mastering her emotion, however, by a strong effort, she at last exclaimed :

" Hearing nothing from Kampei, I thought he had used the money

---

* " Kabe ni mimi, tokkuri ni kuchi," walls have ears and bottles have mouths.
† It is hardly necessary to comment upon the cold-blooded and selfish ferocity here exhibited  But "Chiushin" was the supreme virtue of the *samurai* of old Japan, and to it, just as to the nobler sentiment of patriotism among the ancient Greeks and Romans, all the tender feelings were required to be sacrificed.

paid for me, and had set out to join Yura, and I was angry with him for not coming to say good bye to me first. Oh me! what a miserable fate is mine! Though 'tis wrong to say it, my father was old when he was murdered, while my husband was not thirty—that makes it so pitiable, so pitiable! Oh that I might have seen him once ere he died! Why were we not brought together? I knew nothing of their sad fate, and have never mourned for them, for my father and my husband, both now no more. O, what have I to live for! But I must not die by your hand, brother, or our mother will be angry with you. Let me end my life myself. You can still take my head, or my whole body if you like, and show one or the other in proof of your devoted loyalty."

"Farewell, brother, farewell," she concluded, after a pause, taking up the sword he had thrown away, and placing the point against her throat. At this crisis Yuranosuke suddenly came upon the scene. Perceiving how matters were, he hastily caught Karu's arm, exclaiming :

"Patience, patience ; this must not be."

"Let go, let go," cried the girl excitedly, while her brother stood by transfixed with astonishment at the unlooked-for appearance of his chief—"I will, I must die."

"Ho, there," replied Yuranosuke, forcing the sword out of the girl's hand. "Brother and sister, listen to me. You have cleared away all doubt from my mind ; you, sir," turning to the brother, "shall accompany me to the Kuwantô, while your sister shall not die, but live, and duly mourn the dead."

"Mourn them," said the girl, "I will join them on the dark path," trying to seize the sword as she spoke.

"Your affianced, Kampei," exclaimed Yuranosuke, keeping a firm hold on the sword, "is one of us, but has not yet had the luck to slay a single one of our enemies ; and now that he is among those who no more are, he will be at a loss what to say to our lord; but he shall be at a loss no longer. Look here."

And jumping on the floor of the adjoining room, he thrust the sword between a division of the matting and through the planking beneath, piercing the writhing rascal Kudaiu, who lay hidden there, through the back.

"Drag the fellow out," cried Yuranosuke, at last.*

Heiyemon flew to obey his chief, and, seizing Kudaiu's blood-stained form, pulled the wretch roughly out.

"*Yah!*" cried the soldier, "that rascal Kudaiu? This is a piece of good luck, indeed"—flinging the miserable man down at his chief's feet as he spoke.

Yuranosuke, to prevent his prostrate victim from rising, caught hold of his side-hair, and forced his head roughly back, exclaiming :

"Villain ! Thou hast played the part of the vermin in the lion's belly, who seek to destroy what gives them food and shelter. Well rewarded by our lord, and honoured by his especial favour, thou hast become a dog of a follower of his murderer, Moronaho; secretly informing the enemy of our clan of everything, true or not true, that thou couldest get wind of! Listen. Forty and more of us have left our parents, abandoned our families, and given our wives, with whom we thought to pass our lives, to be harlots, that we might take vengeance upon our dead lord's enemy. Waking or dreaming, the scene of our lord's death was ever present to us, our bowels were twisted with grief, and our eyes ever wet with tears. This very night, the very eve of our lord's death-day—ah, what evil things I have been forced to say about him with my lips; but at least in my heart I heaped reverence upon reverence for his memory,—this very night was

---

* Yuranosuke, it is said, on rolling up Kawoyo's letter, after Karu had been detected in reading it, found that a portion had been torn off, and, always mistrustful of Kudaiu, was led by this discovery to guess at the latter's place of concealment. According to others, the *Karô* saw his former subordinate's face reflected in the mirror, by the aid of which Karu contrived to make herself mistress of the contents of the dowager's missive, at the moment when, startled by the fall of one of the girl's hair ornaments, he looked up and caught her in the act of reading the letter.

一 カ 酔 覧 ノ 場

VILLAINY DEFEATED.

it thou chosest to offer me flesh. I said nor yea nor nay as I took it, but O! with what shame, with what anguish did I, whose family for three generations have served the house of Hanguwan, find myself forced to let food pass my lips on the eve of my lord's death-day! I was beside myself with rage and grief, every limb in my body trembled, and all my bones* quaked as though they would shiver in pieces. Villain that thou art, devil, hellmate——" and twisting his hand more firmly in the wretch's hair, the infuriated *Karô* dragged his victim roughly along the ground, and flung him heavily on the stones, exclaiming:

"Ho, there! Heiyemon, I left a rusty sword in yonder room; away with this fellow, and hew him in pieces with it; make his death a long and painful one."

"So will I, my lord," answered the soldier, readily; and fetching the weapon, he rushed upon his prey, and hacked at him until he was covered with wounds.

"Sir soldier," cried the miserable wretch, endeavouring to creep towards his assailant, and clasping his hands pitifully. "Intercede for me, lady," turning towards Karu. "I entreat you, ask his lordship to have mercy upon me." Thus was the haughty Kudaiu reduced to seek the aid of a common soldier, to implore the assistance of one who in former days he would scarcely have deigned to see, bowing his head repeatedly in the extremity of his shameful agony.

"Stop, Heiyemon," cried Yuranosuke, suddenly bethinking himself; "it might be awkward if we killed the fellow here; take him away with you, as if he were simply dead-drunk."

He threw off his mantle as he spoke, and cast it on his half-dead victim, so as to cover up his wounds.

At this juncture, the partition was suddenly pushed back, and Yazama, Senzaki, and Takemori entered from the adjoining apart-

---

* Lit., "my forty-four bones."

ment. "Sir Yura," they cried, "we humbly crave your pardon for our error."

Yuranosuke, paying no heed to them, continued : "Heiyemon, this fellow is dead-drunk, take him to the Kamo stream yonder, and give him a bellyful of water-gruel; away with you."

END OF THE SEVENTH BOOK.

# BOOK THE EIGHTH.

———

### THE BRIDAL JOURNEY.

### TRANSLATOR'S NOTE.

THIS is simply a description in verse of the journey of the wife and daughter of Kakogawa Honzô from the eastern capital to Kiyôto, the object of which is sufficiently indicated in the succeeding Book. An attempt at a metrical rendering of this portion of the text will be found in the Appendix, it being thought that an insertion of it in this place would interfere with the action of the story.

# BOOK THE NINTH.

———

### THE REPENTANCE OF KAKOGAWA HONZÓ.

ON the morrow of the day when the events recorded in the Seventh Book took place at the tea-house in the Gi-on Street at Kiyóto, Yuranosuke, whom a heavy fall of snow had detained through the night, returned to the wretched dwelling in the obscure village of Yamashina, where he had found a retreat, attended by some servants of the tea-house.

He seemed to be still under the influence of *saké*, and on entering the gate fell to heaping up the snow that lay in the yard, in a helpless manner, as if he had lost his wits.

"Ah, your honour," cried the servants, with a simultaneous note of admiration; "how beautiful everything looks this morning!

> 'See how yonder bamboos low
> Bend beneath their load of snow.'

How apt the lines are; 'tis quite a picture, a fair scene indeed!"

"Ah! in truth," cried a woman-servant who had come out to meet them; "you need only see this place once never to wish to go elsewhere, I am sure."

" Eh ! what?" exclaimed Yuranosuke.

" ' From the shores of Sumiyoshi.'

You know the song, don't ye?—

> ' From the shores of Sumiyoshi,
> Rising o'er the rippling sea,
> High into the morning sky,
> High into the evening sky,
> Lo ! the hills of Awaji.' "*

" Let the wench boast of the place as she likes ; for my part, I would rather empty a pot of *saké* in the Gi-on Street than finish a dozen here.   You're but a stupid lot, after all—into the house with ye, into the house with ye !   Hallo ! wife," he continued, in a louder voice, " where are you?—here are some visitors."

Jerking the words out in a drunken fashion, the *Karô* staggered towards the house, where he was greeted by his wife Ishi.   "You are back, husband," she cried, pouring out tea with a pleasant smile ; " what a cold morning it is," she continued, showing no sign of ill-temper or jealousy† as she handed her husband the fragrant infusion, to which she had added a little salt to assist in clearing away the fumes of the *saké* he had been drinking.

Yuranosuke, however, merely took a sip and then threw the rest away, exclaiming : " Wife, wife, what stuff is this? do you think this will refresh me after such capital liquor as I have been drinking yonder ?   Ah, ah ! how the snow has fallen, to be sure !"

"Well, why stand there out in the cold?" cried Ishi; " see how the snow drives in, like flakes of carded cotton."

"Ah, wife !" exclaimed Yuranosuke, as they all entered, " you women begin to lose your charms when the children come and household cares press upon you.   I am somewhat remiss in my duty to you of late, I confess.   O, what pretty girls there were

---

* A large island, some distance to the south of Sumiyoshi (a portion of Ohozaka).

† The two vices most dreaded by Japanese husbands in their wives.

yonder, with complexions pink as Ise prawns! and what capital *saké*, too! True enough the proverb, 'love goes out with the red petticoat.'" •

"Wife, wife," he resumed, after a pause, throwing himself on the ground with an expression of sudden pain, "quick, I have the cramp in my foot, pray chafe it . . . . . . Ah! it is better now; that will do, that will do"—thrusting his wife, who was complying with his request, rudely away, as he spoke.

"Enough of this, husband," she cried; "have a care, have a care; you are not yourself yet.— I fear,' continued Ishi, addressing herself courteously to the attendants—"I fear he must have been a great trouble to you."

Just then, Rikiya appeared, and enquired after his father.

"He seems asleep, mother; had we not better put a pillow under his head?"

Now, if we were to look a little below the surface, we should find this conduct of the three all a mere pretence, cloaking the reality like the varnish on the pillow concealing the common *Kiri* wood it is made of. † They put the pillow, however, under the *Karó s* head, who muttered a sleepy disapproval of the act. Ishi then dismissed the attendants, who, after leaving their respectful duty for the master of the house, and endeavouring, but in vain, by expressive glances to induce Rikiya to return with them, reluctantly withdrew. As soon as they were out of hearing Yuranosuke rose to his feet.

"Rikiya, you see yonder mass of snow I have been pretending to amuse myself by heaping up? There was a meaning in it—can you guess what it is?"

"I think I can, father. Snow is so light that the least breeze blows it away in dust; yet when heaped up into a mass, as you

---

* A red petticoat was worn by unmarried girls only.

† For a description of the Japanese pillow, see Appendix. The Kiri tree is the *Paulounia Imperialis*. The wood is soft, light in texture and colour, and peculiarly dry.

have done there, it may roll down from some mountain-top and
crush even huge rocks, just as if it were a boulder. So our force
is in our united loyalty, in the weight of our affliction. But that
mass of snow will melt away in time under the sun's rays, and . . . . "

"Nay, not so," broke in the *Karô;* "we forty-seven plotters,
myself, you, and the others, are all masterless men, in the sun of
no one's favour.* In the shade, that mass of snow would take long
enough to melt. Let it be removed, by-the-by, into the inner court,
where the sun's rays cannot beat upon it. As for us, we must
persevere and do the best we can, like the sage Sonko † of the old
story, who, being so poor that he could not buy oil for his lamp,
gathered fire-flies and studied by their light; or that other philosopher
Riuto,‡ whose poverty compelled him to be content to supply his
need with the dim light reflected from a heap of snow."

"Let yonder mass," he resumed, "be taken at once into the
small court at the back. I must away, and write to Sakai; if any
messenger comes let me know."

"Your honour's orders shall be attended to," cried a woman-
servant who was standing by.

Yuranosuke, pushing back a partition, then withdrew.

Presently appeared the wife of Kakogawa Honzô, the *Karô* of
Momonoi Wakasanosuke, seeking out the retreat of the deep designing
councillor of Yenya. In her girdle she carried her husband's long and
short swords, and ordering the bearers to set down a *norimono* which
preceded her, she composedly demanded admission at the *rônin's*
hermitage. A woman servant, letting down her long sleeves §—in
Yuranosuke's better days it would have been a lackey—came
forward crying in a loud, vulgar voice : "Who is there ? "

"I believe," said the visitor, "this is the dwelling of Yuranosuke
Sama ? If I am right, pray let him know that Tonasé, the wife of

---

* "Hikagemono," lit., " person in shade," *i.e.,* " under a cloud."
† A Chinese sage; see Appendix.
‡ A Chinese sage ; see Appendix.
§ That is a mere scullery wench, with her sleeves tucked up.

Kakogawa Honzô, is here. It is long since I had the pleasure of seeing your master, and I should be glad if you would tell him that I have come a great distance in the hope of being allowed an interview with him."

The wife of Honzô then turned to the bearers of the *norimono*, and bade them bring their burden up to the gate.

"Come, daughter," she cried, as her order was obeyed, "you can alight now."

Konami, for the occupant of the *norimono* was none other, accordingly stepped forth, gladsome as the *uguisu** at sight of the wild plum's bloom in the valley-bottom.

"And is this then the home of Sir Rikiya!" cried the girl, whose face was concealed by the white head-dress of a bride. "O, mother, how shall I meet him!" The servant, meanwhile, mending a little the disorder that was apparent about the mean entrance, and affecting a soft manner, invited the new-comer to follow her within. Tonasé accordingly, dismissing the *kago*-bearers, passed into the house, Konami clinging timidly to her mother's arm.

They had hardly seated themselves on the matting when Ishi entered with a graceful step.

"Welcome, welcome, Tonasé Sama," she exclaimed; "and you too, Konami; this visit is most kind on your part. I ought long since to have presented myself to you, but you doubtless know our situation; really, your attention makes me feel quite ashamed of myself."

"Pray, O Ishi Sama, do not make such strangers of us. True, we meet each other to-day for the first time, but your son and my daughter were betrothed long ago; we are both of us mothers-in-law, and, I am sure, need stand upon no ceremony with each other."

"Your kind expressions fill me with confusion. How did you manage to leave your husband, doubtless occupied as usual with his lord's affairs, and journey, this cold weather, all the way to the

---

* The Japanese nightingale. *Herbivox cantans.*

capital? To you, madam, Kiyóto is probably familiar enough; for your daughter, however, it may have some novelty. She must see the famous Gi-on Street and the temple of Kiyomidsu, the great Buddha at Nara, the Hall of Chion, and I can get you admittance to the Temple of Kinkaku."*

The bride, overwhelmed with shyness, could only meet her hostess' kind words with a faint "*Ai, ai.*"

But her mother composedly replied:

"No other than this is the reason of our visit. After the betrothal of our children, an unexpected turn took place in the fortunes† of your lord Yenya-dono, and your son, together with his father, became without a fixed home. Ah me! such changes are too common in this world of ours; but my husband's purpose remained still unaltered, and we sought after you everywhere for a long time, but without success. At last we heard you were living here; and as my daughter had arrived at a marriageable age, we were desirous that she should come to you without delay. I trust, therefore, you will not consider us as intruders. My husband intended to have come in person, but could not; and in lieu thereof gave me his two swords, which, as you see, I carry in my girdle, to represent him, so that at present I play the part of father as well as that of mother. I should be glad to talk over the matter with your husband, for I am very anxious the marriage should take place. To-day is a lucky day, fortunately, and if you would kindly order the necessary preparations to be made—— "

"What you say takes me quite by surprise," replied the wife of Yura. "Unfortunately, my husband is away just now; if he were at home, I am sure he would thank you most warmly for your kindness. But, as you know, when the betrothal took place he was, by the favour of our late lord, honoured with excellent appointments, and could well aspire to the hand of your daughter for his son. Now everything is

---

* The "lions" of Kiyóto, of which a brief description will be found in the Appendix.

† Politeness required the death of Yenya to be referred to in this indirect manner.

very different : he is but a *rônin*, without a single follower ; while your
husband is high in his lord's service—and though your daughter was
promised to our son, to ask for her now would be as out of place as if
one were to demand a temple-bell in exchange for a paper lantern.
Thus, then, we think the marriage ought not to be consummated. And,
as the betrothal has not been ratified by the customary exchange of
bridal presents, my husband says it will be no slight if your daughter
should find another bridegroom."

"Indeed, madam," exclaimed Tonasé in a tone of surprise ; " I
hardly understand you ; but, I can assure you, you are not just to
yourself. As to any difference in position between your husband and
mine, why, the disparity is all on our side. When your husband, as
councillor of one of the higher nobles, had appointments of 1500 *koku*,*
mine, whose lord was only a member of the lower nobility, was allotted
500 *koku* by the year, and no more—1000 less than what your husband
received ; yet, did you refuse our alliance on that score ? Sir Yura,
compelled by misfortune to become a *rônin*, has nothing,—my husband
has—what ? only 500 *koku* more."

"*Iya !*" answered Ishi ; "you are in error. The difference of 500,
or even 1000, *koku* would not matter—if only your husband did not
differ so much from mine in disposition ; we should not refuse your
daughter because her father is high in his lord's service."

"What do you mean," replied the wife of Honzô, "by your talk
about your husband and mine differing in disposition ?—tell me, I am
all ears."

"Our lord's self-dispatch," said Ishi, "was brought about by his high
spirit ; and it was his refusal to dishonour himself that resulted so
fatally for his house ; while Honzô, though of *samurai* rank, stooped
to bribe Moronaho with money and gifts. Yura does not serve two
masters, and cannot receive your daughter as a bride for his son."

---

* A koku of rice (a little over five bushels) was worth about two thirds of a
sovereign. Hence, 1500 koku would be worth about £1000. This estimate,
however, makes no allowance for the different purchasing values of money in
Japan, under the old régime, and Europe.

Tonasé, starting angrily to her feet, interrupted the wife of the *Karô.*

"Stooped to bribe?—of whom talk you? As matters are, I cannot escape your insults; for my daughter's sake I shall pass them over, for the side of the wife must always give way to that of the husband. But whether you allow the marriage to be consummated or not, my daughter is your son's wife, before all the world."

"Pfuh!" answered Ishi, "all that is but fine talk; and, at all events, if she is my son's wife, he can put her away at will; and I, his mother, acting for him, do accordingly put her away from this very moment."*

As she ended, the wife of Yuranosuke suddenly pushed back a partition and disappeared.

"O, mother!" cried Konami, bursting into tears, "I was full of anxiety when I was betrothed, and you promised me that I should be united to Rikiya, and—and so I am here with you; never imagining that my mother-in-law would drive me thus cruelly away. Ah, mother, soothe her, and prevent my marriage from being broken off."

And the poor girl clung to Tonasé, who gazed upon her wistfully.

"Perhaps 'tis a parent's partiality," she said at last, "but you always seemed to me to possess more elegancies than any ten girls together; and so I sought anxiously for a good husband for you, and, thinking I had found one in Rikiya, I caused you to be betrothed to him, and came to seek him here; it cannot be all for nothing. I do not know what O Ishi means, but she cannot put you away without his consent; no mother-in-law can do such a thing, the

---

* The husband could, and still can, divorce his wife at pleasure, the only check on the practice being that imposed by public opinion. He must also, as a rule, return any dowry he may have received. The wife can in no case avail herself of a like privilege. In Japan, even at this day, the *patria potestas*, in its completest form, governs all social relations. An acquaintance of the translator got rid thus of three wives in less than three years; but it is fair to add, his conduct did not meet with the approval of his neighbours.

notion is preposterous. Perhaps it is that, *rônin* as they are now, they are at their wits' end to support themselves, and so have hit upon marrying their son to some rich citizen's daughter, exchanging their good blood for money, and shamelessly breaking their faith with us. Daughter, when such people reject you, you can throw the insult back in their faces. There are plenty of families who will be glad enough to receive you as a bride—why should you not marry elsewhere? Come, answer me, daughter, and with firmness."

The poor woman could hardly restrain herself from giving way to her own grief, as she implored her daughter to master her distress.

"Mother, mother," cried the latter, after a pause, "you are cruel to me. When we left home my father told me that I was most fortunate in meeting with such a husband as Ohoboshi Rikiya, who, though now a *rônin*, was of excellent parts and elegant manners. He said that no virtuous woman could love two husbands, and enjoined me never to marry a second one if circumstances should separate Rikiya and myself, for no married woman ought to think of such a thing. Above all, sleeping or waking, I was not to forget a tittle of my duty to my husband, and never to omit to treat my parents-in-law with the utmost respect and tenderness. 'Always cherish your husband most dearly,' he added, 'never show a jealous disposition even by way of joke; and if you should become in a condition to make me anxious do not conceal it, but let me know the moment you find that you are after the manner of women.' I recollect my father's very words. If I am put away I cannot help it, but I will not add grief upon grief to my father, come what may, say what you will, mother, by becoming the wife of any one but Rikiya."

As Konami concluded, her mother felt her heart swell, almost to bursting, with affectionate sympathy, and, unable to restrain her emotion, gave vent to it in a flood of tears, half unsheathing, in her despair, the sword she carried in her girdle.

"Hold! mother," cried the girl, laying her hand on the weapon and looking up in Tonasé's face; "what would you do?"

"What would I do!" cried Tonasé, "what am I to do? As you
said a little while since, your father is anxious that your marriage with
Rikiya should be concluded as soon as possible, desirous, as fathers
are, of looking upon the face of his first grandchild, and of seeing his
daughter happy, and now the marriage is become an impossibility;
you are rejected, and I shall have to take you back home,—how shall
I show my face to your father, and tell him you have been driven
away! I do not know what to do, or where to turn for help.   And the
truth is, you are not my own child, but your father's daughter by
a former wife, and as I have not brought about the marriage, I shall be
reproached as like all stepmothers and careless about your happiness.
What have I to live for? let me die, let me die, and let your father
know afterwards why I sought death."

"No, no, mother," cried Konami, "'tis not you, but I, who am
hated by my husband, who ought to die.   Alive, I am but a trouble
both to my father and to you, and cause you nothing but grief, unfilial
wretch that I am!   Mother, take my life, I beseech you; I would fain
die here on the threshold of the house from which I am driven away,—
quick, mother, do not delay!"

"Well said, daughter!" exclaimed Tonasé; "you have a brave
heart, but you shall not die alone.   We will together fare by the three
roads;* your mother will do as you bid her, but will not be long after
you.   Are you ready, daughter?"—restraining her tears with splendid
fortitude, and preparing to give the fatal stroke.

The shrill notes of a pipe arrested her hand.   "Ha!" she cried,
"did you hear that, daughter?   'Tis some beggar, I suppose, and the
air is that of the 'Crane and her little ones.'†   Though only a bird,
she loves her young.   What a terrible fate is mine—that I should have
to take the life of my innocent child!"

Distracted with grief, Tonasé could with difficulty stand firm, while
with trembling hand she raised the blade aloft under which Konami,
kneeling on the ground, with a resolute expression, repeated, with

---

* *Vide* Appendix. "Shide Hill."          † A popular song, so called.

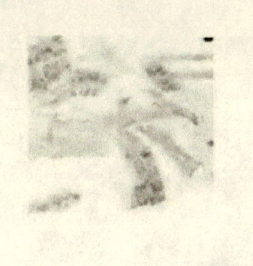

THE DESPAIR OF KONAMI.

clasped hands, "*Namu-amida Butsu*," and calmly awaited the death-stroke. Ere the blow descended, a voice called out loudly, "No more!"

Astonished at this unexpected interruption, Tonasé looked round irresolutely. Her grasp on the fatal weapon relaxed, and the sound of the pipe ceased.

"Ha! the *komusô* is being sent away. Would that some help came to us; but courage, daughter, we must not falter, if a thousand voices cried 'No more!' or the whole world will laugh at us as a pair of cowards."

"Are you quite prepared?" she resumed, after a pause, raising the weapon a second time.

She was on the point of delivering the blow, when the sound of the pipe again made itself heard, and the voice repeated, "No more!"

"What can this mean?" exclaimed Tonasé, in perplexity. "Is it only to send the *komusô* away with his dole, or is it to stay my hand?"

"*Iya!*" exclaimed another voice, from within, "it is to stay your hand; my son Rikiya shall marry your daughter."

"*Yeh!*" cried Tonasé, in a tone of astonishment. "Whose voice is that? Can it be yours, O Ishi Sama? Oh, madam, are you in earnest?"

> "O the pine trees twain!
> Like years, like love attain,
> O joy no bounds restrain!"

sang Ishi, as she made her appearance, bearing a small white-wood four-cornered stand upon her uplifted palm.

"I saw you were thoroughly in earnest, Tonasé Sama," said the wife of Yuranosuke, "in your purpose of taking the life of this young lady, your only daughter—for such she is in effect, if not in blood—whose modest behaviour has called forth my admiration as much as her unfortunate position has excited my compassion. This marriage, distasteful though it is to me, shall take place. In return, I must ask for a bridal gift of a very different kind from what is commonly bestowed on such an occasion as the present. And I have brought this stand for you to place it on"—setting the stand down on the

matting before her guest, who, after some hesitation, returned her
sword to its scabbard with an expression of relief.

"Your wish shall be gratified, lady," replied Tonasé, after a slight
pause. "This pair of swords I carry in my girdle are heirlooms in my
husband's family. The long one is of the workmanship of the famous
swordsmith Masamune;* the short one is of the handiwork of the
equally celebrated maker Yukiyasu;† there is nothing, believe me, my
husband values more highly. . . . ."

"You are laughing at us *rônin*," broke in Ishi, "with your precious
swords. What help would they be to us in our need? No, no, that
is not the bridal gift I want from you."

"Then, pray, lady, what is it that will satisfy you?"

"The head of Kakogawa Honzô, placed upon this stand—that will
satisfy me," cried Ishi.

"The head of Honzô?" exclaimed Tonasé, in astonishment.

"Yes," replied Ishi. "When our lord, the Baron Yenya, in
his high-spirited eagerness to revenge himself upon Moronaho, drew
his sword upon his enemy within the palace at Kamakura, your
husband, whom luck would have present, threw himself upon our
lord and prevented him from fully satisfying his wrath, so that the
destroyer of our house got off with no more than a slight scratch.
None can tell how terribly the recollection of his unfulfilled vengeance
embittered the last moments of our lord! though no word could
pass his lips, well we knew how great was his agony, and how
intense was the hatred he felt for your husband, as the shades of
death were closing-in around him. We are still liegemen of our
ill-fated chief; if you would that the daughter of Honzô become
the wife of our son, you must present us with your husband's
head on this stand; if you would not willingly be separated from

---

* Masamune flourished about the end of the thirteenth century. A very
cleverly written and interesting essay on "The Sword of Japan," by T. H. R.
McClatchie, will be found in the Transactions of the Asiatic Society of Japan,
from October, 1873, to July, 1874.

† His full name was Nami-no-hira Yukiyasu.

him, with both your heads. As soon as we shall have feasted our eyes on this sight, the marriage shall take place without further delay. *Sah, sah ;* what say you—yea or nay? yea or nay?"

Confounded by Ishi's sneering tone and strange request, mother and child hung their heads in confusion, unable to utter a word. In the midst of their terrible perplexity, a voice, apparently that of the mendicant, was heard, exclaiming loudly :

"'Tis the head of Kakogawa Honzô you demand—here it is, take it."

As the words were said, the beggar presented himself, and, throwing off his deep-brimmed hat revealed the features of Kakogawa Honzô.

" *Yah !*" exclaimed Tonasé, in astonishment, "it is your father! Honzô, husband, what means this disguise? Why have you come here? Tell me——"

"A truce to your chatter," interrupted Honzô. "I have heard all that has passed. I came here, secretly, for a special purpose, of which more anon—for the present forbear from questioning me."

"And so," resumed the *Karô* of Momonoi, addressing Ishi, "you, lady, are the wife of Yuranosuke Sama. I foresaw matters would take this turn, and therefore, without saying a word to wife or child, I came here to see for myself whether the state of things was such as I anticipated; nor have I been disappointed. And now you would have my head, as a bridal gift. Ha! ha! why, your husband, lost in dissipation and enervated by debauchery, has become an imbecile, and must have quite given up the idea of avenging his chief's death, which no true *samurahi* would ever cease to cherish. Abandoned wretch! Yura is a perfect model of a spiritless lout. And as a frog's spawn can only be expected to produce frogs, doubtless Rikiya is not far behind his father in imbecility and cowardice. Do you think my neck is in any danger from the blunt-edged swords of *samurahi* of that stamp? Pshaw! do not talk nonsense."

Setting his foot upon the stand, as he concluded this insulting speech, the *Karô* of Momonoi broke it to pieces.

"Pick up the pieces," he resumed, "what want we with your son?"

"Ah!" interrupted Ishi, "you are insolent, sir; we will see whether the sword of a *rónin*, unused though it be, is not keen enough to strike the head off your shoulders. The wife of Yuranosuke, awkward as she may be in handling a weapon, is willing to try her skill with you, so defend yourself, defend yourself"—gathering up her dress as she spoke, and snatching a spear from the wall, with which she made a hurried thrust at Honzô. At this sight Konami and Tonasé started back in affright, and threw themselves upon Honzô, who cast them off with an angry exclamation, and seizing the spear close to the point, twisted it away from his body. Ishi, placing her feet firmly together, endeavoured to force the weapon out of her adversary's hand, but the latter, giving it a sudden kick, caused it to fly into the air. Without troubling himself further about the spear, Honzô next seized Ishi by the dress and threw her on the ground. This done, the dexterous *Karô* set his knee upon the prostrate form of the wife of Yuranosuke, who gnashed her teeth in the extremity of her rage.

The wife and daughter of Honzô looked on in fear and distress, not knowing what to do.

At this juncture Rikiya unexpectedly presented himself, and, seeing at a glance how matters stood, seized the spear which was lying on the ground, and, without a moment's hesitation, ran Honzô with it through the chest. The latter uttered a deep groan and fell heavily to the ground, while his wife and daughter, their eyes blind with tears, caught hold of each other, beside themselves with terror.

Suddenly Yuranosuke came upon the scene, and seizing his son's arm, prevented a repetition of the thrust.

"*Yah!* Rikiya, what are you about? You are overhasty, overhasty."

And turning to the wounded man, the *Karô* resumed :

"I am rejoiced to see you again, Sir Honzô, after so long an interval. In falling by the hand of your son-in-law, you have, I know, met with the fate you most desired."

THE REWARD OF KAKO-AWA HONZŌ.

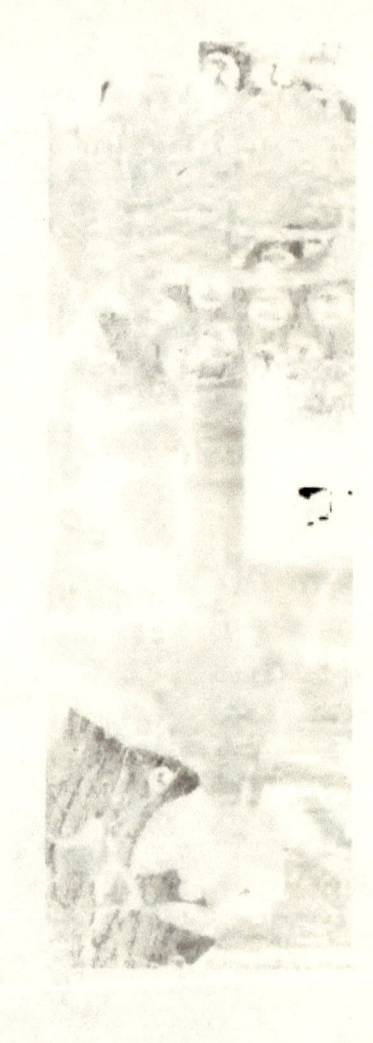

As Yuranosuke, who had divined Honzô's real wishes, concluded, the latter opened his eyes, exclaiming :

"I knew from the first that you had never swerved from your purpose of avenging your chief's death, and that your seeming dissipation was a mere device to throw Moronaho off his guard, while you collected your band together. Ah me! would that I had acted as you are now acting. At the inauguration at Tsuruga-oka, last spring, my lord Momonoi was publicly affronted by Moronaho, and, writhing under the insult, sent for me. After much angry talk, he declared that, the next day, he would throw himself upon his enemy and slay him within the very precincts of the palace ; and I could see from the expression of his face that my youthful and headstrong chief was not to be moved from his determination. Now, I knew that Moronaho's treatment of my master was due to the fact that the latter, who was a member of the lower nobility only, had made but a trifling present upon receiving his appointment ; and, accordingly, without letting my lord know, for I felt I was acting shamefully, I went, most unbecomingly, to Moronaho, and gave him gold and silver and silk robes, and other things. Thus I got my lord out of what seemed to me a great peril, by bribing—for what I did was nothing else—his powerful adversary, who, on next meeting my master, made full apology for his insolent conduct ; so that all thought of revenge had to be dismissed from my lord's mind, and he was forced to let his anger be appeased. It happened otherwise with my lord's colleague, Yenya Sama, whom I prevented from slaying his antagonist because I thought by doing so I might render self-dispatch unnecessary. In this I erred grievously, and, ever since, I have never ceased to repent of the fault I then committed, and of which my daughter's present wretched condition is one of the consequences. As an atonement, I have travelled here to offer my gray head to my daughter's betrothed. I sent on my wife and daughter in advance, and, after fully confessing how I had bribed Moronaho, obtained leave from my lord, and, journeying hitherwards by a different road from that which these women followed, arrived two days before them. I had learned to play on the pipe in my youth and I now found the knowledge of use. After arriving here, I hung about the neighbourhood for four days, and thoroughly penetrated your designs. It then seemed to me that if I fell by your hand your hatred of me would cease, and you would consent to the union of my daughter with your son. If that hope should be realised I shall be infinitely grateful to you for all time to come, and most earnestly do I implore you not to make my journey fruitless. When I failed in my duty as a loyal retainer, I did not, it is true, quit life as I ought to have done, but now I abandon it for my child's sake.    Sir Yura, you cannot refuse to comply with the last prayer of a father." Choked by his tears, the wounded man could utter nothing more, while his wife and daughter, overwhelmed at the terrible sight, could only repeat mournfully :

"Alas! alas! how could we foresee this! 'Tis our delay, husband, father, that has resulted thus miserably! How terrible to know that our cowardice has been the cause of your death—pardon, pardon!"

With these words the two women threw themselves at the feet of the dying man, while Yuranosuke, with his wife and son, stood by, speechless with horror at the frightful scene.

At last, Yuranosuke found utterance. "Honzô-dono,* we are told that the superior man hates the crime and not the criminal.† Your desire to form alliance with us, and our repugnance to it, are not matters to be talked of at the same moment. It is true that we disliked you, but now, as you are not long for this world, I will lay bare to you my most secret thought." Pushing back, as he spoke, the sliding windows of the room, which looked upon the inner court, the *Karô* displayed to the dying man's view two tombs of snow, fashioned with ornaments depending from each of the five corners of the entablature, and thus revealing the future, showed

---

\* " Dono," lit., " palace." is a title of great courtesy, equivalent to "your excellency."

† A quotation from the analects of Confucius.

what the final result of his designs would surely be.   Tonasé at once comprehended him.

"Ah!" she cried, "they will slay their chief's enemy, but will serve no second lord; they will perish, as yonder snow will perish, rather than prove disloyal to the memory of Yenya-dono. It was with such a thought in his heart that Rikiya sought to put away my daughter, not from harshness, but out of a most tender compassion. O Ishi Sama, I would fain recall the wrathful words I have spoken to you."

"Ah! Tonasé Sama," cried Ishi, sadly, "there will be none of that married happiness you hoped to see, that was to be without end,* like the greenery of the *tamatsubaki*.† To receive a bride so soon to become a widow—can a more miserable mockery of joy be conceived! How cruel you must have thought me when, with feigned roughness, I told you the marriage was impossible."

"Nay," exclaimed the mother of Konami, "you have nothing to reproach yourself with; but I, when I recollect how you must have overheard me telling Konami that you were seeking for some rich citizen's daughter as a bride for your son, breaking the faith you had plighted to us, I am so penetrated with shame and distress that I hardly dare lift my eyes to you, O Ishi Sama."

"Your daughter, Tonasé Sama, in birth and beauty is all that we could desire in a bride for our son; alas, under what evil destiny has she been born!"

Ishi's tears checked her further utterance.

Honzô, mastering his emotion, exclaimed :

"Now I am happy, now my hopes will be fulfilled. The devotion of Goshisho,‡ who received with a smile the news of his

---

* Lit., "for eight thousand ages."

† The "tamatsubaki" is probably a species of *Euonymus*, and consequently an evergreen.

‡ An ancient Chinese sage, minister of the King of Wu, whose story will be found in the Appendix.

disgrace by the King of Go for the loyal advice he had tendered, is less admirable than the rare fidelity of Ohoboshi, who will henceforth be cited throughout all Japan as a mirror of loyalty to succeeding generations, with a pride equal to that with which China has for so many ages boasted of her hero Yojô.* In becoming your wife, Sir Rikiya, worthy son of so unique a father, my daughter is a hundred times more fortunate than if she were chosen as the bride of an emperor. To you, the betrothed of my daughter, —the most honoured in being thus accepted by you among the daughters of *samurahi*,—I crave leave to present the bridal gifts of which this is a list." And drawing a folded paper from his bosom, the dying *Karô* gave it to Rikiya.

"*Kowa !*" cried the latter, in some astonishment, as he unfolded the paper, after having lifted it courteously to his forehead— "this is no list of gifts, it is a detailed plan of Moronaho's castle ; porch, barracks, quarters, water-gate, magazines, down to the very wood-sheds ; every portion is minutely delineated."

"Hah !" exclaimed the *Karô* of Yenya, delightedly, as he snatched the paper from his son's hands, "a thousand thanks, a thousand thanks. This is just what I was in need of. For some time past we have been all prepared, but for lack of a guide like this could not advance a step in our enterprise. This plan will be to us as the secret books of Son and Go ;† will be our *Six steps and Three Methods.*‡ We had previously arranged to make an attack by night, getting over the wall here by scaling ladders, then creeping up to the porch and forcing open the outer rain-shutters, to rush in and make our way to our enemy's apartments,—ha ! here we can divide ourselves and then attack thus—— "

As Ohoboshi concluded, he exchanged a look of satisfaction with his son, but Honzô, who had listened attentively to what had passed, exclaimed :

---

* See Appendix.
† Ancient Chinese writers on military tactics.
‡ An old Chinese work on the art of war.

"Nay, nay, your attack must not be made in that manner. Moronaho is a most cautious man, and every shutter and slide in his castle is well furnished with bolts and bars and inside fastenings. You cannot prize them open, and to break them open with mallets would, of course, make far too much noise."

"True," cried Yuranosuke: "but I have provided for that. They say that too much pondering over a difficulty makes it harder than ever to get over; and so it was that, on my return from amusing myself at the tea-house, the sight of the bamboos yonder in the courtyard, bending under their load of snow, suddenly made me think of a plan of forcing open the shutters, which I will explain to you."

So saying, the *Karô* went out into the courtyard, and going close up to a bamboo bending under the weight of snow that had become heaped upon its branches, asked Honzô's attention.

"This bamboo, you see, is weighed down by its load of snow. I shall procure a number of bows, and after bending them in like manner by stringing them, I shall cause their ends to be inserted into the upper and lower grooves in which the shutters slide. Next, upon a given signal, all the strings will be cut through, and the bows suddenly straightening themselves—thus," shaking off the snow from the bamboo, which, relieved of its burden, immediately resumed its natural position, "will prize out the edge of the upper slot, so that the shutters will all fall outwards with a clatter, and we can rush in upon our enemy in the confusion."

The wounded man, delighted with the device, for a moment forgot his condition.

"Good, good," he cried, at length. "How could the Baron Yenya, miserable man, be so shallow-minded * as not to have applied to you in his difficulties, to a retainer so fertile in stratagems, so loyal of heart."

And as he looked back on the past, he could not refrain from

---

* There is here in the original an untranslatable pun, based upon the name of the real personage, of whom Yenya is the fictitious representative. The pun is explained in the Appendix.

I

# BOOK THE TENTH.

---

### THE PROOF OF GIHEI.

AND so muttering to himself, Ryochiku went away.*

It was past the hour of the hog,† and the night was dark, the moon being hidden by clouds, when a patrol of several men, iron mace and bundle of cord in hand,‡ and darkened lantern hanging at hip, crept slowly along one of the streets of Sakai, scanning each house closely as they advanced. One of the number went in front, like the dog scenting game for the hunter. Him the one who seemed to be chief of the patrol motioned to approach, and, as the former obeyed, whispered a word or two in his ear, to which the man immediately nodded an assent.

The party then stopped before a certain house, at the door of which the one who acted as scout began to knock vigorously.

"Who is there—who is that?" cried a man's voice from within.

"*Iya!*" said the chief of the party. "I am master of the ship

---

\* The present book begins thus abruptly in the original. The following pages will make clear who Ryochiku was, and whence he went away.

† About half-an-hour after midnight.

‡ Usually carried, for obvious purposes, by policemen.

that arrived this evening.  There is some error in the freight account—
let me in, I must have a word with you."

"You're making a mighty fuss," answered the voice, "about what
is a small matter enough, I dare say.  Can't you let it rest till the
morning?"

"Why, no," said the first speaker, "the ship ought to get away
to-night, and the account must be settled before she leaves."

Fearing lest the loud tone in which his interlocutor spoke should
awake his neighbours, the man of the house came to the door, and
opened it, utterly unsuspicious of any trickery.

Hardly, however, had he pushed the door back, when two of the
patrol threw themselves upon him, exclaiming :

"You are our prisoner !  Do not attempt to move—we arrest you
on authority !"

The remainder of the patrol then closed round their prey, and
dragged him into the house.

"*Kowa !*" cried the prisoner, throwing his eyes round him in
amazement.  "What means all this ?"

"What means this?  Darest thou ask, villain !" exclaimed the
chief of the patrol.  "Thou art Gihei, art thou not—living at the sign
of the Amagawa,\* in this town of Sakai,† —and by order of
Yuranosuke, a *kerai* of the late Yenya Hanguwan, hast got ready
for him a quantity of arms and horse-gear, enough to load a good-
sized ship with ; which thou art about to send at one dispatch to
Kamakura.  Our orders are to arrest thee, and doubtless thou'lt be put
to the torture—nay, thou canst not escape,—bind his arms, men."

"This is a strange charge, sirs !" cried Gihei, for the prisoner was
none other.  "I know nothing whatever about what you accuse me
of—you must have hit upon the wrong man !"

"*Yah !*" interrupted the chief.  "Hold thy peace and make no
noise, there is proof enough,—now, men !"

---

\* Lit., "The Heaven-stream"—the name given by the Japanese to Tho
Milky Way.

† A considerable seaport town, in the province of Idzumi or Senshiu.

Upon this, his subordinates brought forward a travelling-box, wrapped in matting, that had been stowed on board that night, at the sight of which Gihei appeared somewhat disturbed.

"Stir not!" cried the chief to him, while the men rapidly undid the covering and were beginning to open the box, when Gihei, freeing himself by a sudden effort, kicked a fellow aside, and leaping upon the lid, took up a firm position.

" *Yah*, you ill-mannered boors!" he cried.   "This trunk is full of articles ordered by a noble lady, the wife of a *daimiyô*, and contains various small things and *warahi* books and objects, such as are kept in the secret drawers of armour-coffers, together with the letter ordering them all.  If you open it, the name of a most illustrious and noble house will become public; and you must take the consequences upon yourselves, if you persist in disclosing it."

"Ah! a likely story," exclaimed the chief.   "Thou hadst better confess the truth, without further trouble,—wilt not?  Good!

"You know what you have to do," added the chief, addressing one of his followers, who, with a gesture of assent, immediately left the room, and returned, after a few moments' absence, dragging in with him a child, a little over a year old, the only son of Gihei, and called Yoshimatsu.

"And now, Gihei," resumed the chief, "for the moment we won't trouble ourselves about the contents of yonder box.  You know that Yuranosuke and the other *rônin* of Yenya's following have got up a plot against the life of Moronaho, of the details of which you cannot be ignorant.  Reveal them to us and all will be well; refuse, and your boy here—you shall see what his fate will be."   Drawing his sword as he uttered the last words, the speaker placed the point against the child's throat.

Gihei looked on unmoved, and said scornfully:

"Do you think you have to do with a woman or a child, that you hope to terrify me into making some confession by threatening me

---

* *Vide* Appendix.

through the boy? You will find no coward in Gihei of the sign of the Amagawa. No fear for my child will make me say I know something, when I know nothing—nothing, I swear it by the lowest hell. If, however, you are simply enemies of mine, my boy there is in your hands, and if you choose to kill him I cannot help it."

"Faith!" cried the chief admiringly, "you're a stout-hearted fellow enough! Why, yonder chest contains spears, matchlocks, suits of chain-armour, etc., together with some forty-six devices for the use of the conspirators against Moronaho—and you dare to tell us you know nothing about all this! You would do better to en1 such talk, and make a clean breast of the whole matter. If you don't, you will be killed by inches; hewed at, until your body is hewed into shreds. How like you that?"

"Do not think you frighten me," cried Gihei, "with your threats. I deal not in weapons and armour only, but also in *yeboshi* caps for court and feudal nobles, in all sorts of things, in fact, down to straw sandals for servant lads and wenches. If there is anything unusual enough in that to need enquiry, everybody in Japan will be pestered out of their lives. If one is to be hewed in pieces, or scourged with the threefold cat, for following a trade, why, life is not worth having. Slay me, then; thrust your sword through the child's throat! Why don't you set to work upon me? Where would you like to begin—hew off my arm, or tear open my chest, or slash me on the shoulder or on the back?" *

As he uttered the last words, Gihei, quitting his position on the chest, made a sudden rush upon his captors, and snatched the child from their grasp.

---

* Allusion is here made to the practice of hacking at the dead bodies of criminals, by which the young *samurahi* was wont to perfect himself in swordsmanship, under the old order of things. Treatises exist upon this repulsive art—for an art it seems to have been considered—and one of the commonest of picture-rolls used to represent the various cuts, distinguished by special names, by practising which the aspirant could best learn on the dead subject to qualify himself for mangling the living one.

THE PROOF OF GIHEI.

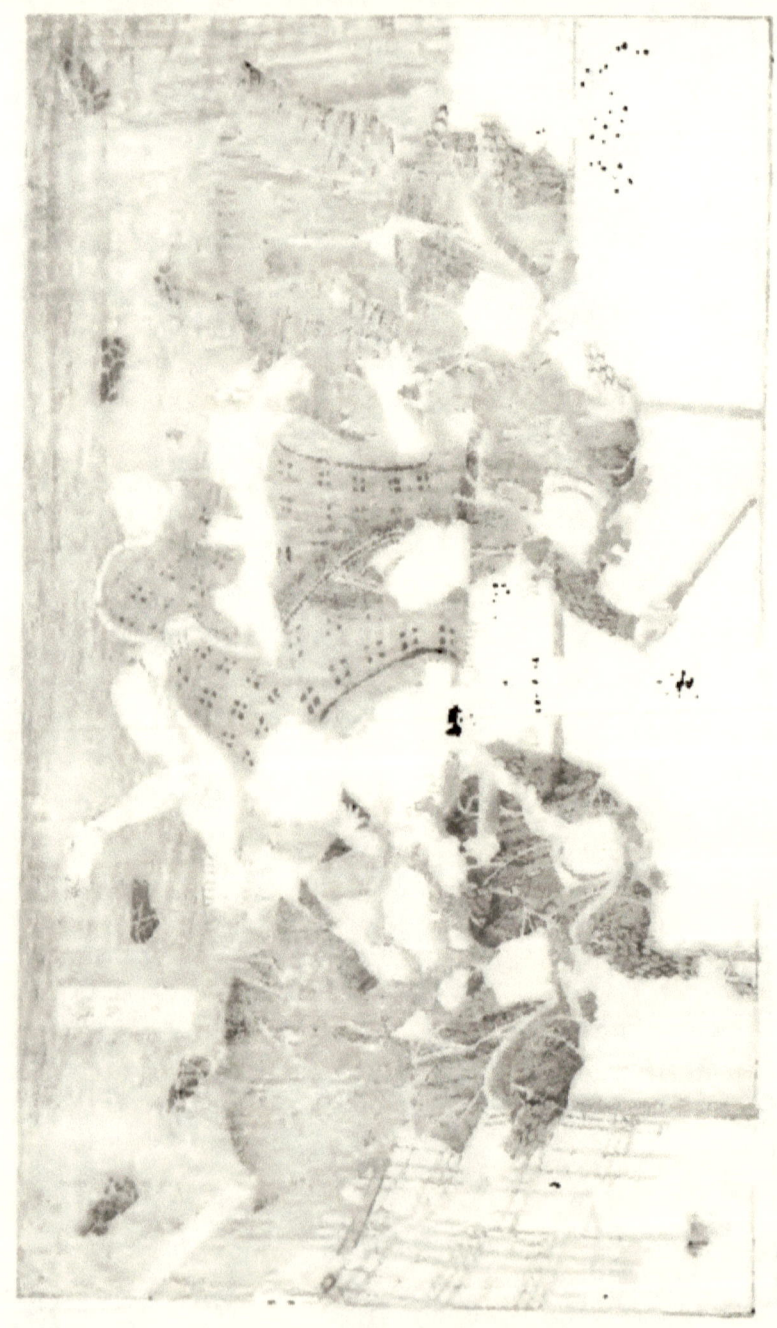

"You shall see," he cried defiantly, "how far your threats are likely to influence me!"

The firm expression of his face shewed that he would not recoil from any extremity, and he seemed on the point of strangling his own child, when the lid of the chest was thrown open, and Yuranosuke, who had lain concealed in it, stepped suddenly forth.

"*Yah!*" cried the *Karô*, "hold your hand, Gihei, hold your hand!"

Filled with astonishment at this unlooked-for appearance, Gihei stood speechless, while the chief and the other members of the seeming patrol threw away their maces and bundles of cords, and, taking up a position at a little distance from their captive, assumed a respectful attitude. The *Karô* of Yenya, with a dignified and grave air, then advanced a step forward, and prostrating himself before the wondering Gihei, exclaimed :

"Sir, I hardly know how to express my admiration for you. Your devotion marks you out among the mass of men, as the brilliance of its flower reveals the lotus in the muddy marsh; as its glitter shows the grain of gold in the sand of the sea-shore. For my part, I knew well how loyal a heart was yours. The *Karô* of Yenya never for a moment doubted your fidelity, but to my comrades here you were a stranger, and some among them thought that since you were a *Chônin** your fidelity ought to be proved; and would not rest until it was settled that you were to be seized, and your loyalty tried, by taking advantage of a father's natural love for his child, and putting you to the proof—by threatening

---

* There were two main divisions of society—excluding the priestly class and peasantry—in old Japan, the lines of demarcation between which are still far from being obliterated. These were the *Bushi* or *Samurah:* (lit., servers, like the Saxon "thegn"; then retainers and fighting men), originating in the soldiery of the early days of the Shôgunate; and the *Chônin* (lit., "street people"), or citizens and artisans. The first class had the right of wearing *hakama* (a species of wide, loose trowser), and of carrying two swords, a short one and a long one, in their girdles; the latter could only wear one short sword, and the ordinary *kimono*, resembling a dressing-gown, with hanging sleeves.

the life of your darling and only boy, unless you divulged our secrets. To show my comrades how brave and true a heart yours was, and to put these companions of mine at their ease, I have joined in the proof, though I knew what a cruel trial it would be to you. And now I do most humbly crave your pardon for what you have been made to suffer. They say that we *Bushi* are the bloom * of mankind, but never, never, has any *Samurahi* equalled you in generous devotion, and the hero who should withstand the onset of a thousand foes would display a courage inferior to what you have just revealed. Would that we could borrow your brave heart! With your noble conduct as our model, could we possibly fail in fulfilling our vengeance upon our enemy; even though he should betake himself to some precipice-fenced fastness in the mountains; or should enclose hinself within walls of iron and brass! Among men, true men are scarce, they say. Those that exist, it would seem, must be sought for among the ranks of the *Chônin*. For what you have done for us, if we did not bow down before you with reverent thanks, as before our village and household gods,† we should be wanting in gratitude to you for the favour you have shown us. 'Tis in the hour of need ‡ that the hero reveals himself. Our lord, who is no more — alas, alas, how sad, how pitiable his fate! — had he known your true and valiant heart, would have advanced you to high military and civil rank, § and never would have repented him of his bounty. The eyes of my companions were blinded, as it were, to your worth; the courage you have displayed this night has acted like the infallible specific of some famous doctor, and they can now recognise your high qualities, thankful that you have caused the scales to fall from their eyes."

---

* Lit., " the wild-cherry blossom."
† *Vide* Appendix.
‡ Lit., " 'tis not in peaceful times that the hero reveals himself."
§ *Vide* Appendix.

Yuranosuke and his fellows then withdrew a little, thrice bowing their heads to the matting, and exclaiming :

"We humbly crave your pardon, sir, for our violence."

"Nay, sirs," cried Gihei ; "I have done nothing to merit the honours you heap upon me; pray rise. The proverb says, 'Judge a man as you do a horse—after you've tried him.' And seeing that I was unfortunate enough to be unknown to you, it was necessary that you should put me to some proof. At first I was but a mean fellow ; but since I have had the honour of transacting the business of your lord's clan, I have become of some consequence. When I heard of the calamities that befell your noble chief, I shared your terrible distress. I racked my brains to devise some plan of exacting vengeance upon your lord's enemy, but with no more success than a tortoise might hope for trying to strut,* like an actor, upon its hind legs. It was then that his honour here, Yuranosuke, came to me; and I did my best, without troubling my head about the consequences, to obey the commands I was favoured with. Oh that I were not a mere *chônin !* If I were a *samurai*, were my rations no more than a handful of rice a day, I might have asked to be one of you, following humbly after you† in your enterprise. I should have been content if I could only have been allowed to draw water for your tea when wearied; but it could not be, mean *chônin*, O how mean ! as I am ; while you, sirs, by the favour of your lord, enjoy the distinction of wearing swords, and are permitted to devote your lives to his memory,—would that a like fortune were mine ! At least, when in attendance upon your lord upon the dark path, you will not fail to let him know how gladly the fellow Gihei would have accompanied you !"

The companions of Yuranosuke, deeply moved by these earnest words, burst into tears, and ground their teeth in sympathetic rage, as they saw how bitter was the distress of Gihei at finding himself unable

---

* Lit., "strut about" with the conventional, and, to Europeans, ridiculous gestures of a Japanese tragedian.

† Lit., "following close at your sleeves, and at the hem of your garments."

to give full vent to his loyal feelings. The *Karô*, however, restrained himself, and immediately addressed Gihei as follows:

"We shall leave for Kamakura to-night, and ere long * we hope to have achieved success. They tell me that you have gone so far as to send your wife away, in your care to preserve our secret. 'Twas well thought of, but you shall endure the discomfort of separation from her for a short time only; she shall soon be called home again. And now I must say farewell."

"But let me wish you a fortunate issue to your undertaking in a cup of *saké* ere you start, sirs," cried Gihei, as Yuranosuke prepared to depart.

"Nay, we must——"

"Pray do not refuse me; here are hand-struck buckwheat cakes—they will bring you luck."

"Hand-struck,† are they? lucky indeed," cried Yuranosuke.

"Ohowashi and Yazama," resumed the *Karô*, turning to his companions, "you two can remain with me; the rest of you may depart, and, picking up Goyemon and Rikiya on your way, get forward as far as Sadanomori."

"Will your honour please to come this way?" said Gihei to Yuranosuke, and the two men who remained with him, after the rest had left.

"It would be rude to refuse you," answered Yuranosuke, as, together with Ohowashi and Yazama, he followed his host into an inner room.

At this juncture a woman came up to the house—Sono, the wife of Gihei; who, either at the instance of her father Ryochiku, or by the will of her husband—she was puzzled between them, as one might find it hard to tell whether the moon, just above the horizon, was rising or setting—had been thrust out of doors.‡

She was alone, and carried a small lantern in her hand, and as she knocked at the door she trembled with fear, confused with the pitch darkness and full of anxiety about her child.

---

* Lit., "in not more than one hundred days."

† The Japanese word translated "hand-struck" means also an attack or encounter.

‡ This portion of the text is disfigured by numerous word-plays, and a general rendering of the meaning is all that has been attempted.

"Igo, Igo," she cried, after having knocked several times, "are you there?"

"What's that," muttered the servant-lad from within, in a sleepy tone, as he stumbled up out of bed, only half awake. "What's that calling me—some wandering spirit or tricky goblin or other?"

"*Iya*, no. It is I, Sono, your mistress; open the door, quick."

"Ah, but in spite of what you say I am rather frightened; you must not shout at me if I let you in," cried the lad, opening the door as he spoke.

"*Yeh!*" he exclaimed, delightedly, as he saw Sono. "It is the mistress; I am so glad to see you back. Why, you are all alone—you might have got bitten by some wild-dog."

"I might as well be, and die from the bite," said Sono bitterly. "I can no longer endure this misery—banished from my own house."

"I don't understand you."

"Is my husband asleep just now?"

"No."

"Is he out?"

"No."

"Well, then, where is he; what is he doing?"

"I am sure I don't know. Just after nightfall, a lot of men came up here, shouting 'caught, caught,' like a cat might do that had just got hold of a rat; and when I heard the noise I covered my head with the bed-clothes and went to sleep. The men are now in the house, drinking *saké*, and enjoying themselves."

"Strange! I wonder what my husband has in hand," said Sono, half to herself.

"And baby," she added, addressing the lad, "is he asleep?"

"Ay, he is fast asleep enough."

"Has he been sleeping with his father?"

"No."

"With you, then?"

"No, all alone; rolled up by himself."

" Why, hasn't he been nursed to sleep, then ? "

" No; master tried, and so did I, but we could not give him any milk, so he did nothing but cry all the time."

" Poor little fellow," cried Sono, leaning against the door, and bursting into tears. "Of course, he would cry, what could he do else ? "

Gihei, who was near, no more noticed her tears than heaven regards the patter of rain upon the earth beneath, and her sleeve was soon drenched with the flow.

" Ho, there, Igo, Igo," he shouted, making his appearance and looking round. "Where is the fellow ? "

" Here I am, sir," said the lad.

" Blockhead ! " cried Gihei, looking aslant at him, with a scolding expression.

" Go and wait upon my guests, yonder."

Storming at the lad, the husband of Sono left the room, and was about to close the slide behind him, when his wife prevented him.

" Husband, husband, do not shut the door; I want so much to speak with you."

" I can neither listen to you nor talk with you. You and your father, I find, are a pair of miserable wretches; away with you," cried Gihei angrily.

" You take me to be like my father," said Sono, " but I am not ; look, this will prove it to you beyond a doubt," throwing a paper, through the half-opened door, at her husband's feet, as she spoke.

As Gihei stooped to pick it up, his wife made her way to his side.

" What is this ? " exclaimed her husband, in a tone of astonishment ; " 'tis the letter of divorce I wrote some time since ; I don't understand your bringing it back."

" You don't understand my bringing it back—how can you say so ? " cried Sono. " You know well enough how ill-disposed my father, Ryochiku, is towards you.* What could induce you to give that

---

* Ryochiku was a doctor, in the service of Kudaiu, and a man of mean and parsimonious character. Dissatisfied with his son-in-law, on account of the latter's connection with Yuranosuke, as well as by reason of certain pecuniary

divorce-letter into his hand? As soon as he got back with it he wanted to marry me to some one else, there and then, to my utter astonishment. However, I put a good face on the matter, so as to lull my father's suspicions, and watching my opportunity, stole the divorce-letter out of his pocket-book, and ran back home with it."

"Surely you love your child," continued the poor woman, with her tears flowing fast. "How could you be so cruel as to send me away, for him to hang at a foster-mother's breast?"

"Oh!" cried Gihei, "the complaint comes from the wrong side, I think. Did you not heed what I said to you when you left, that I did not send you away for any fault of yours, but simply wished you to stay at your father's for a short time, and could not give you my reasons because he was formerly a follower of Kudaiu, and I did not know which way his inclinations tended. I told you, too, to feign illness, and to put on an indisposed look night and morning, and neglect your hair, so that you might run no risk of being troubled with offers of marriage—for who would think of asking a woman to be his wife who neglected her hair? Why have you disobeyed me? And as to your child, Yoshimatsu, think you that you alone were distressed about him? During the day that lad Igo could coax and wheedle him into being quiet, but when night came he kept crying out continually for his mother, and however much we tried to pacify him by telling him his mother would be back soon he would not go to sleep, and when we sought to make him, by scolding or slapping him,

---

transactions on the occasion of the marriage, in which the doctor conceived himself to have been ill-treated by Gihei, he had done his best to annul the union with his daughter. Gihei, on the other hand, fearful of Yuranosuke's secret being betrayed, through Sono, to Ryochiku, with whom he had had an interview just before the arrival of Yuranos ke and his party, had sent his wife home, under a letter of divorce, which, however, he intended to be of only temporary force : so that she might be out of the way until Yuranosuke's designs had been successfully carried out.

Such is the explanation generally given of the conduct of Gihei on this occasion, but in the text followed in the present translation the reader is rather left to infer, than expressly told, by what motives the husband of Sono was actuated.

or making faces at him, he did not cry, but whined and moaned so
pitifully that I could hardly bear the sight of his misery. I now
understood the force of the saying 'your children will teach you how
your parents loved you;' and remembering how often I had behaved
ill to my father and mother, I was filled with remorse, and wept almost
the whole night through. Last evening, I several times took up the
boy in my arms, with the intention of bringing him to you, and even
got as far as the door with him, but recollecting that for you to have
him for one night only would be of no use at all, and that I did
not know in the least how long you might have to remain away from
me, I thought it would make matters worse to take the child to you,
and so walked about with him, dandling him and patting him till
he at last fell asleep in my arms, when I lay down with him nestled
close to me, and rolling his head about as he sought for the breast.
I never intended to separate you from your darling for the rest of your
life, but only for a short time, and, under the circumstances, I could
not avoid writing the divorce-letter. Your father, Ryochiku, would
never forgive me were I mean enough to get back the letter I gave
him, in this underhand manner. I cannot receive it therefore, and
you must take it back with you. The gods have decreed our union
thus far; we must now be to each other as if the one of us had died."*

As her husband ceased, Sono was silent for a moment. Knowing
well the resolution of his character, she felt that he could not be
induced to alter his determination, and when at last she found courage
to speak, her tone was sad.

"How wretched a fate is mine! If I remain here I am in your
way; if I go to my father's house I shall surely be forced to marry
again. Oh, husband, won't you let Yoshimatsu be awakened, and
brought to me for a few moments? Perhaps this is a last parting!"

---

* In the tenth month of each year, the God Iyahiko is supposed to assemble
the eight hundred and more remaining gods at the *yashiro* or shrine near Namiki
in Idsumo, where all the varying destinies of men, their deaths, births, marriages,
&c., are arranged for the ensuing year. The gods being thus absent from their
usual abodes, the tenth month is called "Kamina-dsuki," or "godless month,"
during which the Japanese avoid forming new connections.

"Nay," replied Gihei, "to see him for an instant, and then to have to leave him, would but make the pain of parting from him harder than ever to bear. And now away with you—I have guests here to-night."

"Let me see the child," said the mother, "if only for a moment."

"Come, come," cried Gihei, soothingly, "have a little courage. Did you not hear what I said just now about the harm of seeing him, even for a moment only?"

And putting the letter into his wife's hands, he forced her to the door, and, steeling his heart against her entreaties, pushed her out, exclaiming:

"If you really love your child, return to your father's at once, and get him to afford you hospitality until the spring—when I hope I shall be able to come to some determination—if you will not do this, then all had better end between us."

"Ah, if I could only be sure that my father would not force me into marriage with some one, I might bear the parting," cried Sono, from without.

"Cruel husband!" she continued, "to send me away in this manner, who have done nothing wrong—not to let me see my child's face even. How can you be so hard-hearted!

"For pity's sake," she continued, knocking at the door, "open; let me have a look at him, even if asleep, just once, I entreat you with clasped hands, I beseech you; cruel, cruel!" and overcome with grief, she sank on the ground, and burst into tears.

"Ah," she cried, after a time, collecting her energies, "I will restrain myself—I will say no more. Let my child but catch one glimpse of me, I know he will cry out 'Mammy,' and cling to me so that none can separate us. If I return to my father's to-night he will force me into a betrothal ere a day passes. Oh, husband, what have I to live for? Adieu, husband, adieu for ever!"

The wife of Gihei, however, did not at once go away, but placed

K

her ear against the door, hoping to hear her child's voice, or perhaps
that her husband might relent enough to let her have a look at
him, but there was not a sound in the house.

"Alas, alas," she cried, mournfully; "must I then go without
one look at him!"

She turned to depart, when a couple of stout fellows, their faces
concealed all but the eyes, suddenly blocked up her path.  Ere she
could utter a cry, they rushed upon her—was it not outrageous?—
and while one of them held her fast, the other gathered her hair
(which was dressed Shimada fashion) in his hand, and cut it off
close to the roots, deftly possessing himself at the same moment of
everything she had in her bosom.

The next instant the pair had vanished, no one could tell whither.
Brutal ruffians they must have been, to attack a woman!

"Ah, wretches!" cried Sono.  "Ah, villains!  What means this
violence?  You have cut off my hair and seized the paper I had in
my bosom; if you are common thieves,* why don't you kill me at
once?"

His manhood† roused by his wife's cry of distress, Gihei could
hardly refrain from rushing to her assistance, and the gnashing of
his teeth showed the struggle that went on in his breast.

While the husband of Sono stood thus irresolute close to the door,
Yuranosuke entered from the inner apartments, shouting out loudly
for his host.

"Ah," cried the *Karô*, as he caught sight of Gihei, "we are
infinitely obliged to you for your kind and courteous hospitality;
you shall have news from Kamakura—what other gear we may
require I will let you know of by a swift messenger.  And now we
must bid you farewell—we should be on our way ere dawn breaks."‡

---

* Lit., "robbers of combs and hair ornaments.
† *Vide* Appendix.
‡ Lit., "ere night opens," *i.e.*, grows clear.

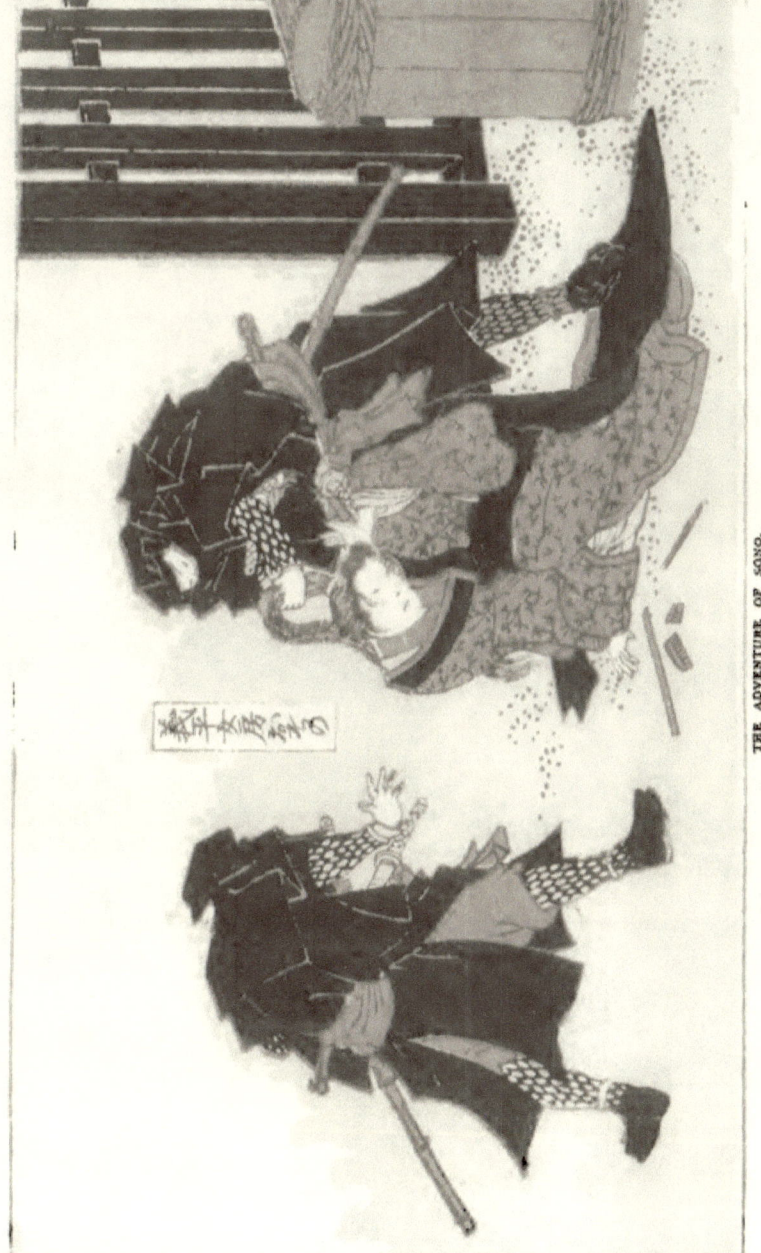

THE ADVENTURE OF SONO.

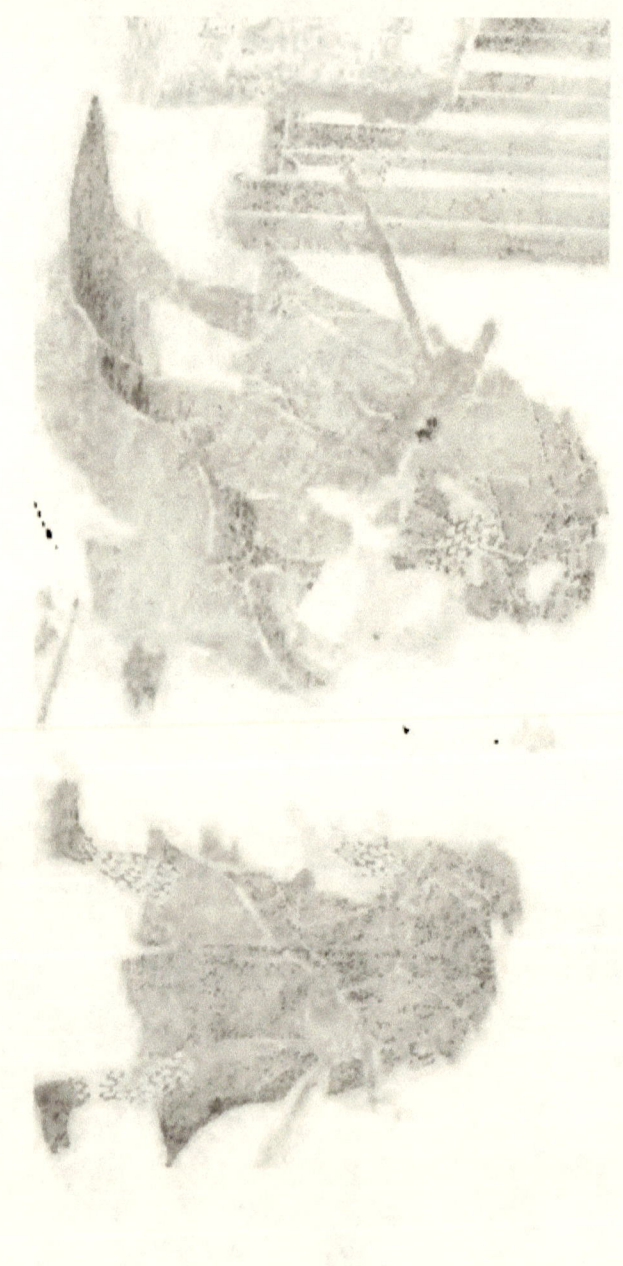

" Well, sirs," cried Gihei, " this is not an occasion on which I dare detain you ; may your journey be a safe one, and may success attend your enterprise."

" As soon as we get to Kamakura, we will send you tidings of us," replied Yura. " Search as we may, we cannot find words in which fitly to express our heartfelt thanks to you for the services you have rendered us."

" Yazama, Ohowashi," continued the *Karô*, turning to his companions, " present Gihei with the parting gift you have ready for him." The two men immediately stepped forward, one of them bearing an outspread fan, used for the nonce as a presentation stand, upon which was laid a paper parcel.

" We beg that you, sir," resumed Yuranosuke, " and your wife, will deign to accept these trifling gifts from us."

A cloud came over Gihei's countenance. " I should not have put my neck in peril," he cried, " simply to get a present from you, sirs. You despise me as a mere citizen, and think I shall be pleased by having my mouth filled with gold pieces." *

" Nay, not so," exclaimed Yuranosuke. " We are taking the last farewell of you we shall ever take in this world, where the gods have decreed that you should remain, and it is by desire of the Lady Kawoyo that we lay these poor gifts at your feet."

" It is plain, sirs," exclaimed Gihei, with increased vexation, " that you do not know me, and treat me with contempt. Your gifts are hateful to me," spurning the fan away from him as he spoke. The paper packet opened out, as it fell to the ground, and its contents escaped. On seeing them, Sono uttered a cry of astonishment.

" Why, these are my comb and hair ornaments, and my hair that the men cut off just now."

---

* Lit., "by having Koban ears clapped on my cheeks." The Koban was a gold coin of an oval shape, and about the size of a human ear, value nearly five shillings.

Gihei, meanwhile, had picked up the paper wrapping.

" And this," he exclaimed, " is the letter of divorce I wrote ! What is that about some one's hair being cut off," he added, turning to his wife—" whose hair ? "

" I will explain," said Yuranosuke. " I sent Ohowashi and Yazama here, round by the back of the house, to seize your wife and cut off her hair, so as to make her like a nun, which will prevent her father from forcing her to marry. Ere her hair grows again, I hope we shall have attained the object of our enterprise, and after our vengeance shall have been fully accomplished, you will be reunited—may you live long and happily together !   Then you, lady," addressing the wife of Gihei, " can take these ornaments, and, using these tresses as a cushion, dress your hair in the *Kōgai** fashion—no one happier in the three kingdoms.†  Only till then will you be, as it were, a nun. And however long it may be ere she be reunited to you, Gihei, we are all sureties for her that she will divulge nothing, and I myself, from the dark path, will act as intermediary in effecting your reunion."

" How can I be sufficiently grateful for the favours heaped upon me ! " cried Gihei.   " Wife, wife, speak your thanks to his honour."

" I can only say that I owe my life to you, sir," said Sono, softly.

" *Iya !* I deserve no thanks," replied Yuranosuke—" none whatever. And were Gihei not a citizen we should be overjoyed to have him with us. When we determined upon making our attack by night, our good fortune made us choose the name of your house, Amagawa, as our watchword. When we shall be within our enemy's gates, ' Ama ' will be our sign and ' Kawa ' our countersign, and as we shout to each other ' Ama, there,' ' Kawa, there,' in the struggle, it will be as if Gihei were with us. And the first character of your name means 'rectitude' and the last means 'level'; happy the omen, our

---

* In which the hair is kept in place on either side of the head by a comb.
† Japan, China, and India.

THE CONSPIRATORS' FAREWELL.

difficulties shall be levelled for us, and a complete success achieved! And now, again, farewell." With these words, Yuranosuke rose, with his two companions, and the three then took their departure.

The fame of Yuranosuke's deeds has come down to posterity, and the watchword "Ama" shall be "Yama."* In the loyalty of his heart he found his tactics of Son and Go,† and the double-meaning language of the world tells us in his name how inexhaustible that loyalty was.‡

---

* Probably the Buddhic "Yama," the "heaven of perennial light," is meant.
† *Vide ante.*
‡ The puns in the text render anything like a literal version of the passage impossible. The name of Yuranosuke's prototype was Kuranosuke (see Appendix), and "Kura" signifies "a storehouse, magazine, treasury, &c."

END OF THE TENTH BOOK.

# BOOK THE ELEVENTH.

### RETRIBUTION.

HAT the soft may overcome the hard, the weak may overcome the strong, was the secret revealed by Sekikô to the hero Chôryô.*

Ohoboshi Yuranosuke, the liegeman of Yenya Hanguwan Takasada, mindful of this maxim, got together his fellow-plotters, forty odd brave fellows, and, embarking with them on board a couple of fishing-boats, in which they lay concealed under straw mats, started for Cape Ina-

---

\* The tale is as follows. In the reign of the Chinese emperor Riuko, Chôryô filled the post of Commander-in-chief. One day, passing over a bridge known as the Bridge of Hi, he met an old man on horseback, who dropped his sandal and somewhat surlily told Chôryô to pick it up for him. Though annoyed at the tone in which the request was made, the great man, seeing the age of his interlocutor, complied with it. Thereupon the old fellow told him to be at the bridge at dawn on the fifth day from that, and he would meet with due reward. Chôryô accordingly presented himself on the bridge on the fifth day, but was reproached by the old man as being late, and told to come again at the end of another five days—which he did, and was again dismissed in a similar manner and for a similar reason. The third time, Chôryô took care to be at the bridge by midnight, and this time was well received by the old man, who bestowed upon him a book treating of the art of war, the Rikuto Sanriyaku (previously mentioned in the Ninth Book), and, telling him that he would meet him once more that day seven years, suddenly disappeared. Chôryô visited the bridge in the seventh year, but found

mura,* in the neighbourhood of which they hoped to find their landing as little guarded against as their enterprise was unsuspected by their enemy.†

They arrived in safety at Cape Inamura, and as the first boat was brought alongside a huge rock on the beach, Yuranosuke leaped ashore, followed by Hara Goyemon, after whom came Rikiya, succeeded by Takemori Kitahachi, Katayama Genta, and others. From the next boat there landed in regular order, Kakuyama Mago-shichi, Sudagoro Katsuta, Hayami, Tomonori, the famous Katayama Gengo, Ohowashi Bungo, carrying a huge wooden mallet, Yoshida, Ohokazaki, Kodera, and others, Kowase Chiudaiu, holding under his arm a number of small bows, the renowned Ohoboshi Sehei, and others, including the eldest son of Kodera, rising up together like the lift of the morning mist, Shinoda and Akane, carrying halberds aloft, with Nogawa, armed with a cross-bladed spear, while several men provided with ladders brought up the rear. All wore mantles bearing for devices different letters of the " Iroha "—a different letter for each man.‡ Yuranosuke, not in the least dissipated now,§ had caused his *aide*, Yazama, to bring with him a number of eight-foot bamboo poles,

---

nothing there but a huge yellow-coloured stone, and thus came to know that his mysterious aquaintance was a spirit sent to try his patience and good manners. The name Sekikô is an abbreviation of Kôsekikô ("the lord of the yellow-stone"), the appellation by which the seeming old man was afterwards known.

\* Near Kamakura.

† There is here a pun in the original which is not capable of being rendered in the translation. The whole meaning of the passage is, however, given.

‡ In the text followed, the forty-six letters of the Japanese syllabary are here enumerated in their usual order, with the names of the adventurers interspersed in such a manner as to allow of a thread of meaning connecting the whole passage.

§ There again occurs one of those *jeux de mots* which the Japanese apparently mistake for wit. There are, however, equally poor ones, both in conception and application, to be found in Aristophanes, and even in the mouths of Homer's goddesses, as in the speech of Athênê, Od. A. 62 :

　　" * * * δι τοσον οἶνσαο Ζευ."

The last letters of the Iroha or Japanese syllabary may be read as forming a phrase meaning " not to be overcome by drink."

for the purpose of putting the plan of forcing open the shutters I
have already described, into execution. At a little distance behind
his chief, followed, humbly enough, Teraoka Heiyemon. In all, the
party consisted of forty-six men, wearing for device each a letter of
the alphabet on their sleeve, chain-armour on their thighs, on their
breast the cuirass of loyalty—of a truth, a lesson-book, as it were, of
the alphabet * of faithful duty.

"Comrades," cried Yuranosuke, turning to his companions, "do not
forget the sign and countersign, 'Ama' and 'Kawa,' the names of
Gihei's house. As has already been settled, Yazama, Senzaki, Kodera,
and their party, headed by my son Rikiya, will make their way in
by the front gate, while Goyemon, with myself, will press round to
the rear entrance. At the right moment, a loud whistle will be heard—
let every one then rush to the attack; there is but one head we have
to take."

The men listened respectfully to their chief's command, and as they
came in sight of their enemy's castle their eyes were ablaze with
fury, while, filled with hatred of their foe, they separated into two
parties, one to attack by the rear, the other by the front gate.

The great lord of Musashi, meanwhile, his suspicions lulled by the
account he had received of Yuranosuke's dissipated life, spent his
time in drinking and debauchery, assisted by the wretch Yakushiji,†
whom he had taken into high favour.

On this very night, exhausted by his excesses, the murderer of
Yenya had only just fallen asleep, when Yuranosuke and his party
approached the castle. A profound stillness reigned, broken only
by the occasional rap-rap of the clappers of the sentinel going his
rounds.

The plan of attack having been finally settled between the two

---

* There are forty-six letters in the Japanese syllabary, excluding the final
nasal sound.

† One of the commissioners officially present at the *seppuku* of Yenya,
described in the Fourth Book, who signalised himself by the brutality with
which he executed his duty.

parties, Yazama and Senzaki, like a couple of bold fellows as they were, crept up to the front gate, and, peeping through a chink, took a survey of the interior. As soon as the faintness of the sound of the clappers showed that the sentinel or watchman was pretty well at the farther end of his round, they caused a ladder to be carefully and noiselessly placed against the wall, and, mounting it rapidly, with the agility of spiders climbing up their web, presently found themselves on the top. The sound of the clappers now became more distinct, and showed the approach of the sentinel ; to elude whose notice they at once dropped to the ground on the inner side. But in vain ; the man saw them drop, and uttered an exclamation. Before he could repeat it, however, they rushed upon him, and, throwing him down, bound his arms tightly. "You must guide us, and truly too," they cried, gagging their prisoner as they spoke, and attaching him by a cord to the person of one of them. Seizing the fellow's clappers, they then went the rounds, forcing him to show the way, and clapping, clapping, just as the sentinel himself might have done. Were they not a couple of stout-hearted blades?

Presently the sound of a whistle is heard. Yazama and his companion know that the moment for action is come.

Clapping loudly, they shout "Ama," "Kawa," and, drawing back the bolts, throw wide open the great gate, through which Rikiya is the first to rush, followed closely by Sugino, Kimura, and his brother.

"Here we are, here we are," cry the men of the party, as they crowd tumultuously in.

Rikiya, meanwhile, scans closely the line of outer shutters, without being able to alight upon a weak spot. Remembering, however, his father's device, suggested by the snow-laden bamboo, he deems the occasion a fit one for putting it into execution, and, ordering the unsplit bamboos they had brought with them to be strung with stout cord, causes the ends to be inserted in the upper and lower grooves in which the shutters move.

"Once, twice, thrice," and all the strings are cut at the same moment ; the bamboos straighten themselves suddenly, and all at

the same time, so prizing out the upper framework and pressing
down the lower crosspiece that the row of shutters fall in with a
simultaneous clatter.

"Now for the attack," shout the leaders, while cries of "Ama,"
"Kawa," fill the air. The retainers of the house, aroused by the
uproar, begin to show themselves, carrying torches and lanterns. The
rear attacking party, having made their way through the rear
gate, now appear, one company headed by Goyemon, the other by
Yuranosuke. The *Karô*, seating himself upon a camp-stool, gave
his orders. His followers, few in number as they were, fought with
desperate courage, and displayed to the utmost their skill as swordsmen.

"Have no eyes for aught but Moronaho," cried Yuranosuke, "'tis
his head that we require."

Aided by Goyemon, the *Karô* directed the struggle on every side,
while the young men, vieing with each other in bravery, kept up a
constant clashing of weapons.

To the north of the mansion of Moronaho lay that of Nikki
Harima-no-kami; * to the south, the residence of Ishido Umanojô.†
On either side, the roofs of the buildings were crowded with men
carrying lanterns, twinkling in the darkness of the night like the
stars in heaven.

"*Ya, ya,*" they cried, "what means all this uproar and confusion,
clashing of weapons, and hurtling of arrows? Are you attacked by
rioters, or by robbers, or has a fire broken out somewhere? We
have been commanded to find out what is going on, and inform
our masters of the cause of the disturbance."

"We are liegemen of Yenya Hanguwan," replied Yuranosuke,
without a moment's hesitation. "Some forty of us banded together
to revenge our lord's death upon his enemy, and are now struggling
to get at him. I who address you am Ohoboshi Yuranosuke, and
my companion here is Hara Goyemon. We are not rising against

---

* *I.e.*, Nikki, Lord or Count of Harima.
† One of the commissioners mentioned in the Fourth Book.

the government, still less have we any quarrel with your lords. As to fire, strict orders have been given to be careful, and we beg you not to be under any apprehensions on that score. We only ask you to leave us alone, and not to interfere with us; if, as neighbours, you should think yourselves bound to assist our enemy, we shall be obliged, despite our inclination, to turn our weapons against you."

To these bold words of Yuranosuke the retainers of the noblemen on either side of the mansion of Moronaho shouted back approvingly :

"Right well done, right well done; in your place we should feel ourselves bound to act as you are acting; pray command our services."

And the next moment the roofs were deserted, amid cries of "Down with your lanterns, there, down with your lanterns."

Meanwhile the struggle with the retainers of Moronaho continued, some two or three only of Yuranosuke's comrades being wounded after an hour's fighting, while quite a number of the enemy were stricken down.

Nothing, however, could be seen of Moronaho, although the soldier Heiyemon ransacked the buildings in search of him.

"I have searched every room," cried Heiyemon, approaching his chief, "and probed the ceilings and floors with my spear, but without coming upon any trace of our enemy. But I looked into his sleeping-room, and found the bed-clothes still warm, so that, seeing what a cold night it is, he cannot have got far away. Possibly he has made for the great gate, so, without further delay——"

The soldier was on the point of hastening away to guard the issue he had referred to, when he was interrupted by a voice crying :

"Ho, there, Heiyemon, not so fast, not so fast."

The next moment, Yazama abruptly made his appearance, dragging with him their long-sought enemy, Moronaho.

"Look at him, look at him," cried the elated captor, "I found him hidden in an outhouse, and dragged him here alive."

The sight of their enemy in their power revived the cast-down spirits of the conspirators, as the dew revives the drooping flower.

"Well done, well done, indeed," cried Yuranosuke. "But he must not be put an end to unceremoniously. He was a *Shitsuji** in the Empire for a time, and must be put to death in due form."

At a sign from Yuranosuke, Moronaho was placed in a prominent position in an adjoining apartment.†

Yuranosuke, addressing the victim, exclaimed: "Though but as doubly humble retainers‡, we have ventured to force ourselves within your walls, impelled by the desire of avenging the death of our lord upon his enemy. We pray you pardon our violence, and beg of you that you will present us with your head,§ according to the usage of our country."

Moronaho, though a vile sort of creature enough, yet managed to keep a composed countenance, exclaiming with forced calmness:

"Right, right, I am ready; here is my head—take it."

Thrown off his guard for a moment, the *Karô* approached his prisoner, who, suddenly drawing his sword, aimed a blow at Yuranosuke, which the latter only escaped by a nimble leap aside, and twisting up his assailant's arm.

"Ha," cried the *Karô*, "a clever stroke that. *Sah!* Friends, upon him—you may slake your thirst for vengeance now."

Another moment, and the body of Moronaho lay on the floor, covered with wounds.

The conspirators crowded round it, wild with excitement, shouting:

"O rare sight! O happy fortune! Happy are we as the *môki*‖

---

* Regent or Viceroy under the Shôgun.

† Such seems to be the meaning of the author, who is here more than usually obscure.

‡ Lit., "retainers of a retainer."

§ The *Karô* wished his enemy to commit *seppuku*, and then to take his head. This was the form of vengence that most approved itself to the sentiments of a Japanese gentleman of the old school.

‖ The *môki*, according to a Chinese fable, was a species of sea-tortoise with one eye in its belly. For three thousand years the monster had longed to see the light, but in vain. One day, while swimming about the surface of

when he found his waif, fortunate as though we gazed upon the flower of the *udonge*,* that blossoms but once in three thousand years."

Cutting off their enemy's head with the dagger with which their dead master had committed *seppuku*, they resumed their orgy, exclaiming :

"We deserted our wives, we abandoned our children, we left our aged folk uncared for, all to obtain this one head. How auspicious a day is this !"

They struck at the head in their frenzy, gnashed at it, shed tears over it ; their grief and fury, poor wretches, beggared description.

Yuranosuke, drawing from his bosom the *ihai*† of his dead master, placed it reverently on a small stand at the upper end of the room, and then set the head of Moronaho, cleansed from blood, on another opposite to it. He next took a perfume from within his helmet, and burnt it before the tablet of his lord, prostrating himself and withdrawing slowly, while he bowed his head reverently three times, and then again thrice three times.

"O thou soul of my liege lord, with awe doth thy vassal approach thy mighty presence, who art now like unto him that was born of the lotus-flower to attain a glory and eminence beyond the understanding of men ! Before the sacred tablet tremblingly set I the head of thine enemy, severed from his corpse by the sword thou deignedst to bestow upon thy servant in the hour of thy last agony. O thou that art now resting amid the shadows of the tall grass,‡ look with favour on my offering." Bursting into tears, the *Karô* of Yenya thus adored the memory of his lord.

"And now, comrades," he resumed, after a pause, "advance each

---

the sea, it came into contact with a piece of drift-wood, to which it immediately clung in such a manner that the belly was uppermost under the wood, a ragged hole in which fortunately allowed the tortoise the opportunity of at last satisfying its long-cherished desire.

* The *udonge* is a plant so rarely seen in flower that it is fancifully said to bloom but once in three thousand years.—*Vide* Appendix.

† *Vide* Appendix.

‡ An euphemism for the grave : a Buddhic term.

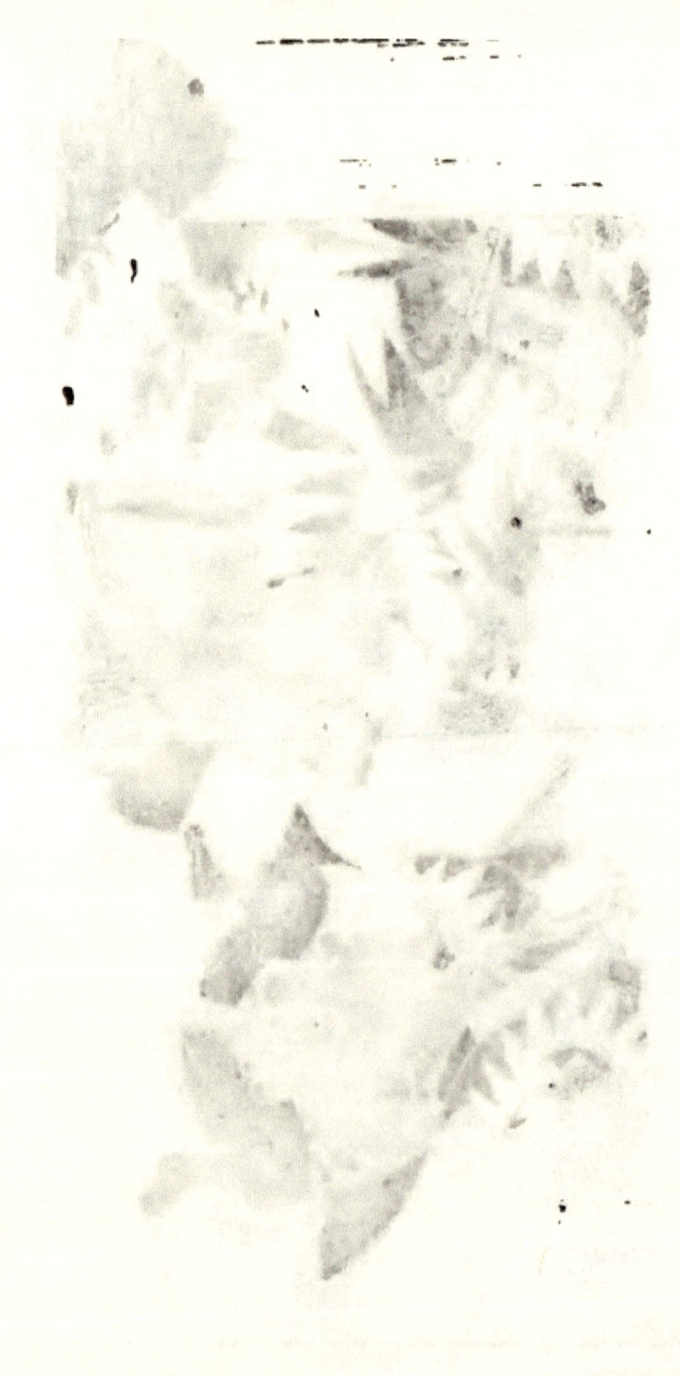

of you, one after the other, and burn incense before the tablet of your master."

"We would all," cried Ishido, "venture to ask our chief first among us to render that honour to our lord's memory."

"Nay," answered the *Karô*, "'tis not I who of right should be the first. Yazama Jiutarô, to you of right falls that honour."

"Not so," cried Yazama, "I claim no such favour. Others might think I had no right to it, and troubles might thus arise."

"No one will think that," exclaimed Yuranosuke. "We have all freely ventured our lives in the struggle to seize Moronaho, but to you,—to you fell the glory of finding him, and it was you who dragged him here, alive, into our presence. 'Twas a good deed, Yazama, acceptable to the spirit of our master; each of us would fain have been the doer of it. Comrades, say I not well?"

Ishido assented on behalf of the rest.

"Delay not, Yazama," resumed Yuranosuke, "for time flies fast."

"If it must be so," cried Yazama, as he passed forward, uttering *gomen* * in a low tone, and offered incense the first of the company.

"And next our chief," exclaimed Ishido.

"Nay," said the *Karô*, "there is yet one who should pass before me."

"What man can that be?" asked Ishido, wonderingly, while his comrades echoed his words.

The *Karô*, without replying, drew a purse made of striped stuff from his bosom. "He who shall precede me," cried the *Karô*, "is Hayano Kampei. A negligence of his duty as a vassal prevented him from being received into our number, but, eager to take at least a part in the erection of a monument to his liege lord, he sold away his wife, and thus became able to furnish his share toward the expense. Thinking that he had murdered his father-in-law to obtain the money, I caused it to be returned to him, and, mad with despair, he committed *seppuku* and died—a most miserable and piteous death. All my life

---

* *I.e.,* "with your august permission."

I shall never cease to regret having caused the money to be returned to him; never for a moment will be absent from my memory that through my fault he came to so piteous an end.  During this night's struggle, the purse has been among us, borne by Heiyemon—let the latter pass forward, and in the name of his sister's dead husband, burn incense before the tablet of our lord."

Heiyemon, thus addressed, passed forward, exclaiming :

"From amidst the shadows of the tall grass blades the soul of Kampei thanks you for the unlooked-for favour you confer upon him." Laying the purse upon the censer, he added :

"'Tis Hayano Kampei who, second in turn, offers incense before the tablet of his liege lord."

The remainder followed, offering up in like manner, amid loud cries of grief, and with sobs and tears, and trembling in the anguish of their minds, incense before the tablet of their master.

Suddenly the air is filled with the din of the trampling of men, with the clatter of hoofs, and with the noise of war-drums.

Yuranosuke does not change a feature.

"'Tis the retainers of Moronaho who are coming down upon us— why should we fight with them?"

The *Karô* is about to give the signal to his comrades to accomplish the final act of their devotion by committing *seppuku* in memory of their lord, when Momonoi Wakasanosuke appears upon the scene, disordered with the haste he had used, in his fear of being too late.

"Moroyasu, the young brother of Moronaho, is already at the great gate," cries Momonoi.  "If you commit *seppuku* at such a moment it will be said that you were driven to it by fear, and an infamous memory will attach to your deed.  I counsel you to depart hence without delay, and betake yourselves to the burial-place of your lord, the temple of Kômyô."

"So shall it be," answered Yuranosuke, after a pause.  "We will do as you counsel us, and will accomplish our last hour before the tomb of our ill-fated lord.  We would ask you, Sir Wakasanosuke, to prevent our enemies from following us."

BEFORE THE TOMB OF YENYA: THE LAST HOMAGE OF THE CLANSMEN

Hardly had Yuranosuke concluded, when Yakushiji Jirôzayemon[*] and Bannai Sagisaka suddenly rushed forth from their hiding-places, shouting :

"Ohoboshi, villain, thou shalt not escape," and struck right and left at the *Karô*. Without a moment's delay, Rikiya hastened to his father's assistance, and forced the wretches to turn their weapons against himself. The struggle did not last long. Avoiding a blow aimed at him by Yakushiji, Rikiya cut the fellow down, and left him writhing in mortal agony upon the ground. Bannai met with a similar fate. A frightful gash upon the leg brought him to his knee,—a pitiable spectacle enough,—and a few moments afterwards the wretch breathed his last.

"A valiant deed, a valiant deed !"

*   *   *   *   *   *   *
*   *   *   *   *   *   *

For ever and ever shall the memory endure of these faithful clansmen, and in the earnest hope that the story of their loyalty—full bloom of the bamboo leaf[†]—may remain a bright example as long as the dynasty of our rulers shall last, has the foregoing tale of their heroism been writ down.

---

[*] One of the commissioners referred to in the Fourth Book.

[†] *Take* (bamboo) formed part of the boy-name of each successive occupant of the throne of the Shôguns during the period in which the so-called temporal power was vested in the hands of members of the Tokugawa dynasty.

END OF THE ELEVENTH BOOK.

# APPENDIX.

HERE are several different texts of the CHIUSHINGURA extant, among which that of the *jōruri*,* which has been chiefly used in preparing the foregoing translation, seems to be the most popular.

The most complete and standard text, however, is that of the "Yehon Chiushingura" (Illustrated Chiushingura), in two parts, each ten volumes, the first part narrating the events that led up to the conspiracy of the forty-seven *rōnin*, and the successful issue of it; the latter part the further fortunes of the conspirators. The work is profusely illustrated with spirited though coarsely-executed woodcuts, and seems to have been published in the twelfth year of the "nengo" *Kwansei* (A.D. 1800-1). It is extremely badly printed, and little use has been made of it in preparing the present translation.

* The etymology of this word is uncertain. It is, however, a Sinico-Japanese compound, and the Chinese characters by which it is represented mean "the pure blue porcelain glaze," or, metaphorically, the genius of tragedy. According to a writer in the *Japan Mail* of March 10th, 1875, this species of composition takes its name from Jōruri Himé, the mistress of the favourite Japanese hero Yoshitsune, the brother of Yoritomo, the founder of the hereditary

The author was one Chikamatsu Monzayemon, who appears to have flourished in the early portion of the eighteenth century. I am not aware of any other important production of his pen.

The edition I have principally used* announces itself as having been printed, partly at Ohosaka, by one Seisuke, at the sign of Kajima, in the Funa-machi ("Ship Street"); partly at Yedo, at a house in the Seto-mono-chô ("Porcelain Street"), near the Nihon-bashi ("Japan Bridge"—the "London Bridge" of the Capital of Dai Nippon).

It is in eleven parts or *livraisons*, the last being double, and is printed in a large thick character known as *kantera*, a term apparently not Japanese, and the meaning of which I have been unable to discover.

The text is written partly in *sôsho*,† Chinese character, partly in

---

Shôgunate (A.D. 1180, *circiter*); and, though afterwards chiefly used in tragic narration, was first employed in telling the tale of the loves of the frail princess. More probably, however, the latter fact has, by a kind of metonomy, invested this Japanese Timandra (Yoshitsune may, without impropriety, be called the Alkibiades of Japan) with a posthumous title which it were not, perhaps, too fanciful to render as " The Muse of the Drama."

A *jôruri*, at the present day, is a sort of dramatic part-prose part-metrical romance, commonly of a tragic cast, of which the dialogue may be recited or sung by actors, with appropriate gestures: the *utaigata*, or song-men of the orchestra, interposing, from time to time, with the narrative, which is often cast in a sort of irregular verse, and thus discharging to some extent the functions of a Greek chorus.

\* The original text of the translation now offered differs somewhat—in places, considerably—from that resorted to for the earlier version.

† *I.e.* " grass writing, " a cursive abbreviated mode of writing, more commonly used in Japan than the ordinary square Chinese. The principal difficulty in the acquirement of the written language lies in the decipherment of this variable and puzzling form, well termed by the old Spanish missionaries an invention *de un conciliabulo de los demonios para enojar a los fideles*, and several years' assiduous study are necessary to obtain a useful command of it, which can be retained afterwards only by constant practice. The advantages that would result to the Japanese from an adoption of the Roman characters—a perfectly feasible change—are simple incalculable. A real foundation would thus soon be laid, on which a true national civilization, very different from the mere imitative and often very laughable travesty of Western forms, beyond

the flowing Japanese syllabic character known as *hiragana*, the *sôsho* forms being not seldom accompanied by a transliteration into *hiragana*.

In addition, the columns of the text are, to some extent, notated musically; various marks indicating where and how the voice should be modulated, and where the accompaniment should be introduced. There is no punctuation, beyond a division into sentences or phrases, shown by a plain circle having nearly the same value as our comma.

A Japanese orchestra generally consists of nine performers (*gakunin*), distributed as follows:

> Two *Taiko-gata*, or drummers.
> Two *Fuye-gata*, or fife-players.
> Two *Shoshichiriki*, or flageolet-players.
> One *Kane-gata*, answering to our triangle-man.
> Two *Utai-gata*, or song-men.

Such an orchestra is called a *kunin-bayashi;* when it consists of only one performer of each kind it is called a *gonin-bayashi—i.e.,* "five-men-grove" *hayashi*, "grove" being the technical term for a musical band, company, or orchestra. The *kane-gata* generally introduces and terminates the whole piece, and each successive movement of the music as well. He is followed by the flageolet-players, and they, in their turn, by the fifers, the drummers coming last. The whole band, except the *kane-gata* and the *utai-gata*, then perform a sextet in concert, the *kane-gata* introducing his instrument from time to time. The sextet finished, the duets—or, in a *gonin-bayashi*, the solos—recommence, and the whole piece thus consists of a succession of movements, in which the instrumentalists follow each other in the order above described; each movement being a series of duets, in a full orchestra, by the different musicians,

---

which the Japanese, for the present, seem unable to advance, might be based; and the land of Dai Nippon, which can at least boast of never having been insulted by the tread of the conqueror within historic times, would rapidly assume a leading position among the ancient empires of the Extreme East.

followed by a sextet of the whole of them, except the triangle and song-men.

The action of the romance is laid in the 14th century, but the events upon which it is founded really occurred at the commencement of the 18th; and must have created a great and lasting interest among the people, for the story is referred to in the commonest epitomes of Japanese history, and is—or, at least, was, some few years ago—familiar to every Japanese with the least tincture of education. In view, however, of the severe penalties that, under the Shôgunate, attached to the publication of recent or current events of a public character, the author found himself forced to adopt the practice, not uncommon with Western writers of a couple of centuries back, of barely disguising the reality by diluting it, so to speak, with a certain amount of fiction, and by so altering names and dates as to evade the law without too effectually concealing the truth. The episode has been given to the world by Mr. Mitford, in one of his admirable *Tales of Old Japan*, that of the "Forty-seven *Rônin*"; but I have nevertheless thought it not out of place to re-tell the tale in the following abbreviation from a popular Japanese version of it, endeavouring as far as possible merely to supply the *lacunæ* in Mr. Mitford's version.

During the reign of the Shôgun Iyetsuna, the President of the *Gorôjiu* (Council of State, lit., "August Assembly of Elders"), about the middle of the 11th month of the 13th year of the period Genroku (A.D. 1701), was officially informed that, in the 3rd month of the ensuing year, three ambassadors of high rank would arrive at Yedo from the Court at Kiyôto. The President, in consequence of this announcement, appointed Asano Takumi-no-Kami (Yenya Hanguwan) and Kamei Sama (Wakasanosuke) special commissioners to receive the ambassadors, with directions to consider themselves under the orders of an official of no very high rank, Kira Kôdskenoske Yoshifusa (Moronaho). The *Karô* of Kamei, Ogiwara (Honzô) by name, on hearing of his master's appointment under Kira Kôdske, who soon began to show his harsh and tyrannical disposition, lost no time in seeking out the latter, and winning his favour by timely gifts. Ohoishi Kuranosuke (Ohoboshi Yuranosuke), the *Karô* of Asano Takumi, refused to act in a similar manner, though much pressed to do so by Ohotaka Gengo (Ohowashi Bungo), a retainer of Asano. Kira Kôdske consequently received Asano with the worst grace possible, and took every opportunity of slighting him. On the arrival of the ambassadors, Asano, who was but ill-acquainted with the duties of his office, committed several grave errors in the discharge of his commission, for which he was severely reprimanded by Kira Kôdske. Anxious to avoid a repetition of his fault, Asano, previously to the coming-off of a grand entertainment which the Court at Yedo gave to the ambassadors, sought advice and instruction from his superior. But the revengeful and covetous Kira Kôdske refused to assist him in any way, and treated him with such violence that the unfortunate Asano at last lost his temper, and drew his sword upon his tyrant within the precincts of the palace, inflicting upon him a severe wound. Kira Kôdske, indeed, would have been slain, but for the timely, or untimely, interference of one Kachikawa Yosobei (whose *rôle*, in the romance, is appropriated by Honzô). By thus drawing weapon within the court-precincts, Asano committed a capital offence, and was accordingly compelled to rip his bowels open, on the 14th of 3rd month of 14th year of Genroku (A.D. 1702).

Meanwhile, Kayano Sampei (Hayano Kampei), a retainer of Asano, in company with a comrade, had, at the commencement of the quarrel between their master and Kira Kôdske, the consequences of which he dreaded, travelled the extraordinary distance of 170 *ri* (420 miles) in 4½ days—ordinarily a journey of 17 days—to find the *Karô* of their clan, Kuranosuke, who was in Banshiu (Harima), and warn him of the danger which Asano ran through the ill-will of Kira Kôdske.

News of the self-dispatch arrived the very day after their arrival, and the retainers of Asano, wild with rage and grief, hardly knew how to act. Kuranosuke next received information

from Yedo that, unless his master's castle and lands were sur-
rendered, orders would be issued that the whole family and clan
of Asano should be utterly destroyed. The *Karô* endeavoured
to avert this disaster, but in vain; and, on the news of his want
of success reaching him, assembled the clan, and after explaining
to them their position, and the impossibility of defending their
lord's castle and lands against his enemies, produced a document
binding them to commit self-dispatch, to the terms of which he
prevailed upon sixty-three of them to signify their assent in the
most solemn manner, namely, by imposing upon it their hands
smeared with their own blood. The rest had discreetly retired
during the delivery of the *Karô's* address.

Having thus separated his wheat from the chaff, he called
the sixty-three together again, and told them that his real
purpose was, not that they should at once commit self-dispatch,
but that they should first of all slay Kira Kôdske, and afterwards
"follow their lord upon the dark path." This was agreed to on
the 11th of the 4th month.

Amano Yarihei (Amagawa Gihei) now comes upon the scene.
He had acted as agent for the clan, and, on hearing of the cruel
death of Asano, had offered Kuranosuke all the aid he could
give towards the carrying out of any design the *Karô* might
entertain against Kira Kôdske. The *Karô* at first declined the
trader's assistance, but, on the latter's devotion being shown by
his attempt to kill himself on being refused the boon he asked
for, Kuranosuke revealed to him the plot to revenge the death
of Asano upon his enemy, and consented to allow the delighted
*chônin* to furnish the requisite arms and fighting gear.

The *Karô* then laid hands on the treasure of Asano, and,
after calling in and paying off the paper currency of the clan,
and reserving a small sum for the expenses of the conspiracy,
divided the remainder equally among his sixty-three fellow-
conspirators, each of whom received 25 *riyô*. This was especially
displeasing to one Ono Kurohei (Ono Kudaiu), who had urged

the *Karô* to divide the money among the conspirators proportionately to their salaries—a proposition to which Kuranosuke would not listen, saying that misfortune had put them all on a level.

The conspirators then separated, promising to assemble upon the signal of the *Karô*.

Kayano Sampei (Hayano Kampei), meanwhile, went to his village, and there found his mother dead. His father besought him to secede from the conspiracy, pleading his age and loneliness; and Kayano, distracted between his love for his father and his sense of honour and loyalty to his lord, sought escape from the dilemma in self-dispatch.

All proper preparations having been made, Kuranosuke, with his comrades—the conspirators had, in the interval, dwindled down to forty-seven in number—forced their way into the mansion of Kira Kôdske by night, and put the enemy of their much-mourned lord to death. This act of vengeance seems to have been accomplished on the 14th of the last month of the 14th year of Genroku (A.D. 1702). The authorities were somewhat perplexed how to act—so great was the sympathy felt for the devoted band—but finally condemned them to *Seppuku*, which they accomplished the following year at the tomb of Asano, in the burial-ground of the Temple of Sengaku at Yedo.

The Temple of Sengaku is close to that of Tôsen, formerly the British Legation—and the tombs of Asano and his forty-seven devoted followers are still shown there.

The marvellous portion of this "ower-true tale" remains to be told. The conspirators, after slaying Kira Kôdske, cut off his head, and offered it with proper ceremonial at the tomb of their lord. As the head touched the stone-work the monument was distinctly seen to quiver.

The following is said to be the "Schwanenlied" of Asano:

Kaze sasou
Hana yori mo,

Nawo mata haru no
Nagori wo
Ika ni to ka sen!

which may be thus rendered—

> \* Tender blossoms strew the ground,
> Flung in wan confusion round
> By the wind's too boist'rous breath;
> More my lot might pity find,
> Forced to leave sweet Spring behind,
> Doomed to an untimely death.

### Page 1. *Shôgun.*

This, the ordinary official title of the former Kubô (known generally to foreigners as Tycoon), is a Sinico-Japanese compound, meaning " General" or " Commander of the Forces."

The full title is Sei-i-tai-shôgun, " barbarian-quelling Generalissimo," and is said to have been first bestowed, about 86 B.C., by the Emperor Shiujin upon his son, the celebrated Yamato-dake-no-Mikoto, who reduced the indigenous Aino tribes of the North and East into subjection to the Imperial power.

The first of the hereditary Shôguns, however was Minamoto Yoritomo, upon whom the title was conferred in A.D. 1190, or, at least, from that date, if, as some writers maintain, it was bestowed posthumously.   Whatever may be the truth as to the date of bestowal of the rank upon Yoritomo, there can be no doubt as to his exercise of the power belonging to it for many years previous to his death, which was caused by a fall from his horse in the last year of the 12th century after Christ.   The predominant position which he had won for the office was maintained by his successors in it, all of whom were direct or collateral descendants from the Minamoto stock—or were adopted as such—up to the year 1868, when the Mikado resumed the power of which his ancestors had

---

\* Asano died in the month of March, when the wild-cherry, so often the theme of Japanese poets and artists, is in blossom—a fugitive beauty soon perishing under the rough blasts of the equinoctial gales.

for so long a period been deprived, and H'totsubashi, better known as Keiki, the last, and apparently the least energetic of his dynasty, retired to the town of Shidzuoka, some 60 miles westward of Yokohama, where, forgetful of the glories of his foregoers, he leads a life of somewhat ignoble obscurity and ease.

Page 1. *The Shôgun of the Ashikaga family had overthrown Nitta Yoshisada.*

The Ashikaga branch of the Minamoto family held the Shôgunate from A.D. 1334 to A.D. 1579, or thereabouts.

When the dynasty of Yoritomo became extinct, in A.D. 1219, the Shôgunate passed, nominally, first into the hands of members of the great Fujiwara house (one of the original eight noble families), and afterwards into those of a succession of Shinwô, or princes of the Imperial blood, but the real power was exercised by the Hôjô family,* connected by marriage, and, probably by blood also, with that of Yoritomo.

During this period, the Mikados seem to have been mere puppets in the hands of the Hôjô usurpers, but towards its close, the Emperor Godaigo—who owed his elevation to the influence of the Court of Kamakura (then the Eastern Capital and residence of the Shôguns—as Yedo, now Tôkiô, was afterwards—now a mere village, distant some 16 miles from Yokohama, and chiefly famous for its grand bronze image of Buddha)—nevertheless made a show of independence, and, in his attempt to free himself from the thraldom in which he was held by his powerful vassal, brought about the war known in Japanese history as the war between the Faction of the North (the Kamakura party) and the Faction of the South (Kiyôto party), which was to be alike ruinous to himself and his rebellious subject.

---

* The town of Odawara, so well known to European residents, was the principal seat of this family, who had a strong castle there, now in ruins and held sway over a large extent of the surrounding country.

The war, which commenced in A.D. 1319, lasted, or rather languished, for 75 years. During it, either party maintained its own Emperor, but since the revolution of 1868 the names of the Emperors of the North have been expunged from the Imperial catalogue, and the Emperors of the South alone are now considered as having been the rightful occupants of the throne.

In A.D. 1330, the Emperor Godaigo was taken prisoner and sent in exile to the island of Oki. A year or two afterwards, however, one of the Imperial generals defeated the Hôjô forces in a great battle, and made himself master of Kamakura. The Imperial exile was re-established upon the throne, but ungratefully gave his confidence, not to the men to whose exertions he owed his return to power, but to a member of the Ashikaga family of the name of Takauji. Disgusted with their treatment, Nitta and his party rose in rebellion against an emperor who knew so little how to requite their services. The struggle was a brief one. Takauji was ordered to march against them, and they were defeated with great slaughter, Nitta himself being among the slain. The rebellion thus extinguished, Takauji was installed as Shôgun at Kamakura, and founded a dynasty that for the next two centuries and a half was virtually to govern Dai Nippon.

Page 1. *Shrine to be erected to Hachiman.*

The etymology or real signification of this appellation of the Japanese Ares I have not been able to trace. The Chinese characters by which it is usually represented mean the "Eight banners," and may possibly imply some notion of the god being a sort of manifestation of the Buddha of the Eight Banners.

The hero deified under this title was the Emperor Ôjin, who died about the commencement of the 4th century of our era. His mother was the Empress Jingu, celebrated as the conqueror of Korea. According to some, Ôjin was the conqueror of Korea, and was, on this account, deified as the God of War. Others, again, assert that he made the Japanese acquainted with the art of weaving, and favoured the adoption of Chinese civilization. He was commonly worshipped by *samurahi*, and was vernacularly known as the Yumiya, or Archer God. The principal temple at Kamakura is dedicated to his worship.

### Page 1. *Nengo Riyakuô.*

Previously to the adoption, some two or three years since, of the European calendar, three systems of chronology existed in Japan, all similar in character to what still exist in China.

The era of the first commenced with the accession of the traditional Emperor Jinmu, in B.C. 600. Thus A.D. 1870 was 2530 of the era of Jinmu.

The second was based upon the sexagenal cycle used in China to the present day. The first of these cycles commenced with the 61st year of the reign of Hwang Ti, B.C. 2637, and the year 1875 is the 11th of the 76th cycle.

The mode in which the sexagenal cycle was used, and each year of it distinguished, was not a little complicated, and for an explanation of it—which would be out of place here—the reader is referred to any work of repute upon China or Japan.

According to the third system, the one most commonly used in books, any year after A.D. 645 was known by its place in the "nengo" (chin "nien hao") or year periods, which from time to time were established and named by Imperial decree. These "nengo" had a duration of from 2 to 15 or 20 years, and were distinguished by such high-sounding titles as "Exalted Virtue," "Celestial Peace," "Great Development," and the like. The present "nengo," which is not to be changed during the life of the reigning Emperor, is called Meiji, "Illustrious Rule," and the year 1879 is the 12th year of it.

The name "Riyakuó" in the text signifies "Uninterrupted Prosperity."

### Page 2.    *Wakasanosuke Yasuchika.*

In Japan, the family name, only used by men, comes first; the individual name assumed at puberty comes afterwards. Under the old regime, the son of a *samurahi* on attaining the age of 15 performed "gembuku," that is, shaved off his forelock, and became a "jak'k'wan," entitled to wear a hat or cap. At the same time he adopted a "nanori," or individual name, generally selected for him, according to certain very intricate rules, by a man of learning, with or without the assistance of a soothsayer, astrologer, or diviner.

Government officials, and *shizoku* generally (the *samurahi* of the "Tokugawa jibun," or old Tycoon days), are now giving up the practice of "gembuku," and wear their hair in the European fashion, as they clothe their bodies in strange-looking travesties of European garments.

### Page 2.    *A Baron of Hakushiu.*

Hakushiu is synonymous with Hôki, one of the former Sanindô provinces.*

### Page 2.    *Seiwa family, a Genji house.*

The usurpation of Yoritomo—for such, in effect, his ascendancy became—towards the close of the 12th century, was the culminating point of the struggle between the powerful Taira, or Hei, and the Minamoto, or Gen, clans, that for a long course of years had spread ruin through the Empire, to end in the establishment of the hereditary Shôgunate in the family of the

---

* *Vide* Mr. Satow's Geography of Japan. Trans. As. Soc Jap., 1872-73, p. 33.

successful chief of the latter faction. The Seiwa was the elder branch of the Gen house, and derived its name from its founder, the Emperor Seiwa, who flourished about the middle of the 9th century.

### Page 2. *Feudatories.*

In the text "Hatamoto," literally, "under the flag" (of the Shôgun). They were the lesser feudatories of the Kubo, and were often known as *Shômiyô* ("lesser names"), in contradistinction to the *Daimiyô* ("greater names"). The main difference, however, between the higher and lower nobles seems to have been less one of birth than of property—the *Daimiyô* being holders of lands of which the produce was valued at 10,000 *kokus* of rice annually, or more; the *Shômiyô*, of lands of which the annual produce was under 10,000 *kokus*.

### Page 3. *The Twelve Naishi.*

A Sinico-Japanese word, meaning "inner attendants." They were noble ladies, daughters of *K'ugé*, who were peers of the Mikado's creation, higher in rank than the *Daimiyô* (who were, in reality, nothing more than deputies of the Shôgun), but possessed only of small estates, and of little direct power or influence. Their duties were to wait upon the Mikado and his consort *(K'wôgo).*

### Page 5. *Yoshida Kenkô.*

A mediocre versifier, who flourished under the Shôgunate of Takauji. Some of the pieces in the well-known *Kokinshiu* ("Songs, New and Old") are attributed to him. He was also the author of a collection of essays on all sorts of subjects of very little intrinsic interest or value, known as the Tsure-dzure-gusa.

### Page 8. *Ôgon.*

Ôgon should be translated "barred gold pieces." The coins referred to were probably Ôban. Ôban, Koban, and silver coins seem (according to the Kingin-dzumoku) to have been first issued in the *nengo* Tenshô, (A.D. 1573-1596); though in the same work we find hints that coins were in use as far back as the *nengo* Tengiyô (A.D. 938-947). The "ôban" was a thin plate of gold (or heavily-gilt silver) of oval shape, about 6 inches long by 4 inches broad, marked with various stamps and seals, rough on the one face, generally on the other covered with an elaborate design, consisting of rows (commonly seven) of transverse shuttle-shaped depressions. The Tenshô ôban contained 44 momme of gold (a momme was, I believe, about 58 grains troy). On the ornamental face are written the characters "ten riyô," by which are meant, says the Kingin Dzumoku, ôgon, or fine gold, riyô, so that each ôban was worth 420 momme of silver. The seal was a paraph of the characters "yei-jô," which signify literally "glory and order."

Page 20 (note). *The Japanese "abacus" or calculating board.*

The reader is referred to the article on Arithmetic in the "Encyclopædia Britannica," where a full account of the abacus in use in China, (*swanpan*), and in Japan (*soroban*) will be found.

Page 26 (note †). *The word "suma" is a misprint for "tsuma."*

Page 37. *Kamishimo.*

A sort of outer ceremonial dress, of stiffened material, curiously shaped about the shoulders so as to present a winged appearance. The trader-class, as well as the *samurahi*, seem to have had the right of wearing it on certain occasions. A peculiar *Kamishimo*, without any device or crest, was worn by a *samurahi* when committing *seppuku*.

Page 45. *Example set by the falcon.*

"Taka wa shishite mo ho wa tsumadzu."—The falcon even at the point of death will not peck at an ear of rice. Of such a noble nature is the bird, that it would rather die than rob the peasant of a single grain of rice.

Page 47.   *I am as fortunate as if I were to come upon the Udonge in bloom.*

In the great Sinico-Japanese Encyclopædia—*Wa Kan Sansai-dzuye*, "Japanese and Chinese Illustrations of the Three Powers (Heaven, Earth, and Man),"—vol. 94, part 1, under the heading of *Basho*, we are told that the *Udonge* is a kind of fig-tree. In vol. 88, under the word *Ichijiku*, the *Udonge* is again declared to be a kind of fig. The popular notion is that the *Udonge* blooms but once in three thousand years, a notion derived, doubtless, from the fact that, in figs, the flowers being within and not without the receptacles, are not externally visible; and hence the tree appears never to bloom.

In the *Nehankiyo*, a Buddhist doctrinal work said to have been composed shortly after the death—or perfection—of Sakya Muni, the manifestation of Buddha upon earth is announced as a most rare event—rare as the blooming of the *Udonge*.

In the century of poems collected by Kiu-an, there is a stanza referring to the *Udonge*, of which the following is a literal rendering:—

> The reign of our Emperor,
> May it be as the *Tama-tsubaki*,
> Everlastingly green,
> May his days be so long in the land
> That he may behold the *Udonge* bloom a hundred times.

The *Tama-tsubaki* is a hardy ever-green shrub, apparently identical with the *Euonymus Japonicus*. The *Ficus Indica*, it will be remembered, is reverenced by the Southern Buddhists as a sacred tree.

Page 52.   "*Namu Amida Butsu*," or "*Namu miyôhô renge kiyô.*"

Introductory phrases of Buddhist prayers. The words are neither Japanese nor Chinese, but are altered Sanskrit. The first is said to mean "O aid me, thou everlasting Buddha," or "Buddha of boundless

light." Amida, Amita, or Amitâbha, is a personage of the later
Buddhism, especially honoured in China as the king of the paradise in
the Western Heavens. " Namu " is the Sanskrit "namoh," Pali " namo
used in invocations. The second, translating the Chinese characters
in which it is commonly written, would seem to signify: " O precious
law and gospel of the lotus-flower." It is commonly used, if I
remember rightly, by members of the Nichiren sect. Good souls are
supposed to live for ever, perched upon a lotus-flower. Sadakuro
tells his victim to choose whatever prayer he may prefer, and die
without further delay.

Page 54. *In the text, the teeth of Karu are said to have been unblackened,*
*which evidence of her youth has been erroneously omitted from*
*the present version.*

The extraordinary custom of blackening the teeth and shaving off
the eyebrows was originally practised by legally-married women only,
but gradually came to be adopted by all women who had attained
their twenty-second or twenty-third year, whether married or not.
The practice of shaving off the eyebrows is said to be falling into
desuetude, and the teeth are now, it is believed, blackened by married
women alone, and even by them only after having given birth to a
child. The material used in blackening the teeth is a preparation
of gall-nuts and oxide of iron. The custom is said to have arisen
in the reign of the Emperor Daigo (10th century), but I have not
been able to find any satisfactory explanation of its origin or meaning.

Page 55. *The Bon month.*

That is, the 7th month, when, on the 13th, 14th, and 15th days,
the *Bon* festival, or feast of lanterns, is held. The Chinese characters
representing the word *Bon* mean "demon or spirit-period," but the
etymology of the word is unknown to me. The popular term is
*Tama-matsuri*, for *Tamashii no matsuri*, "feast of ghosts"—All Souls'
Day, as we should say.

A shelf is erected in the principal chamber of each house, on which rushes are laid, and over which the *ihai*,* or tablets of the departed, are suspended, in the hope that their spirits will revisit the scene of their earthly life. A cord is carried across the shelf (*Tamadana*, or spirit-shelf), from which depend various fruits, such as millet (*Panicum italicum*), Hiye (*Panicum cruscorvi*), water-bean nuts (*Nelumbo nucifera* of Gœrtner), chestnuts, and egg-apples or brinjals (often called aubergines, fruit of *Solanum melongena*). Various boiled cereals are also placed upon the spirit-shelf, laid on leaves of the water-bean.

On the 13th day, about sunset, an *ogara*, or hemp-stalk dried after having been peeled, is lit. The flame, which lasts only a short time, is the *Mukai-bi*, or "greeting-flame," welcoming the spirits on their arrival. On the evening of the 15th, the ceremony is repeated, and the *Okuri-bi*, or "speeding-flame," signifies the farewell of the living to the departing ghosts of the relations or ancestors whose *ihai* are suspended over the spirit-shelf.

### Page 56. *Inari.*

Name of a *Shintô* deity, the patron of rice-farmers. The Chinese characters of the name mean "the bringer of rice." The name *Inari* itself is Japanese, and is probably connected with the word *ine*—growing-rice, paddy. The fox (*Kitsune*) is supposed to be attached to the service of the god.†

### Page 59. *Niogo Island.*

Said to be inhabited entirely by women. An account of it is given in the *Yumi-hari-dsuki*, a sort of romance founded upon the adventures of Yoritomo on a supposed visit to the island, which

---

* *Vide post.*

† A different explanation is somewhere given by Mr. Satow, but the translator is, unfortunately, unable to say where it is to be met with.

is placed in the neighbourhood of the Loo-choo group.* The egg-plant (*Solanum melongena*), or brinjal, is described as growing there to such a prodigious size that ladders are necessary to get at the fruit.

Page 67.  *We shall climb together the Shidé Hill.*

In the mythical geography of Buddhism, a hill over which souls have to pass on their journey to hell or paradise. Some distance beyond it, they arrive at a place where three roads (*San-dzu*) meet, one of which leads to hell (*jigoku*), another to paradise (*gokuraku*), and the third from the world. Before continuing their journey—to hell or to paradise, as may have been decreed— the ghosts strip off their clothes, and give them up to an old woman whom they find stationed there to receive them, under a pine-tree. The old woman is known popularly as *San-dzu no obásan.*

Page 68.  *That you may take it with you on the dark path.*

The dark path is an euphemism for death. Ghosts are supposed to go under the world, where both hell and paradise seem to be situate; hence the expression, "to go on the dark path."

Page 76.  *Jinseng medicine.*

Jinseng or Ginseng is the aromatic root of a species of Panax, a member of the Ivy family, much esteemed in China, and to some but a less extent in Japan, as a tonic and a stimulant. The plant is said to live for a thousand years, and then to assume a human form. The infusion, if given to a moribund, is supposed to prevent decomposition.

---

* The Japanese commonly identify this mysterious island with Hachijo, notes of a visit to which island will be found in Vol. vi. part iii., of the Transactions of the Asiatic Society of Japan.

### Page 77. *A high Kagura feast.*

There are two kinds of *Kagura* festival, both connected with Shintôism, commonly celebrated in Japan. That referred to in the text is known as a *Dai-dai Kagura*—lit., "great great *Kagura*" —and is essentially a solemn adoration of the Sun-goddess (Amaterasu no Ohongami, or Tenshokô Daijin), followed by a sort of banquet, of which the expenses are defrayed by subscription. The solemnities, which are conducted by *Kannushi* (Shintô priests, guardians of shrines), take place in the hall of a Shintô *miya*, or temple, previously guarded from evil influences and from intruders by a roughly-made rice-straw rope carried round its walls. First, the *O-harai* (august purification) of the Sun-goddess is placed upon a stand, and proper offerings are set before it. The *O-harai* is a kind of box containing a fragment of the staff wielded by the priests of the temple of the goddess in Isé, at the festival there held in her honour twice every year. Each *Kannushi* then takes a branch of *Sakaki* (*Cleyera Japonica*), which he holds in one hand, while with the other he commences to beat upon a small drum. The attention of the goddess being thus aroused, the assembled clergy, who have previously disposed themselves in a semicircle in front of the stand upon which the *O-harai* was placed, chant, in a monotonous drawl and to the accompaniment of the drums which they do not cease to beat, a special liturgy (*norito*) to the Queen of the Plains of High Heaven (*Takamaga-hara*). The liturgy ended, *O-harai* inscribed with the name of the Sun-goddess are bestowed upon the laity,* who, ranged in front of the shrine, have assisted at the ceremony, and the proceedings, passing, pleasantly enough, "from grave to gay," terminate with an entertainment, in which those who have

---

* Strictly upon the *Ujiko* only—that is, upon the dwellers in the district over which the local deity, worshipped at the shrine where the *Kagura* is celebrated, is supposed to extend his protection.

subscribed to the expenses, no doubt, duly play their part. One of these *O-harai* ought to find a place upon every domestic *Kami-dana*, or god-shelf—a small model of a Shintô temple to be found in almost every house, labelled with the names of various deities, one of whom must be the Sun-goddess —for it affords protection to the believer's household—only, however, for a period of six months, when it must be changed for a new one brought or fetched from Isé.

For the above description I am in part indebted to Mr. Satow's account of the Shintô temples in Isé, contained in the 1873-4 volume of the Transactions of the Asiatic Society of Japan, where a vast amount of information on the subject of Shintôism will be found. The following specimen of a Shintô prayer, which I quote from Mr. Satow's admirable essay on the "Revival of Pure Shintôism," printed as an appendix to the first part of the third volume of the Transactions already cited, will, it is believed, be read with interest.

"From a distance I reverently worship with awe before Ame no Mi-hashira and Kuni no Mi-hashira, also called Shinatsu-hiko no Kami and Shinatsu-hime no Kami, to whom is consecrated the Palace built with stout pillars at Tatsuta no Tachina in the department of Heguri in the province of Yamato.

"I say, with awe, deign to bless me by correcting the unwitting faults which, seen and heard by you, I have committed, by blowing off and clearing away the calamities which evil gods might inflict, by causing me to live long like the hard and lasting rock, and by repeating to the gods of heavenly origin and to the gods of earthly origin the petitions which I present every day, along with your breath, that they may hear with the sharp-earedness of the forth-galloping colt."

The other kind of *Kagura* is a kind of mystery or musical pantomime, enacted at the shrine of a local deity, in a sort of raised building or theatre accessory to the shrine and called *Kagura-dô*. The celebration may be in honour of the local deity, and then takes place upon his death-day, or may simply be intended to propitiate heaven generally. The expenses are usually defrayed out of the offerings of pilgrims, and by contributions from the *Ujiko*—the dwellers under the protection of the god to whom the shrine is dedicated. Before the mystery opens, a particular kind of *sudzu, Kagura-sudzu,* and two *gohei* are placed in front of the *Kagura-dô.* The *Kagura-sudzu* consists of twelve small bells, resembling those fastened round the tails of pack-horses in Japan, or those attached round the necks of mules in European countries, curiously strung together. A *gohei,* the proper Japanese term for which is *mitegura,* is a kind of wand, from one end of which depend, on either side, strips of paper, notched or slit in a particular manner, so as to present a twisted appearance. Woodcuts and descriptions both of the *Kagura-sudzu* and *gohei* will be found in the 15th volume of the *Wo Kan Sansai-dzuye.* The object of the bells is to call the attention of the god to what is about to take place; and the *gohei* represent—according to Mr. Satow—offerings of rough and fine cloth, which are supposed to attract the god to the shrine. The mystery is then inaugurated by a *Miko,* a sort of virgin priestess, generally a daughter of the *Kannushi,* presenting herself, carrying sometimes the *sudzu* and *gohei,* sometimes a sword, and going through a series of conventional gestures, which have the effect of purifying the spot from all uncleanliness, and of keeping all evil demons at a proper distance.

These preliminaries over, and the place thus made fit for the reception of the god, the dance commences, regulated by the music of a small band, consisting of drums and fifes. The dancers accompany their movements by significant gestures by which the plot or tale is told, no singing or shouting being permitted. The number of performers varies considerably: all are clad in antique costumes, with tall caps on their heads, long sleeves and preposterously lengthened *hakama,* or trousers, which turn up under their feet and are trailed behind, and all wear masks—one simulating the head of a fox, another the fierce look of a robber, a third the countenance of a mild genius, a fourth that of a demon, while others have the expression of a clown or natural, or are provided with horns, or show a protuberant snout like that of a pig, or have the cheeks prodigiously swollen and the forehead absurdly dimished.

The pantomime is various, but the following always forms a part of it. A dancer wearing the mask of a gentle genius is attended by another wearing that of a clown and carrying in his hand a bow and arrows. The former represents Hikohoho no Mikoto, one of the demi-god rulers of Japan. Their dance is grave and solemn, but is soon interrupted by the advent of a sturdy performer, who comes to the front strutting and stamping with great energy. This is Honosusori, a demon, wearing an appropriate mask and provided with a fish-hook and line. On approaching Hikohoho, he drops his swagger and humbly salutes the superior genius, intimating by gestures that he can make no use of the fish-hook and line, and begging to be allowed to barter it for the bow and arrows carried by the god's attendant. His request being granted he retires in triumph; and Hikohoho tries his luck with the hook and line, but the first fish he catches breaks the line and makes off with the hook. The angler and his attendant thus discomfited, pray to the dragon-deities of the sea, who recover the hook and line, and present them to Hikohoho, who immediately returns both to Honosusori and takes back his bow and arrows.

The dance ended, the *Miko* dips a bamboo branch (*Arundo bambos, Thbg*) in warm water—according to some, the water of a bath which she has previously taken—and flirts a shower of drops over the assembled *Ujiko*. As the deity is supposed to have become incorporated with her body for the nonce, each drop so flung has a miraculous power, and those who are fortunate enough to be within their range may expect to be cured of all their ills.

The pantomime of Hikohoho and Honosusori is intended to commemorate the invention of angling; and the mystery, as a whole, is, according to Japanese tradition, a representation or imitation of the efforts made by the gods of old to induce the Sun-goddess to sally forth from the cavern to which she had betaken herself in a fit of dudgeon.* And, indeed, it seems probable enough that it is a relic of the sun-worship which appears to have been the earliest definite form of religion in the country, and simply signifies the joyous welcome with which the rising of the sun over the illimitable waters of the Eastern Sea was hailed by the primæval fishermen who dwelt on the shores of Dai Nippon. The etymology of the word is uncertain. Some derive it from *kami*, a god, and *eragi*, to laugh, and this derivation is countenanced by the fact that the Chinese characters by which the word is ordinarily represented mean " the pleasing of the god." To my mind, however, the more probable derivation is that from *kami* and *kura*, a seat.

The legend of the withdrawal of the Sun-goddess is a good example of the Japanese myth ; and the following account of it, taken, in great part, from Mr. Satow's description of his visit to the Shintô temples in Isé, cited above, will not be without interest to the curious reader.

After the consummation of the marriage of Izanagi and Izanami, the first male and female deities and the immediate creators of Japan, the god Izanagi underwent a long purification by washing in the sea, in the course of which the Sun-goddess Ama-terasu no ohongami, " the mighty goddess brilliant in heaven," was developed from his left eye, while from the right orb was produced Sosa-no-o no mikoto, or the Moon-god. Of all the numerous progeny of Izanagi these two were the most dear to him. He therefore resolved to make the Sun-goddess the ruler in heaven, and she accordingly climbed up the pillar on which heaven then rested, to assume the place assigned her. The Moon-god, on the other hand, was given the sovereignty over the blue sea ; but the god neglected his kingdom, and the earth became desolate in consequence. On being asked the cause of his evil temper, the Moon-god replied that he wished to go to his mother Izanami, who

---

* It is no objection to this theory that the shrine at which the *Kagura* is enacted may not be dedicated specially to the Sun-goddess, for the latter, as the Queen of Heaven, is supposed to have a general right of tenancy of any shrine, and all local duties are more or less under her control.

was under the earth, and his father thereupon made him the ruler of the night. This, however, does not seem to have satisfied the god, for he committed various offences—among others, that of flaying alive a piebald horse from the head to the tail, and then throwing the carcase at his sister, who was seated at her loom, so alarming the goddess that she injured herself with the shuttle, and, full of fear and wrath, retired into a cave, the mouth of which she closed with a door of solid rock. Heavens and the earth were thus plunged into utter darkness, of which the more turbulent of the gods took advantage, filling space with a buzzing noise, and the general disaster was great. The gods then assembled in the dry bed of the Amenoyasu River—the River of the Peace of Heaven—and consulted as to the best means of appeasing the goddess. After much deliberation, the following device was hit upon. Iron was obtained from the Celestial mines, and the god Ishikori-dome, with the assistance of the divine blacksmith, Amatsumore, after twice failing, succeeded in forging a large and perfect mirror. " This, according to the legend, is the august deity in Isé."

Other gods meanwhile planted " Kodzu" (*Broussonetia*) and " Asa" (Hemp), and from the bark of the former and the fibre of the latter coarse and fine clothing was prepared for the use of the goddess. A palace was also built for her, ornaments made to adorn her person, and a sacred wand fashioned out of the wood of the " Sakaki " (*Cleyera Japonica*) to place in her hand.

Tearing the bones out of the foreleg of a buck, the gods then set this in a fire of cherry-wood ; the bone cracked in a particular manner, which was considered to afford a favourable omen, and preparations were at once commenced to entice the goddess from her seclusion.

One god pulled up a Sakaki tree by the roots, hanging on its upper branches the mirror, and on the lower the coarse and fine clothing. Another god then took the tree so adorned, and held it in his hand while he praised in a loud voice the power and beauty of the goddess.

A number of cocks were next collected and made to crow in concert. The god Tajikara (strong'ith'arms) was posted close to the door of the cavern. The goddess Ame no Udzume was chosen as a sort of mistress of the ceremonies, and having adorned her head with a kind of moss, and bound up her sleeves with the stem of a climbing plant, commenced to play upon a sort of rude bamboo flageolet, accompanied by another god, who drew music from the strings of six bows, arranged with the strings uppermost (the origin of the " Koto," a kind of horizontal harp), by drawing across them the rough stems of a tall kind of grass and of a rush, while the rest of the gods kept time with wooden clappers.

Bonfires were then lit in front of the cavern, and a circular box, " uke," placed near, on which Udzume mounted and began to dance, singing a song of which the words have been preserved :—

> Hito futa miyo
> Itsu muyu nono
> Ya kokono tari
> Momo chi yorodzu."

These words are said to have been chosen afterwards to express the numerals

> One two three four
> Five six seven
> Eight nine ten
> Hundred thousand myriad.

There is a difficulty, however, in identifying " tari" with " to," ten. But the stanza is susceptible of a totally different interpretation, and may be taken to mean

> Gods ! behold the door,
> Lo ! the majesty of the goddess ;
> Shall we not be filled with delight ?
> Are not my charms excellent ?

The last line is an invitation by the singer to the assembled deities to gaze upon her beauty.

These proceedings excited the mirth of the gods, whose Homeric laughter caused the heavens to tremble. The rest of the legend may be told in Mr. Satow's own words.

" Amaterasu Ohonkami thought this all very strange, and having listened to the liberal praises bestowed on herself, said 'men have frequently besought me of late, but never has anything so beautiful been said before.' Slightly opening the cabin door, she said from the inside 'I fancied that in consequence of my retirement both Ama no Hara (heaven) and Ashiwara no Nakatsukuni (Japan)* were dark. Why has Ame no Udzume danced, and why do all the gods laugh?' Thereupon Ame no Udzume replied: 'I dance and they laugh because there is an honourable deity here who surpasses your glory' (alluding to the mirror). As she said this, Ame-no-futadama no Mikoto pushed forward the mirror and showed it to her, and the astonishment of Amaterasu O-mi-kami was greater even than before. She was coming out of the door to look, when Ame-no-tajikara-o no Kami, who stood there concealed, pulled the rock door open, and, taking her august hand, dragged her forth. Then Ame-no-kogane no Mikoto took a rice-straw rope and passed it behind her, saying: 'Do not go back in behind this.'"

Udzume is commonly called Okame, and is represented in the *Kagura* by the dancer whose mask is a human face with puffed-out cheeks and diminutive forehead.

### Page 83 (note). *Names of Women.*

Women do not use surnames, not even those of their husbands, and are known by one name only. In addressing them the honorific "O" is prefixed, and the honorific "sama" (often contracted into " san ") added. Thus, " Yuki," snow, becomes O Yuki san,—Miss Snow ; " Tsuru," crane, O Tsuru san,—Miss Crane ; " Kane," gold or metal, O Kane san ; " Hana," flower, O Hana san ; " Sono," garden, O Sono san, &c., &c.

### Page 98. *The sage Sonko and the philosopher Riuto.*

Both appear to have flourished under the Tsin dynasty (A.D.

---

* The middle country of reedy moors.

265—317). On looking into their biographies, I find nothing worthy of record beyond the anecdotes in the text.

Page 100. *Gi-on Street, the Temple of Kiyomidzu, the great Buddha at Nara, the Hall of Chion, and the Temple of Kinkaku.*

The Gi-on Street was, and still is, the principal pleasure-street of Kiyôto.

The temple of Kiyomidzu ("the temple of the Limpid Waters") is sacred to Kwanon—Chinese, Kwanyin—the Buddhic Venus of the Far East. It is much visited by women, especially by those who desire children. In the grounds is a famous waterfall called Otowa no Taki, the waters of which are supposed to be endued by the goddess with various healing and invigorating virtues.

Nara is eastwards of the line joining Kiyôto and Ohozaka. Formerly the Tenshi (Emperor) resided there, but it does not seem ever to have been the real capital as some pretend. Mr. Brunton, C.E., in a most interesting article upon native constructive art, printed in the Transactions of the Asiatic Society of Japan (1873-4, p. 81), gives an account of the Buddha, from which the greater portion of the following brief description is taken.

The image is contained in a temple 292 feet long, 170 feet broad, and 156 feet high—that is, to the arête of the roof, which is supported by 176 pillars. The height of the Buddha, which is in the usual squatting position, is $53\frac{1}{2}$ feet, the length of the face being 16 feet, the width of the shoulders 28 feet 7 inches, and the length of the middle finger 5 feet 6 inches. On the head are 966 conventional curls. The glory or halo is 78 feet in diameter, and on it stand 16 figures, each 8 feet high.

Two images are placed in front, each 25 feet high.

The whole is in bronze, cast in pieces, afterwards soldered together, and the "whole construction shows great skill and original genius in the mixture of the metals, and in the methods of casting them."

The total weight of metal is about 450 tons, consisting of the following ingredients:—

| | | | |
|---|---|---|---|
| Gold | ... ... | 500 lbs. Avoirdupois. | |
| Tin | ... ... | 16,827 „ | „ |
| Mercury | ... ... | 1,954 „ | „ |
| Copper | ... ... | 986,080 „ | „ |

This is the largest Buddha in Japan, and was first erected in 743 A.D., but was twice destroyed in the course of the wars that desolated Japan about that time, and the present image was set up in the 12th century. Six times in succession the casting failed, and it was only at the seventh essay that a successful result was obtained. The head is said to be much more modern than the rest of the figure.

*The Hall of Chion (Chi-on In).*—A celebrated temple in Kiyóto of the Zenshu (Buddhist) sect. The name *In* is generally given to a Buddhist temple of a higher, *Tera* to one of a lower, order. An intermediate kind exists, on which the appellation *Ryô* is bestowed. Chi-on In may be rendered as "The Hall of Intelligent Benevolence."

*The Temple of Kinkaku.*—Erected by Taiko-sama, more renowned for its decoration, internal and external, than for the beauty of its situation. In fact, the temples of Kiyóto have been overpraised. None are comparable to the Shiba temple, lately destroyed by fire, in Yedo, or to the great Tôshô-gu at Nikko. Kinkaku may be translated "Golden Palace."

Page 111. *The devotion of Goshisho.*

Goshisho was a minister of a king of Go (Wu), who, despite his remonstrances, neglected the affairs of the state and engaged in a long and disastrous war with the state of Yets (Yueh). Upon Goshisho strongly advising his master to have nothing to do with a beautiful girl sent to him as a present by the king of Yets, the king of Go became so enraged that he ordered his faithful minister to be decapitated and his head exposed. Shortly afterwards, he was taken prisoner by his adversary and led in chains past the very spot where the head of the unfortunate adviser was exhibited, the features of which were observed to form themselves into a bitter smile as the degraded king went by.

### Page 112. *Hero Yojô.*

Yojô (Yü Jang) was the minister of a king of Shin (Tsin), who was defeated and slain in a war with a king of Shin (Ts'in). Yojô vowed revenge, and in order effectually to disguise himself swallowed varnish (some say, lime), which caused an eruption to break out in his face that completely changed his appearance. One day, hearing that the king of Ts'in would ride over a certain bridge, he stationed himself under it, armed with a sword, and awaited his enemy's approach. As the king of Ts'in came near, his horse refused to cross the bridge, despite the efforts of his rider, who, thinking there must be some cause for such an extraordinary aversion, ordered his attendants to search the neighbourhood. They did so, and found Yojô, whom they brought to their master, to whom he confessed his designs. The king laughed at the presumption of Yojô, and, handing him his mantle, said scornfully, "Stick your sword through that, and imagine that my body is within it. Thus you can satisfy your longings for vengeance." Yojô took the mantle without saying a word, and, wrapping it round himself, thrust his sword through it into his body and fell back dead.

### Page 112. *The secret books of Son and Go.*

Son (in Chinese, Sun Wu or Sun Tsz) was a celebrated Chinese commander of the 6th century before Christ, in the service of Ho Lü, prince of Wu. He was also the author of a book on military science still in use. The "Three Steps and Six Methods" is the book bestowed upon Chôryô by the genius Sekiko. (*Vide post*, "Chôryô.")

Go (Chinese, Wu K'i), a famous general in the service of Ts'u (a feudal state under the Chen dynasty, flourishing from the middle of the 8th to the latter third of the 4th century before Christ). Ordered to march against the state of Ts'i, of which his wife was a native, he put her to death lest she should persuade him to deviate from his duty. He was finally taken prisoner and slain by the people of Ts'i. He wrote a book on strategy, which is still esteemed by military men. (See Arts. 635 and 866 of Mr. Mayers' "Chinese Readers' Manual.")

### Page 113. Note.

Asano Takumi no Kami was the real name of the prototype of Yenya. *Takumi no Kami* was the designation of his office, overseer of works; but *Asano Takumi*, in the common language, means "poor in resources," "shallow in conception," "witless," and the like.

### Page 115. *The thread of his existence was snapped in twain.*

The soul is supposed to be a material substance of irregular bag-like form, kept within the interior of the body by a sinuous prolongation or "thread" attached to some part of the human frame. On this "thread" being snapped, the soul flies forth and life is terminated. The expression in the text *tama no o* may also refer to the rosary used by Buddhist priests, which consists of a hundred and eight beads strung together in the usual way. These hundred and eight beads are said to represent the hundred and eight lusts, cares, miseries, and vanities of the world; and as the sundering of the thread puts an end to the existence of the rosary, so the destruction

of that human consciousness which links together the troubles of
the world puts an end to all human ills and sorrows.*

### Page 115. *Komusô.*

A class of men who, either from remorse or from disgust with the
world, abandoned society to lead the life of wandering mendicants.
They were—for the practice has now fallen into desuetude—generally
*samurahi*, and went about dressed in white, wearing a curious deep-
brimmed hat † which entirely concealed their features, and playing
a sort of rude flageolet as they solicited alms. No special religious
meaning seems to have attached to the custom. But the etymology
of the word points to that contemplative life which leads to absorption
in nirvana, and the practice therefore was, in all probability, more or
less under the sanction of Buddhism.

### Page 119. *Warahi books.*

Lit. "jest-books," but in reality obscene novels and woodcuts, which,
even under the old regime, the higher classes in Japan at least avoided
diverting themselves with in the presence of others, and did not boast
of possessing.

### Page 122. *Village and household gods.*

The household god *(ujigami)* is, strictly speaking, the common
ancestor of the clan, and corresponds with the *Lar Familiaris* of the
Romans, or the *Heròs epônumos* of the Greeks.

---

* " Tama no o " is also an extravagant grammatical term equivalent to "syntax."
The idea being that the latter, as a sort of connecting link between words, may
be fitly designated by such an expression as the "thread of jewels." See
Mr. Aston's Grammar of the Written Language.
† See the woodcut opposite page 103

N

The village gods *(ubusuna no kami)* are the local gods, but just as the *Penates* of the Romans often included, or were synonymous with, the *Lares*, so the *ubusuna no kami* seem to be confounded with the *ujigami.* Thus the inhabitants of a district under the protection of a special deity are commonly called the *ujiko*, or members of the family of the deity, who himself is known generally as the *ujigami.* On this subject much information will be found in Mr. Satow's essay on the " Revival of Pure Shintôism " previously referred to.

Page 122. *High civil and military rank.*

Lit., to the command of his troops and the governorship of his province.

Page 130. *His manhood roused by his wife's cry of distress.*

Allusion is here intended, I believe, to the *otokodate* of Bandzui Chôbei, a sort of Japanese knight errant, or, more properly, benevolent brigand who robbed the rich to aid the poor, and enforced a code of his own against the oppressor in favour of the oppressed.

Page 135. *The Hero Chôryô.*

In Chinese, Chang Liang. One of the principal partisans of the founder of the Han dynasty. He died in the early part of the 2nd century before Christ. (See Art. 26 of Mr. Mayers' work cited above, and the note to page 135 *supra.*

Page 142. *Ihai.*

These tablets are inscribed with the posthumous name *(okuri-na)* of the deceased and the date of his death. When the wife

survives the husband, she often has her name added in red
letters, which upon her death are converted into black ones.
*Ihai* are placed upon the *Buts-dana*, or Buddhist shelf, and also
—as stated in a previous note—on the *Tama-dana*, or spirit-shelf,
on All Souls' Day. The ancestral halls common in China, in
which the tablets of the ancestors of a family, or sometimes of a
clan, for several generations back, are honoured, are not found
in Japan.

The Eighth Book consists of a metrical description, mainly in
the form of a dialogue, of the journey of Tonasé, the wife of
Honzô, the *Karô* of Wakasanosuke, with her daughter, Konami,
from Kamakura to Yamashina, a small village hard by Kiyôto,
where they hope to find Rikiya, the son of Yuranosuke the hero
of the story, who, since the destruction of the house of Yenya, had
withdrawn with his father into an obscurity hitherto impenetrable.
It will be remembered that in the Fourth Book Rikiya is affianced
to the daughter of Honzô.

On the stage, this portion of the romance would be sung or
recited with appropriate gestures, so arranged as to form a kind
of continuous slow dance, to the accompaniment of music.

The following attempt at a versified rendering* claims the
indulgence of the reader. The translator has endeavoured to
preserve, as far as possible, the spirit and even the letter of the
original, although at the risk of roughness being perceptible in
the execution of his task; but as the point of the text often lies
in an untranslatable play upon words, he has been obliged in one
or two instances to omit, and in others to modify or amplify,
portions of the interlude.

---

* A previous translation by the present writer will be found in an Essay
on Ancient Japanese Poetry, contained in the *Westminster Review* for
October 1870.

KONAMI.

" Its name upon this fleeting world*
Who first bestowed, O rapid Aska,† say,
Whose restless waters aye have swirl'd
Thro' changing channels; as changeful is the way
Of Life to us from happiness hurl'd—

---

* More literally, " floating "; hence variable, light, changing, unstable world.
The earth is supposed to be suspended in the ambient atmosphere, as a fish in
water. The following account of the creation, according to the ancient philosophy of Japan, extracted from the above-mentioned essay in the *Westminster
Review*, may be interesting. " Originally all was chaos, matter existed but rude
and formless. Divine influence penetrated the cosmic mass; a process of
differentiation ensued, and the whole assumed an ellipsoidal form. Next the
grosser parts became concentrated towards the centre, and the foundations of
the earth were laid; while the more subtle parts receded and enveloped the
globe with an ethereal fluid, of which the more delicate exterior layers consti-
tuted the sky, and those nearer to the earth's surface formed the firmament.
The notion of the existence of space apart from matter seems utterly strange to
the philosophy of China and Japan, which, besides, never attributes the creation
of the materials of chaos to any Divine First Cause; but owns, though impliedly
rather than expressly, the self-existence of primeval unorganised matter and of
some divine influence, not seldom, indeed, supposed to originate within and from
the elements of chaos itself, by which the original substance of the Universe is
forced to differentiate itself into elementary earth, air, and sky. From such a
divine influence spring a multitude of powers personified as innumerable genii,
who are the immediate creators out of the already partially developed materials
of chaos of the animate and inanimate objects of nature, and to whom are
entrusted the government and regulation of the phenomena and laws of the
Universe." The original text is full of word-plays utterly unsusceptible of
translation, and the present version is, accordingly, in great part an imitation
rather than an exact rendering of the Japanese. It is, however, believed that
the meaning and colour of the text are preserved to the extent to which this is
possible. The metre, which is somewhat irregular, consists of alternate lines
of five and seven syllables—the following text of the first fourteen lines of the
translation will serve as an example :—

Ukiyo to wa, . . This " evanescent " (miserable) world,
Taga ii-somete, . . Who first named it so ?
Asukagawa ? . . O River Asuka.
Fuchi mo chigiyó mo . { Salary / Deep places } and estate.

[*Continued on next page.*

† A stream near Kiyóto, flowing through flat land and constantly changing
its bed. Hence the evanescent character of the banks amid which the river
threads its way, and the propriety of Konami's address to it.

A Wavelet* breaks upon thy famous strand
 Whom Yenya welcomed as the bride
Of his esquire who long had sought her hand,
 Low fall'n with Yenya's fall her pride;
She was betrothed and Kakogawa's child
 Fond hope deep in her being bore,
But Fortune adverse ne'er upon her smil'd,
 No bridal gifts exchang'd,† no more
By lover sought, her soul is sad."

### TONASÉ.

"Peace, daughter, peace; thy mother bids thee haste
 Towards Yamashina, where glad
Thou shalt by bridegroom surely be embraced.
 Alas! a bride-train thus forlorn
Hath never yet in all the world been known,
 With doubt and grief my heart is torn;
Without attendant, mother and child alone,
 On foot must urge their weary way,
And strive Yamato's far-off land to gain."

| | | |
|---|---|---|
| Seto kawari; | { Course of life<br>{ Narrow channels | } how these change ! |
| Yorube ko-nami no | . Of me, Konami, his dependent : (a wavelet touching thy strand). | |
| Shitabito ni . | . To his (Yenya's) underman. | |
| Musubu, Yenya no<br>Ayamari wa, . | ) The contract of betrothal (was allowed) but<br>} (there took place) the error of Yenya; | |
| Koi no Kasegui, , | . The deep foundations of love; | |
| Kakogawa no . | . Of Kakogawa | |
| Musume Konami ga | . The daughter Konami, | |
| Ii-nadzuke, . | . She was promised, | |
| Tanomi mo toradzu, | . But there was no giving or receiving of bridal gifts, | |
| Sono mama ni . | . Under these circumstances. | |
| Furi-suterareshi, | . Shaken off and abandoned. | |
| Mono omoi . | . She broods over things. | |

* A pun on the speaker's name, Konami, "child-wave," "little wave."

† Without which a marriage, or rather betrothal, is not looked upon as complete.

## KONAMI.

" My body's white as snow, men say,
The chilly winds with crimson hues it stain
    Such as the wild-plum's flow'r make gay,
My fingers all are sore benumbed with cold,
    Apt name Kogoye* pass is thine;
O'er Satta's ridge our toilsome way we hold,
    Thence gazing back the curling line
All pensive watch of vaguely erring smoke
    That issueth from Fuji's peak
And van'shing in the lofty sky is broke;†
    How sweet if 'twere the bonfire's reek
At threshold lit‡ my welcome home a Bride,
    How 'twould our sadness charm away!
With pines o'ergrown Matsubara's§ plain so wide
    Now travers'd, crowded is the way,
The sea-coast way,‖ by some high Daimiyö's train,
    I know not whose; how blithe and gay
They seem: ah! when shall I know joy again?"

---

* A double pun here—" Kogoye " meaning: 1st. "to freeze, congeal "; 2nd, "the passage of a child."

† They are travelling westwards, leaving Fusi-yama (more properly, Fuji-san) behind them. Fuji-san is, and probably always has been within historical times, completely extinct, so far, at least, as the summit is concerned. But the vapours that commonly wreathe or hover around its high bare peak often have the appearance of smoke or steam issuing from the long since cooled crater. The elevation of Fuji-san is close upon 13,000 feet above the level of the sea. The upper portion is covered with snow throughout the year, except from the end of July to the middle or end of September, when the peak is bare, though even during those months large masses of snow lurk in sunless clefts and crevices. No Japanese poet has omitted to celebrate the picturesque beauty of the mountain.

‡ Alluding to the custom, probably borrowed from China, of carrying the bride over a flame into her husband's house.

§ That is, "the plain of pines."

‖ The Tōkaidō, "eastern sea-way," the high road between the capitals of East and West Japan.

## TONASÉ

"O would that Fortune smiling were
Upon us, proud thy bridal train should be ;
 Than thee none happier, none more fair.
Now yonder may we Sur'ga's Fuchiu* see.

The omen cheers thy mother's heart,
Her child shall yet the marriage pledge exchange,
 By husband yet be led apart
In bridal bower, sweet vows to interchange.

 In tender whispers heard by none.
Narrows the path thro' th' briars hardly seen,
 To parents as to child† unknown ;
Fain would'st thou now on lover's strong arm lean."

## KONAMI

"On Mariko's sunny bank we stand,
His rapid stream shall roll our griefs away,
 Dear mother ; now on our right hand
High Utsu's hill we leave behind, O say

 Shall I a bridal pillow press,
Half-sleeping, by a husband's arms embraced ?
 What mighty cares my mind distress,
Ohoi‡ river! thou whose waters haste

---

* A considerable town in the province of Suruga, some 90 miles westwards of Yokohama. It is now known as Shidsuoka, and is the present residence of Hitotsubashi, the last of the Shōguns. There is a curious word-play here, the sense of which I have endeavoured to give—*suru ga fuchin* meaning in the common language, "the crowning of one's efforts with success."

† They are now supposed to be passing through a place called Oya shiradzu ko shiradzu, which name signifies "unknown to parent, unknown to child.' and involves probably some local story or tradition.

‡ *Ohoi* means "great," "vast." The River Ohoi is one of the largest in Japan, and the bed of it, at the point where a ferry carries travellers on the Tōkaidō across it, must be some hundreds of yards wide. But, except occasionally during

In rapid tumult onwards sped,
As fleeting often is the love of man,
Yet 'tis not fickleness I dread
In him I love, but 'neath misfortune's ban
Our love's full flow'r can hardly blow.
Our feet upon Shiradsuka's bridge now stand,
Past Yoshida we further go
To Akasaka; our wearied limbs demand
Repose; the beckoning women * cry
That throng the door of every inn,† 'Fair Bride,
To Kyomids' ‡ far-famed temple hie,
To Otowa's § plashing fall pray choose a guide,
And there, fair Bride, some space delay,
Adore the temple's deity and view
How to Kwanon ‖ the pilgrims pay
With sacred dance and music homage due,
Then join in the applauding shout
And share the merry throng's loud happiness.'
'Not so, my tale of tender doubt
To my chosen lord alone I shall confess.' "

the heavy autumn inundations, the stream is not much more than a hundred yards in breadth, occupying a sinuous channel in the middle of the dried-up stony bed of the river's course.

* These are servants who tout for guests.

† What follows seems to be a portion of an ancient song, to be found, I believe, in the *Shinzenden* of Bakin, and as old, probably, as the time of the Ashikaga Shōguns.

‡ Kyomidzu. See *ante.*

§ Otowa. This is a petty stream of water falling over the ledge of a rock in the grounds of the temple of Kyomidzu, supposed to have peculiar restorative qualities.

‖ Kwanon is the Buddhistic Venus, and like the *hominum divomque voluptas, Alma Venus!* of the great Latin poet, is regarded by some not only as the goddess of mercy, but as presiding over the continuous sustentation of the world and all its living creatures;

> "—— per te—genus omne animantum
> Concipitur, visitque exortum lumina solis.

She is the Avalōkitēs'vara of Northern Buddhism, first mentioned in the

### TONASÉ.

"Right, daughter; were thy lover here
Three suppliants we would Isé's * gods revere."

### KONAMI.

"Thus we our clownish verses sing.
To Nar'migata's † town we come.   Success
    The happy name, I trust, may bring.
Ha! Atsta's shrine descry we yonder—yes,
    Full seven leagues across the bay;
Haul taut the sail, bend, fellows, bend to th' oar
    With measured stroke—away, away—
Haste, haste, for distant still looms yonder shore.
    Hark! how loud the rudder's creak!
Meseems the chirp of some small *sudsu* ‡ fly,
    Or the grasshopper's unceasing shriek,

---

Sutras of the fourth century after Christ.  But Avalôkitês'vara was a male deity, and Eitel gets over the difficulty by supposing that the Buddhist apostles to China in the fourth and ninth centuries of our era, incorporated a native female deity (Kwanyin) having similar attributes with those of the Buddhist god, with the object of their own devotions.  Kwanyin is said to have a disobedient daughter of Chwang of the Chow dynasty, B.C. 690 *circiter*.  She was condemned to be beheaded, but the executioner's sword broke, and she was put to death by being smothered.  Her soul descended to hell, which thereupon became a paradise.  But Yama, the Pluto of Buddhism, fearful of losing his kingdom, rejected her, and she reappeared upon earth in time to cure her father of an illness by cutting off the flesh of her arms.  As a mark of gratitude he ordered a statue to be erected to her "with arms and eyes complete (tsien)," but by a misunderstanding of the word "tsi'en," which means either "complete" or "a thousand," the statue was made with a thousand arms and a thousand legs; and the goddess is often so represented at the present day, both in China and Japan.  *Vide* Eitel, "Handbook of Chinese Buddhism."

* Isé is supposed to be the favourite abode of the primeval gods of Japan, the chief of whom is the Sun-goddess, known commonly as Daijingû Sama.

† Narumigata, in the common language, may mean "the place of establishment of oneself."

‡ A sort of small insect, making, by attrition of its wings, a somewhat pleasant sound, and for that reason often kept in bamboo-bark cages, and fed upon bits of cucumber or melon.

The grasshopper that, as the old song tells,* doth cry
  Thro' the chilly nights when the hoar-frosts lie."

### TONASÉ and KONAMI.

"How fierce the hail drives thro' the windy air!
  Our heads before its pelt we bend,
We lead, we follow the crossing boats that dare
  Still with the howling storm contend.
Next Kamé's hill we pass, awhile
At Seki halt, where from the eastern way
  Parts stretching south for many a mile
The road to distant Isé,—the merry play
  Of packhorse bells we hear as thee
We view, Sudzuka, † Tsuchi's lofty peak, ‡

---

* Kirigirisu
  Naku ya, shimo yo no
    Samushiro ni
  Koromo katashiki ;
    Hitori ka mo nen!

I spread my garment on the ground
  Whereon the night hoar-frosts lie.
Through the gloom pierces the shrill cry of the grasshopper.
  In the chill solitude
How can I find repose on my lonely couch?

† *Sudzu* is the name given to the string of bells generally hung round the tail of the animal. The pass of Sudzuka—Sudzuka-tôge—is of considerable height, but the traveller who climbs it is well rewarded by the succession of picturesque views it affords him.

‡ Allusion is here made to the old song—

"Saka wa teru-teru,
Sudzuka wa kumoru,
Aino-tsuchi yama,
Ame ga furu."

Which may be thus rendered—

"The sun shines fair on Saka's peak,
While clouds veil Sudzuka's summit bleak,
And Tsuchi's top that lies between
Is through the shower hardly seen."

Saka, Sudzuka, and Aino-tsuchi are three conspicuous and contiguous hills, forming part of the range crossed by the Sudzuka-tôge, on which the phenomenon referred to is often observed during the showery days of early summer.

Rain-hidden, hardly may we see ;
Rain ever hides, men say, the summit bleak,
   O Minaguchi ! *—the rocky vale
Of Ishibé † we next fatigued toil thro',
   Pass Ohoctsu, Mii's ‡ temple hail,
The hillside skirt, our further way pursue,
   And now a petty hamlet nigh
Yamashina, § our journey's end descry."

---

* Meaning, strictly, "the outflow of the waters," but by a pun signifying 'the mouths of all men," that is, common report.

† Literally, "the stony place."

‡ From which the finest view of Lake Biwa is to be had.

§ Yamashina is the last village on the road, being close to Kiyôto.

## THE BALLAD OF TAKASAGO.*

A wanderer's staff he grasps now erst
   On distant journey bent:
Must many a weary, weary day
   On per'lous track be spent.

TOMONARI.

"Of Aso's shrine in Higo land,
   Within broad Kiushiu's sway,
The guardian, Tomonari, I ;
   Now list ye to my lay:

---

* Takasago is the name of a coast district in Banshiu (Harima), washed by the waters of the Inland Sea, some ninety miles westwards of Ohozaka. The author was one K'wanzei (according to some a writer of the name of Kadsu Mitsuyoshi), a composer of *Nô* (historical lyrical dramas in irregular metre with musical accompaniments, commonly based upon episodes of the long feud between the Gen and Hei families), who flourished about the year 1450 A.D. The ballad is often sung —a portion of it at least—as a kind of epithalamium, the changeless verdure and longevity of the pine, as exemplified in the two trees of Takasago and Sumiyoshi celebrated by the song, forming a theme appropriate to such an occasion.
   The persons of the ballad are:
      Tomonari, a country *kannushi*, or guardian of a Shinto *miya* or shrine.
      The Spirit of the Pine Tree of Takasago in the form of an old woman, with a broom in her hand.
      The Spirit of the Pine Tree of Sumiyoshi (or Suminoye) in the form of an old man, holding a kind of bamboo rake.
   The portions not included within inverted commas are on the stage recited or sung by the *utaigata*, or songmen, who thus, to some extent, discharge the functions of a Greek chorus ; while the dialogue is carried on by actors to the accompaniment of music and with appropriate gestures.
   The term ballad (*ballata*, from "ballare" to dance) is as apt a name for the piece as I could hit upon. The narrative portion, alone, is indistinctly metrical, the dialogue is, more properly, prose ; but the whole is recited or sung in the manner above mentioned. It belongs to the category of *Nô*, and, like its fellows, is written in a language by no means always easy to understand. The present version is a free imitation and not a literal translation of the original ; but with the exception of some obscure passages, the sense is correctly, though not literally, rendered.

" Upon Miyako's wondrous sights
   I never yet have gazed,
And towards the royal city press,
   To feast my eyes amazed.

" And by the way I fain would halt,
   And turn a space aside,
Where Takasago's famous strand
   'Fends Harima from the tide."

O he has girded up his frock,
   Nor fears the distant way,
All eager the stately town to gain,
   No longer will delay.

Well through the surf his bark is launched
   Upon the sparkling sea,
O may fair spring winds waft him on,
   Clear skies above him be!

Still o'er the wid'ning wat'ry waste
   His course he presses on,
Beyond the dim, white, misty line
   Where sea and sky seem one.

Beyond, and far beyond again,
   And leagues still leagues upon,
His bark sails o'er the circling sea
   Ere Harima's shores are won.

O hoar and venerable Pine!
   Thy swaying branches through,
With constant boom, the sweet spring winds,
   And ceaseless murmur, sough.

While from the sounding shore below,
  Where still the mists adhere,
The cadenced roar of the flowing tide
  Delights the wanderer's ear.

O ancient Pine! whose lofty top
  With countless winters' snow
Hath sparkled, is there wight alive
  Thy birth or youth may know?

Amid thy topmost twigs behold!
  The glitterings rime doth lie
Upon the crane's rough-woven nest,
  Ere yet the sun is high.

Each morn, among thy far-spread limbs
  The winds soft greetings sing,
Each e'en, low murmuring farewells,
  Through all this time of spring.

I well could rest beneath thy shade,
  There commune with my soul,
And muse in silent loneliness,
  While by the hours should roll.

For converse should I ever long,
  And seek response from thee,
The rustle of thy wind-stirr'd leaves
  Would softly answer me.

Lo! leaves and twigs the ground bestrew
  And to my raiment cling,
I shake me free, with busy rake
  The brown heap shorewards fling.

浦　ノ　砂　高　橋

TAKASAGO NO URA

O far-famed Pine of Takasago!
 How scarred thy wave-washed trunk!
The waves of time, too, on my brow
 Have rippled wrinkles sunk.

Long, long have clung to thee, hoar Pine
 These leaves now brown and sere,
With greenness aye renewed thou still
 Thy leafy top shalt rear.

### TOMONARI.

" I thought some peasant here to meet,
 And lo an aged pair
Confront me, yet perchance may they
 Me further wand'ring spare."

### AN OLD MAN AND AN OLD WOMAN.

" What would'st thou of us? Well will we
All that we know explain."

### TOMONARI.

" A stranger your famed Pine would see
 Hath come across the main."

### THE OLD MAN.

" From Takasago's lofty Pine
 The leaves thou see'st us heap,
Are fallen; 'neath the ancient tree
 Our guardian watch we keep."

### TOMONARI.

" Suminoye's Pine and you, men say,
 Are like a wedded pair,
So far apart, how that may be,
 I pray you, sooth, declare!"

### THE OLD MAN.

" Thou knowest the roll, ' Songs new and old,'
 Therein wilt find it writ,
 How Suminoye's Pine and yon
  In wedded bonds are knit.

" Sumiyoshi in the land of Tsu.
 'Twas there I saw the day ;
 This dame of Takasago is :
  Now ask us aught ye may."

### TOMONARI.

" How comes it, ye, so far apart
 Saw light, together dwell
 Beneath yon Pine ?  The mystery
  Ye doubtless may dispel."

### THE SPIRIT OF SUMIYOSHI.

" Thou say'st not wisely, Sir, methinks ;
 From many a distant source
 Down rush the mountain-streams to join
  In the river's mightier course.

" And so, by love or fate, two souls
 Together drawn, make one,
 Although ten thousand leagues may seem
  To bar their union.

" And sooth, Sir, listen to my words,
 And hearken to my say ;
 The Pine Sumiyoshi's strand o'ershadows,
  The Pine o'erhead doth sway,

" Are things without the breath of life,
 Yet from remotest time
 Hath fame them joined in constant love,
  Despite wide-sundered clime.

" And shall we twain, whose pulses beat
   With thrill of active life,
Whom many a year hath closer knit,
   From discord free and strife,

" Since first I left my earlier home,
   And here sought my dame,
Not still more rightfully to be
   United lovers claim?"

### TOMONARI.

" How pleasantly thou tell'st the tale,
   Ne'er told before, I ween,
How have the bonds of love been knit
   These stately pines between."

### THE SPIRIT OF SUMIYOSHI.

" Of old, men spoke of them, and said,
   A happy omen here,
Now peace throughout the land shall reign
   'Thro' each succeeding year."

### THE SPIRIT OF TAKASAGO.

" Long, long ago the ancient fame
   Have olden poets sung
Of Takasago's lofty Pine
   The ' Myriad leaves' * among."

---

* The "Manyôshiu," or "myriad leaves," is the most extensive, and at the same time the most ancient, collection of Japanese poetry known. It seems to have been compiled about the commencement of the 9th century, and no doubt contains poems of a much older date—all in pure archaic Japanese, free from any admixture of Chinese. See the article in the *West. Rev.*, cited *supra*.

o

### THE SPIRIT OF SUMIYOSHI.

" Great Daigo on Sumiyoshi fair
  Bestowed its name, men say,
O blest are those who live beneath *
  Our Emperor's gentle sway."

### THE SPIRIT OF TAKASAGO.

" The Pine, ne'er bared of leafy dress,
  Still green stands 'gainst the sky,
Unfaded still long years shall stand
  Sign of eternity."

### THE SPIRIT OF SUMIYOSHI.

" Unchanged through ages be the glory
  Of Sumiyoshi's tree,
Fair emblem of the constant peace
  These happy days shall see."

### TOMONARI.

" O sweet your speech, a calm so sweet
  My troubled mind doth bring;
O clear my soul from vexing doubts,
  O clear the day of spring."

### THE SPIRIT OF SUMIYOSHI.

" O clear the sunny day of spring,
  Lo! o'er the western sea,
Sumiyoshi's shores we may descry
  From 'neath Takasago's tree."

---

* There is here in the original a play upon words difficult to render.
  Sumiyoshi " means " fair are our abodes, happy our lives."

### THE SPIRIT OF TAKASAGO AND TOMONARI.

" Whose green leaves sparkle set so fair
 Against blue sea and sky;
Ah! sweet, full sweet, the spring time is,
 Bright shines the sun on high."

How calm our land embosom'd mid
 The four encircling seas;
How soft the murmuring awaked
 By the lightly blowing breeze.

So lightly felt in our happy land
 Our mighty Emperor's sway;
O constant Pair your gladness add,*
 And join in my poor lay.

Though poor it be, for how shall any
 In fitting couplets sing
Of all the joys our gracious Lord
 Doth to his people bring.

### TOMONARI.

" The story of yon lofty Pine
 Well have ye told to me:
Tall trees and lowly herbs, men say,
 But lifeless things these be.

" Yet well tall trees and lowly herbs
 Their appointed seasons know,
The Spring's mysterious power obey,
 Sunward their blossoms show." †

---

\* When sung as an epithalamium, the ballad usually ends with this stanza.
The text here is utterly untranslatable, owing to the word-plays, and I have
therefore not been able to give more than the bare idea of the original.

 † " ———— Vere rosam, frumenta calore
  Viteis auctumno fundi suadente videmus. — LUCR. I. 174.

## THE SPIRITS OF SUMIYOSHI AND TAKASAGO.

" The Pine no change of season owns,
  Its foliage ever green
In summer heat, 'neath winter snow,
  For a thousand years is seen."

### THE SPIRIT OF SUMIYOSHI.

" Explained the tale of Takasago,
  Suminoye's story told,
The antique legend now thou may'st
  To all the world unfold.

" All living things from mother earth
  Their life and being gain,
And nature, nowhere voiceless, sings
  An universal strain." *

Tall trees and lowly herbs, stones, sand,
  The soil our feet do press,
The winds and waters, everything,
  A soul divine possess.

The murmuring of the gentle zephyrs
  Amid the woods of spring,
The hum of insect 'mong the dews
  Autumn abroad doth fling.

Are these not strains of Nature's song !
  Her universal voice
In sigh of breeze, in purl of stream,
  We hear and rejoice.

---

* This stanza is a quotation from a poem contained in the collection known
as Kokinshiu.

Sublime its lofty top uprears
    The peerless Pine on high,
For a thousand autumns still hath flung
    Against the azure sky.

Its far-spread branches, vestur'd e'er
    With dress of changeless green ;
Well Shikô's* favour were here bestowed,
    Well men's loud praise I ween.

---

* The allusion is explained in the following song :—

Shin no Shikô
Mikari no toki,
Ten niwaka ni kaki-kumori,
Tai-u shikiri ni furishikaba,

Mikado ame wo shinogan to,
Komatsu no kage ni
Tachi-yoreba,
Kono matsu tachimachi taiboku to nari,
Yeda wo tare, ha wo kasane ;

Kono ame wo morasazarishikaba Mikado
Ta-iu to iu shaku wo
Kono matsu ni okuri
Tamaishi yori
Matsu wo Ta-iu to môsu to ka ya.

A spirited translation of the above appeared in the *Japan Weekly Mail* of March 10th, 1875, on the basis of which the following version has been attempted.

Shin no Shikô
Once a-hawking did go ;
All at once the clouds lowered,
And down the rain poured,
    Ho ! the Emperor must not get wet.

An ancient pine-tree
Seemed good shelter to be,
And 'neath it did he go,
When the branches grew so
    Thro' the thick leaves the rain could not get.

'Twas the Emperor's whim
That the tree should from him
Have a *shaku* with Ta-iu writ on,
'Twas no sooner said than 'twas done,
    And the pine-tree's called Taiu e'en yet.

The wind booms through the stiff-set leaves
   Mid which the morning rime
Glitters, the deep green hues shall still
   Endure throughout all time.

Aye morn and eve the leaves fall thick,
   Yet still the ancient tree
With all its leafy glory clothed,
   Shall ne'er unvestured be,

Ne'er bared of its dress of deep, deep green,
   As by the long years roll;
E'en to the leafy Kadsura* nature
   Doth briefer being dole.

And ever monarchs of all trees
   Shall either hoary Pine
Through happy ages reign supreme
   Of constant Love the sign.

Well merit ye, tall Pines, your name,†
   Ye seem with pride to say,
Your peers may fade and pine and die,
   Ye ne'er shall pass away.

---

The point lies in a word-play upon 'Tai-u' and 'Ta-iu'—the former signifying "great rain," the latter being the name of a certain high rank.

A *shaku* was a sort of tablet on which memoranda were noted. The word also means a degree in rank.

Shin no Shikô is the Chinese Emperor Chêng or She Hwang-ti, who flourished between B.C. 259 and B.C. 210, and first consolidated the petty feudal states of China into one vast Empire. (See Mayers' "Chinese Reader's Manual," Article 597.)

* Masaki no Kadzura. It is uncertain what is meant here. *Masaki* is the Euonymus Japonicus, *Kadzura* may be Uvaria Japonica Thbg. or a kind of wild vine, Vitis Pentaphylla.

† The word *matsu*, "pine," means also "to wait, endure," and the compound *matsdai* signifies "to the end of time."

### THE SPIRIT OF SUMIYOSHI.

"Sir Wanderer, hearken to my words,
    Twain guardian spirits we,
Of Suminoye's tall Pine, I,
    Of Takasago's, she."

### TOMONARI.

"Full strange the tale ye tell, meseems,
    A land of marvels this,
Of either Pine ye would reveal
    Some deep mysterious bliss."

### THE SPIRITS OF SUMIYOSHI AND TAKASAGO.

"Tall trees and lonely herbs possess
    Of soul divine a share,"

### TOMONARI.

"O wise mankind are grown beneath
    Our Emperor's fostering care."

### THE SPIRITS OF SUMIYOSHI AND TAKASAGO

"Our lord is lord of all the land,
    Of all the land bestows,
O long beneath his gracious sway
    May men enjoy repose!

"Towards Sumiyoshi, abode of Peace,
    Come, Wanderer, turn thy feet,
There pleasantly shall glide the hours
    In various converse sweet."

A fisher-bark they launch, aloft
    They hoist the narrow sail,
Far o'er the evening waters speed
    Before the favouring gale.

Towards where Awaji's isle looms high
   Above the heaving sea,
And leagues on leagues they sail ere that
   Suminoye's on their lee.


### THE SPIRIT OF SUMIYOSHI.

"Thou Pine that rearest thy lofty top
   On Sumiyoshi's shore,
Ne'er since—ah me how long ago!
   Thy stately form I saw,

"Have I thy glory ceased to own,
   Through many a wakeful night,
Or the mem'ry lost of the secret bond
   Doth me with thee unite.

"And thou, Sir Priest, before thy shrine,
   Round fenced with red-stained pale,
May beat of drum at holy feast,
   And sacred mime ne'er fail."

TOMONARI. "Lo! westwards o'er the heaving waters,
   Beyond the purple sea,"

S. OF S. "Still Takasago's shore we view,
   Where stands the lordly tree."

TOMONARI. "Here store of Tamamo* herb wherewith
   At New Year homes are dressed;"

S. OF S. "At foot of yon tall Pine reclined,
   Our limbs we well might rest."

TOMONARI. "The dead leaves of the deathless tree
   Upon me fluttering fall,"

---

* Perhaps "mo" (*Ceratophyllum submersum*).

S. or S. "With wild plum's flowerful branchlet I
My wrinkled brow enthrall."

### TOMONARI.

"Upon my raiment snow-flakes glitter;
Beneath the streaming moon,
With gods in godlike revel to join
How glorious the boon."

### THE SPIRIT OF SUMIYOSHI.

"Hark to the music of the sea,
Sweet as the maiden's song,
Urging the sacred mime before
The temple-crowding throng.

"Behold how yon tall Pine's vast shadow
Trembles with ceaseless quiver,
Upon the moonlit waters mirrored,
At every wavelet's shiver."

### TOMONARI.

"O blest the land doth heav'n's decrees
And god-gi'en chiefs obey:
To high Miako's lordly town
Still distant is the way."

### THE SPIRIT OF SUMIYOSHI.

"May troops of maidens welcome thee
As chief from victory,
A thousand, thousand blessings ever,
I pray, attend on thee.

"White-robed when thou at holy feast
Invok'st the gods' high grace,
Thine outstretched arms all ill avert,
And every good embrace.

"O for a thousand autumns may
   The people peaceful be,
For full ten thousand years enjoy
   Long life, prosperity."

How softly sweetly sings the breeze,
   O everlasting Pine !
Among thy far-flung leafy limbs
   Whereunder I recline,
And aye could lie, well pleased to list
   To music such as thine. *

---

* This last stanza is sung or recited by the "Utaigata."

*Finis.*

# PREFACE OF THE AUTHOR.

(ORIGINAL TEXT REPRODUCED OPPOSITE.)

———◆———

## KANA TEHON CHIUSHINGURA.

## DAIJO.

Kakô ari to iyedomo shokusezareba sono ajiwai
wo shiradzu to wa, kuni osamatte yoki bushi no
chiu mo buyû mo kakururu ni tatoyeba, hoshi no
hiru miyedzu yoru wa midarete arawaruru tameshi
wo koko ni kanagaki no . . . . . .